THE THIRSTY

HILLS

The Thirsty Hills

By

Marona Posey

Book Two in the Look Away Series

The Thirsty Hills, ©Marona Posey, August 2013
Cover art: Dwayne Adams

ISBN-13: 978-1493501908
ISBN-10: 1493501909

This book is a work of fiction. While reference might be made to actual historical events, existing locations or actual diseases, the names, characters, places, and incidents are either the product of the author's imagination or are used fictitiously and any resemblance to actual persons, living or dead, business establishments, events or locales is entirely coincidental.

Acknowledgements

Many thanks to Erika Contreras, June Moreland, Sara Maddison, and Nancy Riddick for editing this book. To my children; James Walton, Mark Walton, and Melanie Roberts, for their tolerant support along with my husband Joe Hewitt who kept me focused. And, to the vast fan base for the characters in this book, many who see themselves in a similar struggle for survival.

Preface

This novel is the sequel to *Look Away, Dixieland*. This is the second novel in the "Look Away" series, which will consist of four novels that follow Skye Campbell and her family from the bombing of Pearl Harbor in 1941 to the bombing of the World Trade Center in 2001. You will follow their lives for sixty years while the world undergoes vast changes, fights more wars, and enters the space and computer age.

Readers of my first novel identified with the struggles of the main characters and want to know what happened to them. In this novel, a new family is added, ghosts of the past emerge, diseases of the era take lives, the villain is different, the settings distinctive, the tribulations real, and the emotions common to all humankind. They pull at your heart as the two families forge ahead with their lives.

The will to survive is a powerful force. The men and women of these novels are a testimony to that determination. Many people in the South suffered punishing poverty prior to and after World War II, but their struggles go back further. The War Between the States devastated the South and recovery lagged behind the rest of the United States. Then the Great Depression of the 1930s stalled progress. Those years shaped the attitudes of our grandparents who struggled to survive and cemented their attitudes about life. They passed those attitudes on to the generations that followed.

After World War II, the rebuilding of America began in the 1950s when the nuclear and space ages began. The states labeled Dixie were important in these developments and if you have not read *Look Away, Dixieland*, you will not know the entire story that put the characters in the place they are in this sequel. This novel continues with the generation that was alive during World War II, their children, and grandchildren. We return to Dixie for the first part of the book.

Skye Campbell – born 1908

(Skye married three times.)

Children of Skye:

    1.   **Virginia Ross (Jenna),** born 1925. (She changes her name to **Morgan Madison**.)

    She has one son, Clark Madison.

    2.   **Carolina Ross (Carrie),** born 1928.

    She has two children, Amanda and Dave.

    3.   **Ross Campbell,** born 1941.

    He has two children, not named in this book.

    4.   **Phillip Poschett,** born 1951.

    5.   **Josephine Poschett,** (step daughter), born 1935.

    She has one daughter, Colette. Her husband is Clark Madison.

***

David Mayer – born 1911

(He marries twice.)

Children of David Mayer:

    1.   **Emma Mayer,** born 1941 (adopted by David)

    2.   **Grace Mayer,** born 1951

CHAPTER 1

Thursday, July 3, 1980

The call came into the Morgan County, Alabama Sheriff's Department at 4:30 p.m. the day before July fourth, Independence Day weekend.

"Crap, why does someone shoot a person on the beginning of the holiday weekend? I had plans to go fishing," the detective on duty asked the dispatcher.

"I agree that it's highly inconvenient, but I have no control over the crazies in this area. A woman is down in front of Sammy Ridings' trailer. He's holed up inside with a pistol and from what he's yelling, he has plenty of ammo. A black-and-white is out there and they're calling for back up. An ambulance is on the way," the dispatcher replied.

"I'm right behind them," the detective relayed as he ran to his unmarked vehicle.

He sped through the small town of Decatur, Alabama, to Highway 31, turning south toward Velma's Trailer Park where Sammy Ridings, his wife, three kids, two dogs, and an assorted number of cats lived in a broken down mobile home. This wasn't the first time the police had been to a domestic dispute at that address. They'd been out there last week on a complaint that Sammy shot holes in a neighbor's garbage can.

Sammy liked to beat his wife and kids, and when he'd been drinking, he got mean. He also liked to shoot things, any mongrel dog in the trailer park, the windshield of some perceived enemy, the light on the pole at the end of his driveway, the plastic swimming pool next door. But he'd never shot anyone. Until today.

The detective figured that Sammy's wife was on the ground. Too old for her age, battered, wrinkled from years of chain smoking and binge drinking, she had three children who deserved a better life. Rumor had it their youngest child had a birth defect that kept him hidden from public view.

The detective pulled up to the trailer in time to see Sammy being led out the back door of the trailer in handcuffs. A young girl was crying and holding her bloody arm. A body was on the ground, covered by a quilt someone brought to the site. On the opposite side of the road two children were being cradled by a woman, the youngest was a boy with a cleft pallet.

A rookie on the force ran over to him.

"The woman on the ground isn't Sammy's wife. See for yourself. This is tragic, tragic," his words trailed off.

The detective walked over to the body. He exposed the head and took a long look at the face.

"No, oh my God, no, no...she's dead. How did this happen? How did she get involved in this mess?"

"No one knows. Guess you'll have to figure it out and you'll have to tell the judge. A real tragedy here, a real tragedy," the rookie replied as he shook his head.

CHAPTER 2

Thirty-eight years earlier
December 20, 1941

David Mayer gathered his briefcase off his desk and fumbled through the documents inside to make sure he had everything he needed. Several files, a legal pad for notes, and his glasses were there.

"I'm going out to visit Skye Campbell and then over to Madeline Cox's house. Skye wants to sell her property and I'll bet Madeline is in the mood to sell hers now that the war is raging. Call Daisy and tell her I'll be home for supper," he told his secretary, reaching for his umbrella and overcoat.

David threw his briefcase in the backseat of his 1938 Packard parked in front of his office. He noticed the sun had chased away pesky clouds that usually claimed the first part of morning. *It's going to be a clear, crisp day,* he said to himself as he slid into the car.

The eight cylinder engine started with a smooth, deep rumble. He turned east toward the low mountains where the gravel road would take him to the top of Robinson Mountain. A spectacular drive, the narrow road hugged the pinnacle of the mountain where Skye Campbell's acreage spread out from the road.

It will be good to get out of the city where I can visit the thirsty hills of the country, he thought, then laughed when he realized he'd characterized Decatur, Alabama, as a city. You could see from one end of it to the other.

David let his mind drift back to last week when he received letters from Skye and Madeline. He decided to go see them today, a few days before Christmas, since the recent snow storm had finished its business and moved east. Driving due east, he noticed patches of snow dotting the landscape in the shadows and on the backside of rocks. Old Man Winter had announced his presence then lifted his fury. He'd be back.

He knew Skye from legal work he'd done on her first husband's estate. He knew Madeline from her years of working at the courthouse, before she resigned to care for her dying husband. He wasn't sure the women knew each other; they didn't have much in common. Neither of them had a telephone. The telephone lines ended a mile out of town. It wasn't much of a chance for him to take the trip, since neither of them could drive and Skye didn't own a car.

Skye Campbell's letter stated she wanted to sell her farm and move into town. Owen, her no good second husband, had run off to join the Army the day after Pearl Harbor was bombed. In her letter she announced the birth of her baby boy, who would be a couple of weeks old. David had already made a couple of phone calls and had a prospective buyer for her property. He wasn't surprised that Owen left to join the Army. Owen was the type of man that would do this to a woman, leave her stranded with a new baby.

"How do women get mixed up with men like him?" David said to himself, talking out loud in the car. It was a bad habit of his.

David had seen Owen Campbell's hot temper several times. He was a mean character, and in the Army he might meet his match. He might not come home from this war and it might not be the Germans that got him.

David looked out the window as he drove up the mountain. The valley below stretched toward the Tennessee River. Tall pines and oaks hung out over one side of the road where a deep drop-off on the other side yielded to commanding views where the tops of the trees were below the steep road. It would be a mess if you missed a curve and skidded off. He tightened his grip on the wheel.

A lone cloud appeared out of nowhere, dropping rain on the windshield. The inside of the glass fogged from the humidity. David turned on his wipers, slowed down, and wiped the fog with his hand. Suddenly, he dreaded the fifteen mile drive on the narrow, winding road. He looked around to the back seat for his umbrella. It was back there, peeping out from under a pile of paperwork he meant to take into the house last night.

He returned his thoughts to Skye and her predicament. When Carl Ross, her first husband, died from a kick in the head by a horse, David handled the legal work on his estate. He advised Skye to sell her farm and move into town with her two girls. She wouldn't listen, and remained on the mountain raising horses, pigs, cows, and vegetables. Some of the best horses in Morgan Country came from her stock and she was making a meager living.

Skye also made and sold the best fruit cakes in the state of Alabama. Her cakes won first prize several times at the Morgan County Fair. They were three-layered cakes with apples, raisins, and other seasonal fruit that floated in a rich, cinnamon flavored batter. She frosted the cake with a caramel icing and pushed pecans on the top and sides. She baked a lot of them this time of year to sell to the grocery store in town. Maybe she would have one today and he would buy it from her, another reason to see her before Christmas.

David briefly wondered if he could buy Silver, Skye's prize stallion. If he could buy the horse, he could turn a quick profit, maybe make two hundred dollars or more, but he knew Anna, his wife, would pitch one of her fits. As sick as she was, he didn't understand how she had the energy to concentrate on making his life miserable.

Tuberculosis had eaten away most of her lungs. She weighed less than a hundred pounds, different from the sturdy woman he married six years ago, the older sister of the girl his father picked out for him, a good Jewish girl for him to produce sturdy Jewish grandchildren with. That wasn't going to happen. A few days ago, the doctor examined her and told him she had less than three months, if that long. She hadn't been out of bed for weeks and

Daisy, their colored maid, was tending to her every need. David was grateful he had Daisy. She was an angel and a damn good cook.

Anna hated David's clients. She hated everyone, except Daisy. David wanted to tell her that they couldn't afford Daisy if he didn't get more cases, but Anna had her own source of money and he let it go. Over the years, he'd fought many battles with her and lost all of them. When he protested that the house she picked out for them was over their budget, she produced five thousand for the down payment and told him she'd buy it in her own name if he didn't get a mortgage for the rest. He bought the house then they went on to the next battle, the one about the baby. She would never let the matter die.

David continued to drive up the mountain as the humming of the motor kept him in his dreamlike state. He began to hear Anna's accusations.

Suddenly her voice started, "Oh yes, that's right, I know what kind of man you are, I remember now, I remember our baby and what you produced for a child."

In a trance, he saw on the inside windshield of the car a newsreel of the birth of their baby. The little misshapen form popped up in front of him. They had waited three long years for the birth of their child, a little boy, stillborn and horribly deformed. His head was about the size of an orange and there was a hole where his mouth should have been. He didn't have a formed nose and his eyes were small dots on his face. He was small, weighing only two and a half pounds. He never took a breath, staying alive in Anna's womb through the connection of the umbilical cord to her blood supply, arrested in an early stage of development.

From that day, Anna vowed to never have another child of his, his defective sperm would never go into her body again. Several doctors they consulted told them they should try again, that this wasn't a genetic problem. One doctor suggested the deformities might be related to Anna having a case of measles early in her pregnancy. She never believed it. That had been the last of their sex life and the last of what little bit of happiness they shared.

A buck darted in front of the Packard. David swerved to miss it and he popped back to the task at hand, the trance gone, the baby erased, Anna out of his mind. He was almost to the top of the mountain where the shadows of the trees held wider patches of snow.

As David pulled up to the trail that led to Skye's house, he grabbed his umbrella then lumbered out of the car. This was going to be a messy climb and he vowed to get some weight off when the holidays were over. At thirty, he should be able to run up the path, but his desk job had added twenty pounds to his frame and inactivity had taken its toll.

Near the house, David smelled wood burning and something baking. He noticed the primitive log house, not much more than a shack, small and drab with a porch on the front and a barn behind the house where the woods started. A few chickens scattered as he knocked on the door.

Skye's daughter, Carrie, as pretty as her mother and almost as tall, showed him to a chair in front of the fireplace. David sensed she had matured a lot since he had last seen her but he was more amazed at the baby, a perfect little boy, red-headed like his father. He rested in a small basket near the hearth, sound asleep.

Skye was petite with full breasts and a toned body, her waist a little thick from the recent birth. Her dark hair, pulled back and braided, emphasized her Cherokee Indian heritage passed down from her mother. She appeared happier than David had ever seen her. Her eyes sparkled, her smile revealed straight teeth and her light olive skin was smooth with fine lines at the corner of her eyes.

In her younger years, she had probably been a head turner but her clothes revealed poverty that diminished her attractiveness. Dressed in a ragged skirt, a patched blouse, and worn out boots, she appeared older than her mid-thirties. Work in the sun and wind, frequent childbirth, and abuse had pulled her down to a stratum where women die too young, leaving their children behind for a younger wife who would repeat the process.

Skye came to the point immediately. "I want to sell the farm and move to town. I can't keep this place going since Owen left for the war. My sister sent me a letter and said there are jobs at the meat processing plant. Jenna has already left to find work in Mobile."

"I think that's a good decision. I have a friend who's interested in buying your farm, and I'll find you a place to live in town," David assured her.

"Okay, I'm ready this time," Skye replied, reminding David she'd not listened to him years ago.

"I'm sure I can get your asking price. I'll be back in two weeks, so start packing." David gathered his briefcase to leave.

Skye handed him a fruitcake, a sack of black walnuts, a sack of shelled pecans, and a five dollar bill. David asked for another fruitcake, gave her the five dollars back and told her they were even.

Skye smiled and said, "Thank you Mr. Mayer, you're so kind to us."

David lumbered to his car and drove ten miles to his next stop. On the way, he saw the Tennessee River on his right, peeking out between hills and barren trees. Occasionally he caught a glimpse of a barge being pushed by a tug boat as it slowly made its way toward the Ohio River.

David had never been in Madeline Cox's home and he'd not seen her in two years. She had been a clerk at the courthouse but left to care for her sick husband. Cancer claimed him six months later and she remained on the mountain with her children. He'd never met them but had seen photos of a young boy and a cute little girl on her desk. He felt honored she'd picked him to do some legal work. He guessed he got the job because most of the attorneys in Morgan County were gone to war.

David tried to join the Army but his partial club foot decided his fate. He walked with a slight limp and over the years corrective shoes helped, but he wasn't fit for long marches. It wasn't his choice to stay behind, so he decided he'd do as much for people as he could. He reduced his rates and if someone couldn't pay, he'd work out a payment plan or do the work *pro bono*.

David rounded the curve to the Cox house and marveled at the neatness of it. The white, clapboard house had been freshly painted. Blue shutters framed the windows where lace curtains hung. A perfectly crafted white picket fence surrounded the neat yard. A flag stone walk led to the porch with a blue front door. A swing moved gently in the wind as a beagle hopped off a pillow and sniffed at his shoes. Madeline opened the front door. David walked inside to a room filled with French furnishings.

"Hello, Mr. Mayer, so good to see you," Madeline remarked as she shook his hand.

The white streak in her gray hair appeared wider and her face held more wrinkles, but otherwise she looked the same. A girl holding a baby came into the living room, followed by a teenaged boy.

David settled on the green silk sofa. The girl sat in a matching chair, the baby in her arms. The infant was wrapped in a pink blanket. The girl, with long, blonde, curly hair, light blue eyes, and freckles across her nose, was the most beautiful girl he'd ever seen.

"Mr. Mayer, please let me introduce you to my daughter Daphne. She's holding Emma, her baby. This young man is my son Joseph, who turned seventeen on Thanksgiving Day. He'll be returning with you today to join the Army. I have no way of getting him to town since I don't drive, so your being here serves a double purpose. Since Daphne and I will be stuck up here in the wilderness with no man around, I need to sell this place and buy a house in Decatur. I'm hoping you can help me achieve that," Madeline said, as Daphne handed her the baby.

"Tell me about your property," David suggested between sips of mint flavored tea Daphne brought into the living room. A tray of cookies followed.

"There are one hundred fifty three acres in this parcel around the house. I also own three lots in town and a two acre track out on Bluff City Road. I want to sell everything but the lots in town. We hope to move to Decatur, and I hear there's a position at the courthouse open. I'll be applying for that," Madeline revealed as the baby began to whimper.

"Will the father of the baby be moving to town with you?" David asked, surprising himself at the question that popped out unexpectedly.

"No, the father is not a part of the baby's life," Daphne added quickly, leveling her eyes to his.

"It will take a while to sell that much property, but I'm sure I can find a buyer. The lots out on Bluff City road will sell quickly, and that should give you enough for a down payment on a house."

David looked at Daphne as he felt warmth spread from his neck to his face. He had embarrassed the girl and now he was blushing.

Thirty minutes later, he'd retrieved the information he needed but Madeline wanted to hear the latest about everyone they knew in common at the courthouse. Daphne took the baby, put the pink blanket over the bodice of her blouse then slid the baby under the blanket. David heard the baby suckle. He had never seen a woman nurse a baby and it overwhelmed him. He tried not to stare. She acted like it was the most normal thing in the world, so he relaxed.

Idle conversation followed as Joseph brought two suitcases into the front room. David realized it was time to go as Madeline hugged her son. Daphne pulled the baby from under the blanket and wrapped the blanket around the child, laying her on the sofa. The sun began to sink in the winter sky as the two women followed Joseph to the front porch.

"I want a letter every week," Madeline said to her son as tears ran down her cheeks.

"You come home from the war, you hear me? Don't get yourself killed. You're too important to me, to Emma," Daphne said as he picked up his suitcase.

"I promise. I'll come back. It will take a lot to get a big guy like me," Joseph said, trying to be light hearted. Daphne handed Joseph a book of French poems and a small Bible.

"You speak French?" David asked, surprised.

"Yes, we all speak French. It's my native tongue," Madeline replied, wiping away tears.

"I'll come back in a couple of weeks, and hopefully I'll have some proposals for the property," David said as he and Joseph got into the car. Joseph looked back once when they started down the mountain. David took him to the address in town that Madeline gave him.

As Joseph exited the car, he asked, "Will you help Mom and Daphne find a new place to live? They'll need the help of a good man and I wish you could be that man, the one they can call on in emergencies. Mother talks well of you."

"I promise I'll be there for them. Don't worry, I'll find them a suitable home and go by and check on them every week or so," David assured him.

David drove slowly by his office. The closed sign was out and the lights off. Gladys had left early again. He looked at his pocket watch; it was 4:48 p.m. He was going to have to talk to her about leaving before five.

He drove down the middle of town and thought about Joseph going off to war, a mere lad doing his part for his country. It reminded him that he'd been cheated out of the experience, out of the camaraderie of the men, out of his part in the war against an enemy that he knew first hand. He had seen how the Germans treated Jews. His parents had sense enough to escape Poland and leave everything behind, but it had cost his mother her life and the life of his little sister.

His stomach rumbled when he turned down his street. He remembered all he had consumed since breakfast was a cookie and the mint tea. He hoped Daisy cooked something he liked for supper.

As he drove further down the street, he noticed several cars parked at his house. Dr. Roper's car was one of them. People were on the porch, standing outside. Daisy ran out to meet him. Something was wrong. Daisy was crying.

"My Anna has done gone home to be with the angels, she's gone, she's gone," Daisy whimpered.

David hurried inside.

CHAPTER 3

December 30, 1941

The Christmas holidays came and went and David didn't notice. To him, the holiday signified the end of another year and he wanted 1941 to disappear. Anna's death took him by surprise, he had expected her to last longer.

He buried her before sunset the day after she died, in the Jewish tradition. The people in town that knew them would read about her funeral in the obituaries after it was over. A rabbi from Birmingham drove up and did a graveside service. Six people attended, including David. It was hard to see the casket go into the grave and know Anna would never come back to him. He couldn't believe she was gone; she was only thirty-five, a few years older than him.

The day after the funeral, he and Daisy cleaned Anna's room. He took all the linens, pillows, curtains, and the large wool rug out to the back yard. He piled on the feather mattress that reeked of urine and her last hemorrhage. Then he burned everything. Daisy cried and went back into the house. David stayed until there was nothing but ashes.

The next day, he told Daisy to scrub down everything in her bedroom and the bathroom, but to leave Anna's clothes alone. When she finished he opened all the windows.

"The winter winds will do the job. By morning, the stench and the germs will be gone," he mumbled to Daisy as he took her home.

"I loved her like one of mine. She quit breathing after that last coughing spell, she didn't take another breath," Daisy declared as tears rolled down her cheeks.

"Take off two weeks and get some rest. You deserve the break. Consider it a paid vacation," David said when he dropped her off in front of her modest home in Low Town, the small settlement south of town where the colored people of the county lived.

Her husband watched for her to come home every day, waiting patiently on the front porch. He always waved at David and smiled at his wife, helping her up the front porch stairs. Low Town had no building codes. People bought lots and built what they could afford. Some homes were brick, some made of logs, most of them were clapboard, and a couple were from the old days when dog trots were popular. One still had the open space, the other had been enclosed with a crude door in the middle.

The next morning, David started his search in Anna's room. He knew she hid jewelry and diamonds from him, which he suspected were in her bedroom. He didn't have to search for the envelopes, he knew where they were. The envelopes she smuggled out of France came with them on the ship and then by train to Decatur. Each envelope or small box had a name on the front with an address. On some envelopes there were notes and inside the packages were jewelry, diamonds, gold, coins, money; anything people wanted to preserve for a new start when the war ended.

Jewish friends by the hundreds gave the envelopes to Anna and her sister to keep for them until the war ended. Then they planned to retrieve them for a fresh start. They were not the only ones doing this, but with Anna and Eva's connections in Poland, Germany, and France, they smuggled hundreds of packages out, hiding the envelopes in their school books, underneath their skirts, and in their blouses. Then they stashed them in a hidden place for safekeeping. Anna brought a trunk of the envelopes with her to America.

After David and Anna arrived in Decatur, Anna placed the trunk in the attic but the jewels given to her for payment were hidden in her room. She also had a lot of money in various bank accounts, money she'd invested for her family who owned a jewelry business in Warsaw. They bought and traded diamonds with a company in South Africa and were smart enough to move money to New York with bankers they trusted.

Anna showed David some of the diamonds when she was pregnant, when she was in a state of bliss, before the baby was born. Then she hid them and never told David where they were.

I wonder if she would have told me about her hiding place had she lived longer, if she had forgiven me for fathering our

27

deformed child, he reflected. Instead, death slipped in, taking her secret hiding place with her. She had no notice that morning that she had a few hours to live. He knew that because they talked before he left for the office. They agreed on the night's activities, they would listen to the war news on the radio in her room and she would eat supper in bed.

He looked around her room, the bed now a dark hole, no mattress over the slats, the place where they shared their love gone, erased, expunged. David found the smell had dissipated in the frigid room. He closed the windows and began his search. He looked through every drawer, turned them over, looked behind furniture, searched the pockets in her clothes, turned them inside out, opened all the books in her room, emptied her purses, and examined the floor for loose boards. Nothing, he found nothing.

Frustrated, he left her room and the house. He walked around the yard then decided to take a drive. He went north, over the bridge toward Athens. He drove slowly, noticing geese flying in a V formation over the stark cotton fields. An old scarecrow waved at him, its arm catching in the wind. A mile down the road, another scarecrow guarding a winter garden stood tall with a ragged shirt in tatters, a hawk sitting on the top of its head. Bare trees and the bleak landscape stretched to the horizon.

It's December, everything dies in December, he reflected as he arrived in Athens. David found a small café open and realized he was hungry. Inside, he noticed the small dining room where the tables, covered with red and white checked oil cloth, held salt and pepper shakers, a bowl of sugar, and eating utensils. Chairs painted with brown, glossy paint bounced light off the shiny finish. He ordered a bowl of beef stew and drank two cups of coffee. He finished with apple pie then bought the local newspaper.

He took a different route home, one through the country that ended in Moulton. Almost dusk when he pulled into his driveway, he hesitated in the car.

She'll never be there again, she's gone, he said to himself.

He walked around the block, waved to his neighbors, and went inside. He read the paper then listened to the news. An hour later he resumed his search, turning on every light to illuminate the corners.

David looked behind and under the heavy furniture downstairs. Then he pulled a chair out of the dining room and looked over the top of the large china cabinet in the kitchen. On top, he found an old hand bag Anna had used when he met her in Paris. He opened it, then carried it to the kitchen table and poured out the contents.

Inside were three bank books and a small cardboard box. Carefully, he cut the string on the box and poured the contents on a plate. Glittering diamonds and other precious stones fell out, some as large as a marble.

In the bottom of her purse he found three diamond bracelets, another one with three rubies in a wide gold band, three solitaire diamond rings, and other rings, some with diamond clusters, some with emeralds. He reached into a pocket in the back of the purse and found three keys. They probably belonged to safety deposit boxes in the banks in New York City where the bank books revealed she had accounts.

David checked the top of every piece of furniture in the house. He didn't find anything else. He went through her clothes again, feeling all the seams for lumps where something might have been sewn in, but he found nothing. He looked through all the boxes of powder and cosmetics in the bathroom. There was nothing in them.

He went back to her closet and looked into the toes of the six pairs of shoes she owned. They were empty. Next, he pulled down shoe boxes that she had saved. He found three boxes in the back, behind old quilts. Those boxes contained bank statements. He carried them to the kitchen then shut the door to her bedroom. Now all he needed to do was follow the trail Anna left behind. The cancelled checks would make it easy.

Who was helping her and what did they know? Who is her contact? David wrote down the questions because he had seen no instructions on what to do with the envelopes in the trunk in the attic. Until he knew more, he'd leave the envelopes as they were, but the jewelry belonged to him as her heir. All of her assets were his. She'd left him a fortune.

All night he worked on the bank books, statements, deposit slips, withdrawals, and correspondence. She had set up three accounts, one for her parents, one for her sister Eva, and one for her with a pay on death to David. He was convinced he'd found all the statements and had a reasonable understanding of what she left. The unknown was what was in those safety deposit boxes in New York City.

David tried not to think about the fate of Eva and his in-laws. There were reports of movement of Jews out of the ghettos but no one seemed to have a clear answer to where they went. Rumors of work camps and prisons surfaced then were debunked by the Germans. It was too horrific to contemplate.

Anna begged her parents to get out of Poland. They assured her they would, and arranged passage out of Warsaw in July of 1939. They balked at the last minute, waiting on a delivery of diamonds to arrive. Anna received a letter from them in late August. They stated Eva had come to visit and they all planned to leave the next day. Anna never heard from them again. None of them.

Her parent's last letter stayed by Anna's bedside in her Torah. She read it every week, crying each time she held it then cursing them for being so greedy. Most of their money had been moved to New York, to banks in the Jewish sector of the city. Anna went there each spring during the early years of their marriage, before she was too sick to travel.

She took the train to New York on family business, as she called the reason for the trips. She never wanted David go with her, claiming it was her duty to preserve the family assets and that he didn't need to know their business. But he knew her mission, not from her but from Eva, who was afraid Anna would die and the secret with her.

Eva, the girl David's father had picked out for him to marry, had no attraction to David and it showed when they met in Paris. But Anna, her older sister, let him know she would marry him and she wanted to immigrate to America.

"Anna is not healthy, she has advanced consumption," Eva warned him on the eve of their engagement announcement.

"There are cures, treatments in America. I want to marry her," David countered.

After they married, David realized Anna made the right moves to snag him. She gave him a sample of her assets one night when Eva had gone to the opera. One tumble in bed and he knew he wanted more. Did he love her? In his own way he did. Mostly he settled for Anna and she settled for him.

I need to contact her parents and let them know she died, he said to himself, but he had no way to contact them. Letters they sent after Germany invaded Poland were returned. *If they survive the war, they know how to find me. Then I will tell them about Anna.*

David sat at the table fidgeting with a napkin when a wave of exhaustion covered him. He put the jewelry and jewels back into Anna's old purse then carried it to his bedroom. He put the purse in the drawer with his socks and the shoe boxes full of statements on top of his chest.

I need sleep, deep sleep, he acknowledged. The stress of the last few days had taken a toll. He ran the bathtub full of hot water, then poured in a cup of Epsom salts before he climbed in. His muscles relaxed and he felt his blood pressure drop as the water surrounded him.

Exiting the tub, he decided to shave. David noticed his ordinary face in the mirror as he lathered his cheeks. He knew he looked older than thirty. Wrinkles had already formed around his eyes and he had a deep one on his forehead. His mousy brown hair had started to recede. He wasn't tall and tended to slump. His stocky body lumbered when he walked due to his foot deformity. He hated the word *deformity* but it was that. A partial club foot is a deformity.

He searched Anna's medication and found three sleeping pills. He took two, then built a roaring fire in the fireplace, gathered two quilts and a couple of pillows, and stretched out on the sofa. He watched the spits of fire curl over the wood and dart upward, breaking into pointed flames. He inhaled the scent of burning hickory and oak, the aroma like a drug entering his senses. He felt heat hit his face and without noticing, he started to sob. He wept for the baby he and Anna lost, the children he would never have, and for Anna. They had a few good years before it all fell apart.

She never trusted me but I cannot dwell on this. I must let the humiliation she heaped on me fade away and I will erase her cruel remarks from my memory. I must stay busy and I will, there is a war going on and things to do. I have to get back to work, David said to himself, his brain foggy with grief. He went to his bed, crawled in, and pulled the covers over him, tucking the quilt around his neck.

He had never felt so lonely, so alone.

CHAPTER 4

February, 1942

David found a buyer for Skye Campbell's farm with one phone call. He drove out to present the offer. Her face lit up with the news.

"Well, that was a quick sale. I'll take it." Skye smiled as the words gushed out.

"I figured you would, so I rented a house in town for you. It's close to the school Carrie will attend. I'll send a truck to move your things. I know a couple of boys who can load it and you have Owen's old truck you can put stuff in," David suggested.

"I don't know how to drive," Skye reminded him.

"One of the boys will drive it, and once you're living in town I'll teach you to drive. You need to know how if you're going to work at the meat processing plant. It's five miles out of town, too far for you to walk. You're also going to need a car. That old truck isn't reliable. I'll be looking around for one," David advised as he looked at her simple furniture and wondered how much she'd keep.

"Are you sure I can learn to drive? I'm frightened about the traffic," Skye replied with the question.

"Traffic? There's no traffic in Decatur. Rush hour is six cars behind the only red light. You should drive in New York City. They have traffic," David laughed, then changed the subject.

"I heard Colin joined the Army about two weeks after Owen left. Someone said he was at the recruiter's office then they saw him leave on the bus."

Colin, Owen's younger brother, had lived in town at the local boarding house. Owen and Colin were close in spite of the ten year age gap. Until Colin moved into town, he'd lived out in the woods with Owen. Rumor had it they ran moonshine whiskey, which was against the law in Morgan County. David knew they were rough men and stayed away from them.

"Yes, he told us he would. I hope he does well, he's a good kid," Skye added while Carrie held the baby.

"That boy had a rough life with his mother dying so young and Owen raising him out in the woods. They have a brother in town, a half-brother. His father was their mother's first husband. Harold is a decent man with a three children. Do you know him?" David asked, making conversation as Skye packed three fruitcakes in a box for him.

"I met him and his wife once. They were nice to me," Skye said as she handed the box to him.

David placed a parcel on her table.

"Open this after I leave. Be ready to move ten days from today. You need to sell everything you don't want to take to town. All your animals, everything has to go. I'll put an ad in the paper and I expect you'll get people coming up here in a few days. I'll see you on moving day and we'll go to the office so you can sign over the property and get a check. I'll have the utilities turned on for you at the house in town," David instructed her.

"Can you advise me on how to open a bank account? I don't have one," Skye asked.

"I'll get you to the bank so you can open an account and deposit the check. That's an easy thing and it won't take long," David assured her then asked, "anything else?"

"Well, uh, I've never lived in a house with electricity. Is it going to be hard to learn how to use it?" Skye asked.

"It's simple. You'll have the hang of that electric stove in five minutes," David laughed. "By the end of the first week, you'll be baking cakes. I want the first one out of that electric oven. You're going to do fine and Carrie will love being in town. There are some good shops in Decatur and I heard a new grocery store is opening. There's a great park by the river where you can stroll with the baby and watch the trains and cars cross over the bridge."

David left, taking the cakes with him. He thought about Skye as he drove down the mountain. Her life would change dramatically after she moved and he hoped Owen stayed in the Army long enough for Skye to build a new life. He supposed Skye loved him or she wouldn't be his wife. He wondered what women saw in a man like Owen. He guessed some men had an appeal as the "rough and tough" kind. They seem to be magnets to needy women.

What kind of bum would leave a needy wife with a newborn?
he asked himself.

David would help her move, get her settled, teach her to
drive, and the rest would be up to her. She'd have some money for
their new start, thanks to her first husband, a good man who died
too young. As he drove down the mountain, he reflected back to
times he'd seen Skye and the girls come to town to buy supplies
and groceries. On those trips, the family would drive down in
Owen's beat up truck, all four of them crowded in the front seat.
Skye always wore the same denim skirt she had on today, one with
a ragged hemline and stained pockets. Her feet were covered with
frayed socks and run down boots. Her appearance delegated her to
a pauper status she assumed without knowing the status existed.

When Skye began to show her last pregnancy, David saw her
in the grocery store, the girls in tow and Owen outside the front
door, waiting on them to check out. Owen didn't approve of Skye
talking to people, especially men, no matter if she knew them.
Once David saw Owen slap her on the sidewalk, and he knew from
bruises on her face that wasn't the only time. When David didn't
see them for a couple of months he figured the baby had been born.
Then the letter came from Skye.

David didn't want her new life to begin where the old one
left off. He put some gently worn clothes for her and her girls in
the package he left, things that had been Anna's. A life in a better
place was what they needed. He understood her oldest daughter
had moved away to find work in Mobile.

Good for her, I hope she does well, he said to himself as the outskirts of town came into view. Winding through the bare streets to his dark house, he realized he didn't dread going inside the empty structure, a two story house in the historic district of Decatur.

I've started a new chapter in my life, one I have to handle but then, well…I have no choice, do I? he asked himself.

Anna had left him a fortune and all he had to do was go to New York and find the trail. He loved New York in the spring.

He couldn't wait to taste its treats.

CHAPTER 5

March, 1942

Skye knew the move to town would be traumatic. She had never lived in town and didn't want to leave her home, her garden, and the animals, especially Silver, her prized stallion. She didn't want to leave the land where her mother had run through the forest that edged closer to the barn each year.

Leaving the mountain meant leaving the ways of her childhood, her heritage. She grew up in the deep woods of south Tennessee, free and wild, running through the timber, trotting through fast moving creeks, chasing deer, climbing mountains, bathing in the river.

Skye's mother kept her Cherokee ways until the day she died. She could hunt and fish like a man, and skin a deer in five minutes. She kept an outside fire where meat was cooked or smoked. She knew the herbs and plants of the forest, and collected them in homemade baskets. Every June they picked berries, and in the fall they gathered hickory nuts and black walnuts. They knew the places where deep, cool water flowed, where the catfish swam, where the migrating geese stopped on their way to another destination.

Skye was the oldest of the Simmons children. Her sister and two brothers had given into city life years ago, both of them now living in Texas, near Fort Worth. Her sister lived in Guntersville, a nearby town in the mountains of north Alabama.

All of Skye's children had been born on Robinson Mountain in the log cabin her first husband bought from his parents. They added two rooms and enlarged the barn to shelter the horses they bred and sold. Their garden and chickens supplied them with food, and a cow provided milk and butter. Venison, rabbits, squirrels, wild turkeys, and hogs kept meat on the table. They had everything they needed until Carl Ross was kicked in the head by a horse and died the next day.

Skye maintained the farm, scratching out a living, selling horses, cows, eggs, and baking cakes to sell in town. Her two girls rode the school bus to school and Skye encouraged them to graduate from high school, something she had not done.

Her oldest daughter, Virginia, most of the time called Jenna, quit school after the eighth grade and Skye could not persuade her to continue. Carrie, named Carolina at birth, desired a high school diploma and vowed she'd finish high school and wanted to experience college.

Ross, born three months ago, was the product of her second marriage. Now she realized the horrible mistake she made the day she married Owen Campbell, a man she knew a short time. She did not know his abusive manner and had never seen his hot temper before their marriage. Now he was no longer with her, and he wouldn't return to hurt her or her children again.

Once the decision to move to town culminated in the sale of her place, she sold all the animals to two men who drove down from Tennessee. One man bought Silver and the other man bought the cow, the other three horses, and her pig. He paid her three hundred dollars for Silver, a fortune. That morning, she sold the rest of the chickens to a neighbor, then a man from town bought all the tools in the barn, the old wagon, and Owen's guns. He asked about Owen's truck, but she needed it for the move. He promised to come back and buy it when she moved to town.

Skye saved some of her kitchen things, old dishes she'd bought when she married the first time, the handmade quilts from her mother, and the coal shuttle that had belonged to her grandfather Simmons. Now she had to say goodbye to the home where she began her life with Carl Ross as a virgin bride of sixteen.

Surprised at how quick Mr. Mayer found a buyer for her property, she did not have time to reconsider the move. He had advised her to leave the farm after Carl died, but she wouldn't, her fears of living among the people in town guiding her decision. She felt she didn't fit in town. People there avoided her and her girls.

After Mr. Mayer left that morning, Skye opened the parcel he left. Tears flooded her eyes. Inside the box were clothes for her and Carrie, fine things, probably from his wife who had died a few weeks ago. *He doesn't want me to wear my rags to town*, Skye realized. Skye decided she'd burn their old clothes before they moved. They would wear the new things on moving day, then they would go shopping and replace everything from that store she'd seen on Main Street.

She had never had the nerve to go inside the department store in Decatur. She and the girls stood outside and looked at the sweaters, blouses, dresses, and shoes on display from the sidewalk. Other people made a wide berth around them, she could see their eyes traveling to their clothes in the reflection of the window.

None of us will wear rags again, Skye said to herself after sorting the things Mr. Mayer left in the parcel. She held up a pink blouse, turning it in the light, touching the soft fabric and the white lace on the sleeves and bodice.

Skye knew Mr. Mayer loved his wife, it showed in his eyes when he talked about her. He bought cakes for her, their maid, and his secretary. Skye went by their house once, to the back door to deliver a cake. Anna Mayer insisted she wanted to meet her. She went inside and marveled at the furnishings in their home, the large rooms, fancy dishes, the lace table cloth on the dining room table, the patterned rugs with fringe on the ends, the piano in the corner. Anna, bedridden by then, thanked Skye and asked her to bring her girls to see her when she got well.

She will not get well, Skye knew when the sick woman coughed from deep inside her chest. Anna Mayer died six months later.

Skye wished she could tell Mr. Mayer the truth about Owen, her second husband. He did not leave immediately after Pearl Harbor to join the Army. That was a cover for the truth. Owen died the night of December 6th and a few hours later, she and Carrie threw his body in the Tennessee River. Owen died as he lived, fighting violently, assaulting the two women closest to him. She caught him and her oldest daughter Jenna in the barn, Owen on top of Jenna, ramming his penis into her, her legs locked around him, meeting his thrusts with pleasure.

Skye pulled him off her sixteen-year-old daughter. Owen grabbed a skinning knife off the bench in the barn then he ran toward her with the knife, aiming at her belly. Eight months pregnant, she couldn't move fast enough to get away from him. The knife caught her in the top of her breast then he pulled his arm up to stab her again. Jenna screamed for him not to hurt her mother. Jenna picked up a pitch fork. Owen turned on Jenna, holding the knife like he would strike her.

Skye hit him in the back with a shovel and he fell into the pitchfork, the tines going all the way through him. Jenna pulled the pitchfork out and he fell onto the hay. He bled to death. There was no way to save him.

Then Skye shook Carrie awake inside the house and told her to go to the barn to help her sister. She decided they would tie him to the sled, and she and Carrie took him down the mountain path to the river where they threw him in. A foot of snow covered everything and there was no way they could bury him in the frozen ground. On the way back, Skye went into labor and Carrie delivered Ross the morning of December 7th, 1941.

That morning, Jenna rode Silver to town after taking $100 from her mother's jar of money. Jenna left a note and said she would get a job in Mobile and pay her back. They had not heard from her since she left.

When Colin came to see them the next day, he told them about the bombing of Pearl Harbor. The war gave Skye the perfect reason for Owen's disappearance. *He ran off and joined the Army,* was the lie she told Colin two weeks later. The lie seemed plausible, he may have done that had he lived. Then Colin joined the Army, hoping to find Owen. With both of them gone, it made her move to town easier.

But, what am I going to do when Owen doesn't come home from the war? Can I say he was killed over there? Will that work? Can it be checked? And what about Jenna? Will she find me in town? Skye tried to run all the possibilities through her mind.

Skye knew she had failed Jenna. If she hadn't married Owen, if she had listened to Mr. Mayer's advice and moved to town after her first husband died, Jenna would still be with her. She failed Jenna, and now she had another child to raise, Owen's child.

Never again will I fail my children. Carrie and Ross would have the things they need and deserve. They will have the opportunity to graduate from high school, to get a decent job, meet educated people. And Ross will grow up to be a good man, a man like my first husband, Skye said to herself.

Carrie, her sweet Carrie, her thirteen-year-old daughter who helped her drag Owen to the river on the sled, had undergone more than a young girl deserved. Sometimes Carrie asked about Owen's body.

"When do you think he'll float to the top?" Carrie asked her a few days after the river took him.

"I don't know. The cold water will keep him from bloating as fast as warm water would. I hope he floats over to some place where no one will find him. There are hundreds of miles of shoreline on the river," Skye suggested.

"What will we do if they find him?"

"We'll face that when we have to. Until then, we keep telling people he joined the Army. You don't need to worry, you did nothing wrong." Skye tried to reassure her daughter, who had spent the last few days helping her pack their things.

"Everything is ready and I'm going to bed. Give me Ross, he can sleep with me his last night in the house where he was born." Carrie held out her arms for him, snuggling him and kissing his chubby cheeks. Skye watched her daughter and newborn disappear behind a rough wooden door.

She walked into the kitchen and glanced at the wood burning stove, aware that she would never cook on one again. She'd lived in this house eighteen years. Skye felt a few tears escape, then she saw the Montgomery Ward catalog lying in the middle of the table. She turned to the women's clothing section. She wanted to buy a few things for herself, a tailored skirt, a patterned blouse, a leather handbag, and a pair of high heeled shoes. She had never owned a pair of high heeled shoes. She wanted to look *elegant*. She saw that word in the catalog and wasn't sure what it meant. She would ask someone at the meat packing plant when she started to work.

Skye closed the catalog, looked at her calloused hands, worn-out shoes, and her ragged skirt with stains, rips, and patches. Skye closed the catalog and took a small mirror off the wall, one Owen had used to shave. She looked at her face and saw a woman older than her thirty-four years.

"Owen Campbell, you will not defeat me. I'm not ugly and I'm not old. Thirty-four is not old. I can look like a lady. I can be elegant, I know I can."

Skye walked out the back door of the house and took a deep breath. She inhaled the aroma of pine, cedar, and wet earth in the crisp, night air. She heard the swishing sound of tree branches hitting the roof of the house. Smoke from the fireplace drifted upward, carrying sparks from the fireplace that traveled upward then floated downward, mixing with millions of stars in the inky blackness. An owl hooted, a coyote yipped in the distance as a star streaked toward the horizon.

Tomorrow her life would change. She wondered how much. There was no way to know.

CHAPTER 6

April, 1942

David remembered the frigid winters in New York City, how the wind wound around the buildings and sucked you into a stiff gale when you stepped off the curb to the cavernous streets. He had never forgotten the filthy snow, slippery sidewalks, and the cars speeding by, throwing slush on the pedestrians, the drivers never looking back to see if people dodged the icy missiles.

He remembered how the rats would scurry across the streets to find warm pipes in basements, how the bare trees allowed soft light to filter through to the slushy soil where birds tried to find worms tunneling up for a glimpse of sunlight.

During the frigid months of winter, the residents of New York hurried to get off the streets, dashing to a revolving door or to the entrance of their flat. That's why he waited for spring to return to the city he loved.

On his calendar, David blocked out the last two weeks of April and the first week of May for his trip. By the time he boarded the north bound train, he'd helped Skye Campbell and Madeline Cox settle in town. True to her word, Skye brought David the first cake she baked in the electric oven. She seemed to have adjusted to her new life, finding the clothes he gave her and her daughter. He'd seen her wearing a new outfit in the grocery store. She'd had her hair cut in a chin length bob and pink lipstick brightened her face. He looked at her shoes. They were new, patent leather with a two inch heel.

She'll be fine, she's already adjusted, he said to himself as a smile spread over his face.

He arranged the same truck and boys to move Madeline Cox, her daughter and granddaughter to town. He found a buyer for part of her land and she bought a house in Decatur. He noticed a couple of weeks after she moved she had a job as a clerk in the tax collector's office.

Satisfied he had done all he could to keep his promise to watch over people the soldiers left behind, David boarded the train to New York City in good spirits. He settled into a seat by the window and relaxed when the train pulled out of the station. He'd looked forward to the trip for months. He watched the scenery unfold, ate in the dining room, and enjoyed a cocktail and smoke in the club car.

Each day, a newsboy from a different city hopped on the train when it stopped for passengers. News of the war filled the headlines, changes in factories dominated the inside pages, casualties from battles consumed the back pages.

Of particular interest to him were the articles about the changes wrought on America. Factories had been retooled to produce tanks, airplanes, and ammunition for the European war and the American forces. Cars would no longer be produced and he was glad he had his Packard, a reliable automobile that never failed to crank. He read about livestock prices, recruitment quotas, and how rationing had started in some cities. The newspaper predicted American citizens would get ration cards for gasoline, food, cheese, milk, bread, and sugar. Beginning next week, city lights would be dimmed or turned off at night so submarines could not find coastal cities or a stray bomber find a cluster of houses.

When David finished the paper, he would pass it on to another passenger, then pull out *For Whom the Bell Tolls*, a novel he'd found among Anna's books. At night he slept, covered with a blanket he stuffed in his suitcase, his head propped by his rolled up coat. He liked riding the train, the only way to get to New York unless you wanted to drive three weeks over horrible, unpaved roads with gasoline in short supply.

He relished the food in the dining room, where weighted silver sat on top of starched white linens, where stemware sparkled in the overhead gas light, where the waiters served in white gloves and stiff, white linen jackets. He liked that a different person sat with him each night, sometimes it was a business man, sometimes a couple. That provided opportunities for him to converse with someone.

Finally the train arrived at Grand Central Station. David found the men's lavatory, shaved, brushed his teeth, changed his shirt, and hailed a taxi. On the way to his hotel, he remembered why he loved New York in the spring. In Central Park, trees were budding pale green sprouts as tender shoots of grass began to overtake the dormant straw, uncovered as the snow melted and flowed down into the East River.

In Central Park, daffodils danced in the wind as forsythia bloomed beside dark junipers, bordered by a brilliant, pink crab apple. He inhaled the scent of lilacs then saw a few down by the small lake, their lavender flowers sporting white tips.

People were everywhere, men in uniforms headed to the waterfront to embark on troop ships, busy merchants standing outside their doors beckoning people in, street vendors hawking their merchandise, business men rushing to their offices, restaurants full of hungry people, and women in trousers disappearing into the factories to work at the jobs the men left behind.

He saw an older man walking a King Charles spaniel, holding the leash with one hand and his hat with the other one. When the taxi stalled in traffic he heard warblers, swallows, magpies, and a mockingbird singing in the trees, looking for a mate or chasing off an intruder where they had a nest. The city was vibrant, noisy, and busy. David felt more alive here than anywhere.

It was a different city than the one he witnessed when his parents shuttled him through Ellis Island in 1917. Gone were the occasional horse drawn wagons, the snorting mules pulling delivery trucks, the waste of the animals that mixed with the trash and rotten food that added to the stench of decay and filth. He didn't see people in rags with worn out shoes and tattered coats.

The beggars and the drawn faces of the indigent were gone. Absent were dirty children with sunken eyes and hollow cheeks, the torrid headlines of suicides that filled the obituaries each day, even the mongrel dogs that guarded the garbage piles. The time he spent in New York as a boy was a memory too vivid too forget and too horrid to remember.

War changed everything. Now, the city was bustling with new energy, it was marching to a different cadence. There was a new odor in the city, one of frying sausages, grilled onions, baking bread laced with cinnamon or was it cloves? There was a fishy whiff but it was okay, that meant the fish market was still there, selling the catch of the day, the men still throwing the slippery missiles around, sorting them to sell.

David knew the poverty was still there, hidden in the tenements where families struggled to keep warm in the cold water flats. Many of the poor died during the harsh winters when pneumonia, cholera, tuberculosis, and dysentery claimed the elderly, young, and weak. David knew how they lived for he had been one of them. He remembered how hard it was to climb six flights of stairs to a frigid apartment where there was little food and sparse heat.

He even remembered back in Poland the discussion his parents had about taking the steamer to America, then they were on it, in the bunks in the belly of the ship for endless days. Nights slid by as the four of them shared a narrow bed. He still heard the moans, grunting, and snoring in the dormitory where foul air circulated with the stench of spoiled food, body odor, and overflowing toilets. Six days into the journey a blast of frigid wind found its way down the staircase, the fresh air welcomed by the masses. Then a storm tossed the ship and vomit from the seasick passengers added to the stench. Later that day David joined them, dizziness and nausea claiming his body.

Lethargic from not eating, he lay on the bunk and yearned to return to Poland. Then there was a lot of excitement among the passengers and his father took him to the deck and held him up to see the Statute of Liberty as the ship slid into New York harbor. He remembered the date, January 15th, 1917, and how the tears ran down his mother's face as she clutched his little sister, the little sister who wouldn't live through that first winter, whopping cough taking her quickly. His mother would die later that year, heartbroken and beaten, typhoid claiming her frail body.

David and his father had lived in a two-room flat in Williamsburg where the Hasidic Jews with their long black coats, hats, and curly sideburns thrived in their self-imposed ghetto, their mezuzahs on the door posts of their apartments. He knew the area well and decided to stay there during this trip. He went to an old hotel on Graham Avenue, around the corner from the apartment where he and his father had lived. The hotel would have a vacancy; soldiers wouldn't know about the establishment. The rooms it rented were used by Jewish people in town for a funeral or wedding.

He went into a little shop on Graham Street, the one where his father had worked. David bought a pack of cigarettes in the exact spot where his father's desk used to be. Back then it was a haberdashery, and for a minute he saw his father in his rumpled brown suit and heard his lively voice but his father wasn't there. Instead, a young clerk asked him if he was lost.

David checked into the hotel and the next morning he walked to the first bank on his list. He thanked his common sense for bringing his wool coat. A stiff breeze wound its way through the canyons of buildings and located his neck. He turned up his collar and cursed himself for leaving his hat at home.

In his briefcase he carried Anna's bank books, her death certificate, passport, Last Will and Testament, and Letters of Testamentary naming him as Executor of her estate. He also had their marriage license. He didn't want to come up short; he wanted everything to be done on this one trip and not to have to mail papers back and forth. He entered the lobby of the First Fidelity Bank of New York City and asked to see a director of the bank.

Three hours later, with Anna's account closed and a check in his briefcase, he walked to the next bank, eight blocks away. At this rate, it would take him a week to take care of everything. He had four more banks to visit.

"Good planning, Anna," David said to a complete stranger walking down the street. He was glad he didn't have to hurry home. He decided to look at some apartments while he was in town, in case he wanted to live in New York City again.

David saw a For Sale sign in a building on Fifth Avenue, facing Central Park. The building manager told him about the apartment.

"It's a three bedroom flat on the fifth floor. The elevator in this building goes all the way to the roof where the view of Central Park is magnificent. The deposit to hold the apartment is $500 and the total price is $8,500," the salesman stated as he showed him the rooms.

"I want it, and I'll pay cash," David replied as he walked to the balcony that opened from the living room.

"The title documents will be ready in three days and we can close after you examine them," the salesman suggested.

David paid the five hundred on the spot and the realtor ordered the paperwork. David decided he could afford it now that he knew how much money he had. He would come back later and furnish it.

That same afternoon, Mr. Abraham Hoffenstein of the Hoffenstein, Emerton & Selman Law Firm, greeted David as he entered his corner office on the thirty eighth floor of the Empire State Building. Mr. Hoffenstein told David about meeting Anna in 1936 when she was visiting her aunt in the city. That was the year after they married. She had no aunt in New York City, and it amused David that she had concocted the story. She was there to set up accounts for herself for the money and diamonds she smuggled for her parents. Mr. Hoffenstein was visibly upset over the news of Anna's death and briefly David wondered if they had a fling. Then he dismissed the supposition.

It doesn't matter, she's gone. I have to keep my mind on the important issues, he said to himself as he took the elevator down to the street.

David spent the next ten days visiting banks, eating at the best restaurants, seeing current movies, and walking through Central Park. He closed the deal on the apartment and the realtor gave him the keys.

Back at his hotel room, he spread out the statements from all the banks. When he was finished with the calculations of Anna's diamonds, jewelry, and money, he fixed the value of her estate at two hundred fifty thousand dollars. It shocked him that she had smuggled that much out of Poland for herself. The value of Eva's account was sixty-seven thousand and her parents' account was three hundred twenty thousand. The bank agreed they should leave Eva's and their parent's accounts intact until the war ended and they came to claim them.

His business finished, it was time to go back to Alabama. He didn't want to leave. He decided he would go home, close his law office, and move to New York. He relished Central Park being his front yard, museums within walking distance, and restaurants to explore.

Mr. Hoffenstein hinted that David might join their law firm and the salary he quoted was enough for him to live comfortably. He had no reason to stay in Alabama but he had to return to wind up his law practice, sell his house, and then he needed to decide about Anna. She was buried in Decatur. Could he leave her? He wasn't sure.

With him mind bouncing between his home in Decatur and his apartment in New York, David boarded the train to go home. He mulled over his decision during the next three days as he watched the scenery unfurl and warm days prevail.

Exiting the train in Decatur, he inhaled a mixture of flowers and freshly cut grass. He smiled when his Packard that had been sitting idle three weeks started on the first turn. Pulling into his driveway, he looked past his shaggy grass to the fully bloomed plum tree in the front yard. Several robins flew out of it when he slammed the car door.

David inserted his key into the back door but it opened to his touch. Had he left it unlocked, or had someone been inside? He entered the kitchen. Everything was the same, no one had disturbed anything. He guessed he had forgotten to lock the back door.

There are some benefits to living in a small town, he said to himself. He decided he would stay for a few months and think about things.

I can furnish the apartment in New York later. There's no hurry. After the war would be a good time to start over. That's it, I'll move to the new apartment after the war.

David threw his suitcase on the bed and called his office to see what Gladys was doing.

CHAPTER 7

July, 1942

Madeline, Daphne, and Emma settled into a house on a tree lined street in Decatur where century old trees branched over the street, their limbs providing a highway for squirrels to scamper to the next block where a large hickory tree, an oak, and a beech tree lined the alley. Two elms in the front yard sheltered nests of robins, doves, titmouse, and a chatty mockingbird. The two story house, built in 1915, contained six rooms, a bathroom on the second floor, and a toilet in the space under the stairs. Wrapped by a porch on two sides, it sat on a narrow lot with a detached garage in the back.

After Madeline returned to work, Daphne found a baby sitter for Emma and registered for classes at the local college. David started coming over to visit the family the week after he returned from New York.

"I promised Joseph I'd watch over his special girls and I'm going to honor that. Let me know what I can do to help and if you don't, I'll be upset," he told them as Emma reached for him. He smiled when the child landed in his arms.

Madeline wondered if helping them adjust was the true motive for his visits.

"He's a lonely man. His wife died and they had no children," she informed Daphne after his second visit.

"I like him. He seems like a good man, and it never hurts to have a friend."

"He's a lot older than you," her mother reminded her.

"I'm older than my real age. This did a lot to me," Daphne pointed to Emma.

"I know, but you're twenty years old. I'm sure he's over thirty. He may be a good man, but he is boring and not attractive. You should be with younger people," Madeline suggested as she took Emma.

"I don't want to be with younger people. They ask too many questions. It's hard, Mom, very hard."

"Yes, I'm sure it is. We don't want to live a lie but you have to protect yourself, you need to have a response when someone asks." Madeline had told her this before.

"Tell them that I was brutally raped? Is that the story I should tell them? I can't do that. So I say, 'the father is away in the war' and let it go. Since I don't know who the father is that's a possibility, and as good of one as I can muster."

"Maybe someday you will know who did this to you," Madeline commented.

Daphne reached for her daughter, taking her toward the stairs. She looked back at her mother.

"I love her so much. It's true that I hate her father, but I love her. Never would I have believed I could love this baby, but I do. Look at that angel face. About Mr. Mayer, I like him. He walks with a limp and I'll bet that's why he isn't in the Army. Anyway, we'll see what happens. When school starts, I'll be too busy to think about things."

Too busy to think about things, stayed with Madeline. Her daughter had been beaten and raped by two men, and Emma was the result. The horror of the rape had caused her daughter to lose her innocence, robbed her of her last year in high school and changed her life.

Weeks flew by and Emma learned to crawl, disturbing everything, looking into cabinets, lifting the commode cover, laughing, and babbling while exploring the house. Madeline brought home a play pen to confine her. She screamed and yelled. Toys were added and nothing satisfied her.

"Spoiled little brat," Madeline said after two days of the play pen resistance.

"Well look who observed that. You're her number one spoiler," Daphne laughed, taking her daughter when she came in from school.

"Has David been by today?" Daphne asked her mother.

"Oh, so now it's David?" Madeline retorted.

"Yes, it's David. I really like him and he's crazy about Emma."

They heard a rumble in the driveway.

"He's here. We're off to the park. Emma is going with us."

Before they left, Madeline asked David to hang a swing on the front porch and a new screen door. She promised him lunch on Saturday in exchange for the project.

"I can do that. I'll be over Saturday morning. Do you have the things I need to hang them?"

"Yes, everything is in the garage," Madeline answered.

After he finished the project, he picked up Emma and held her in the swing. She fell asleep in his arms.

"I've never held a sleeping baby. It's a peaceful thing."

"Yes, yes it is. She's the light of our lives. I would have never believed being a mother would be this rewarding, especially under the circumstances of her birth. I'll put her down for her nap and be right back." A few minutes later, she joined David on the swing.

"Guess we should try it with two people and see if it will hold," David laughed.

"It will. You did a great job. Thanks David, thanks for everything you do for us. I know you're a busy man and I think sometimes we ask too much of you."

"The three of you are the highlight of my week. I look forward to every minute I spend with you. I'm afraid I have let my emotions get involved. If you think that's a bad thing, you need to tell me now before I put my hopes up too high."

"No, I don't want you to be afraid of us, you and
I...uh...having a relationship. But, well...I need to tell you how
Emma came to be," Daphne stuttered.

"It's none of my business," David replied.

"I want you to know. I want the circumstances of her birth to
be your business."

"When you want to tell me, I'll listen." David reached for
her hand. She didn't pull it away.

"I want to tell you now. It's not a pretty story and what
happened to me is a nightmare. Sometimes I have trouble sleeping
and I'm horrified that I may be assaulted again. In February of
1941, two men grabbed me when I came out of the outhouse
behind our house. One man put his hand over my mouth and one
threw a shirt over my face. Then the two of them carried me into
the woods. It was very cold that day, and almost dark. I saw the
men briefly before they threw me on the ground. One man held me
down while the other one tied my arms and uh...my legs apart,"
Daphne revealed, her voice trembling.

"The red headed man pulled my blouse over my face and
pushed it down into my mouth. He slapped me when I started to
protest. I passed out. When I came to, he was raping me. I felt it,
he hurt me. Then the other one raped me and uh...then...then it
was over." Daphne began to cry.

"I was a virgin. I tried to scream, but there was a part of the
shirt in my mouth and I couldn't. I almost suffocated. Then I heard
my brother calling me and the men started to leave. The dark

haired one came back and cut me loose, and I pulled the shirt off my face. I saw the man who untied me. I saw him up close. I had never seen them before." Daphne's eyes narrowed, her gaze focused straight ahead.

"Joseph found me and carried me home. I didn't want to be taken to the hospital where everyone would know what happened, so my mother took me to our doctor. She told him I'd been raped and he advised her to call the police. I begged her not to call them. The doctor treated my cuts and sent me home. I became ill three days later, sick with pneumonia from being on the frozen ground so long. For two months I stayed in bed, coughing, wheezing, and running a high fever. I missed the last semester of high school," Daphne said as she continued to gaze ahead, her neck stiff, her voice lower.

"Then my mother realized I was pregnant. I didn't have my flow and I began to be nauseated and had all the symptoms. Emma was born, and I had decided to put her up for adoption, but after holding her I couldn't do that. I love her, in spite of the way she was conceived, I love her. It isn't her fault she's the product of a rape. I will never tell her, she'll never know because she would think I didn't want her, and I didn't. The entire time I carried her I despised the baby inside of me. But I changed my mind."

"Did you ever find the men that did that to you?" David asked.

"No, but their faces will be with me all my life. So, now you know. I'm tarnished, and I don't know how I'll react to a man who wants me someday. I don't know if I can trust like I should. I know there are good men and bad men, but I had never been exposed to that kind of violence. My father was a good man, a gentle man, a man much like you. Hopefully, I will not run away from a life of happiness in a good marriage. It's in God's hands," Daphne said.

"I don't feel you're tarnished, not at all. Love heals a lot of wounds. You need a patient man. I don't care that you have Emma, in fact, I consider that a plus. I once had a baby, my wife and I, and he didn't live. The baby was deformed and I'm not sure I can father a healthy child. And I have this foot. It has kept me stateside, not that I wanted that, but here I am while the other men are fighting our enemies. Most women would consider me unlovable, boring, a cripple," David countered.

"You are not a cripple," Daphne replied, searching his eyes.

"I love you, Daphne, I love you and Emma. You're special to me and I hope to be worthy of your love someday." David let the words escape.

"I love you too, but I didn't know if you would want someone like me," Daphne cried.

David slid his arm around her and quickly they were in each other's arms. He found her lips then kissed her cheeks. Then she put her head on his shoulder.

"David," Daphne said.

"Yes?"

"Can we date? Can we do things a couple does, go out, that kind of thing? I've never been on a date," Daphne asked.

64

"Of course we can. We can start tomorrow. How about me taking you to Huntsville to a great restaurant? That is, if you mother can watch Emma."

"She can. I'll be ready by five-thirty tomorrow afternoon. Mother will be home from work by then. Now it's time for you to go home. I've got a lot to think about, and I need to get upstairs and see about Emma."

David left and drove home. He smiled all the way to his back door. He had someone who cared for him, a beautiful young woman who had a lovely child, a child for him to love. He didn't feel lonely for the first time since Anna died.

The next week, David had a telephone installed in their house. It was a four party line, but they didn't know anyone to call so that was fine.

"I want you to have the telephone in case of an emergency, and I can use it when I come over. I might need to call if I'm running late for a date," David reasoned.

Then his visits became more frequent. David feel deeply in love with Daphne but the eleven year age difference bothered him. He looked for signs she could love a man his age, one who had no traits of a younger man, a man who had already been married, one with a limp, a full waist, and less hair than normal. He noticed how her face lit up when he dropped by to see her and Emma, but he still had doubts.

Their Sunday date this week was to let Daphne drive all the way past Huntsville to the top of Monte Santo Mountain and back.

When he arrived for the date, she had pulled her blond hair back with a pink ribbon that matched the pink and white blouse tucked into her navy blue skirt. When she opened the door, David gasped.

"How do you get more beautiful each time I see you?" he asked, and meant it. Emma held out her arms for him.

"There is my darling Emma." David gathered her into his arms and smothered her with kisses. Then he handed her to Madeline.

"Are you ready for an adventure?" he asked Daphne.

"Guess we'll find out."

David backed the car out of the garage and turned east. He stopped at the end of the street where Daphne took over the drive. She pulled onto the highway that led to Huntsville. Daphne grasped the wheel tightly as she drove over the bridge, exhaling a sigh once she was on the other side. David laughed.

"You're over it. We aren't going to fall into the river," he commented with a huge grin on his face.

Daphne kept her eyes on the road, looking straight ahead, observing the traffic and the highway. She drove past cotton fields that stretched toward the horizon on the north and toward the river on the south. The highway carried them due east.

David broke the silence. "Did I tell you Judge Whitt is going to retire? Not because he wants to, he has stomach cancer. His doctor told him he has a year to live, if that long. He wanted me to apply for his position, and I have. I should hear next week if I have the job."

"You would make a great judge," Daphne responded, keeping her eyes straight ahead.

"There aren't many attorneys around with the war raging. I'm the only attorney left in town with enough trial experience to meet the qualifications. It'll be a temporary appointment, and if I get the job I'll run for the office when this term expires."

"You will be a shoo-in, everyone will vote for you," Daphne declared.

"I don't know. Most people wouldn't vote for a Jew."

"I'm sure it doesn't matter to anyone that you're Jewish," Daphne protested as small houses on the outskirts of the little town of Madison broke the endless cotton fields.

"You're so innocent and so delightful," David said with a chuckle.

They continued as David told Daphne about his childhood in New York City, about meeting Anna in Paris, his marriage to her, and about his mother and sister who died after they immigrated. He described French food and the cabarets in Paris. He told her he had an apartment in New York that overlooked Central Park and that he might live in it someday.

"Now, tell to me about your childhood," he said as he pointed toward the mountain looming in the distance.

Daphne told him about growing up on Robinson Mountain, about her father who died three years ago and how she missed her brother who was away in the war. Before she could go further, they turned into the downtown area of Huntsville. David pointed to the bank building that had been there since the 1830s and the big spring that bubbled out from under the rock cliff.

"Did you know the trial of the outlaw Frank James was held in Huntsville, right there where the courthouse stands? The James boys ran with a gang that held up a train in Muscle Shoals and during that robbery Frank James supposedly shot a man. He was probably guilty, but all the witnesses had died and the jury didn't convict him," David said in his "summation to the jury" voice. They drove around the small town, scrutinizing old homes that dated back to the Civil War.

"The reason so many pre-Civil War houses survived dates back to a promise made by the Union commander when their Army occupied the town. He told the citizens of Huntsville if they would feed breakfast to his men he would not burn the city when he left. Also, some of the credit may belong to the numerous Union sympathizers that occupied the northern part of Alabama."

They left the downtown area and drove up the mountain where tall pines, oaks, hickory, elm, and pecan trees loomed over the winding road, deep shadows underneath providing pockets of coolness in the summer heat. They ate a picnic lunch at the park where the old hotel, on a pinnacle overlooking the city, was boarded up, ready to fall with the next strong wind that found its way through the ghost filled rooms.

They left the mountain, leaving behind crumbs for the chickadees, warblers, blue jays, and squirrels. Daphne held the steering wheel with both hands as she made the trip down the curves, driving too close to the middle some of the time and too close to the edge the rest of the way. When they arrived home, Daphne wouldn't put the car into the garage, stopping five feet short of the structure.

"I'll do that later," she said, rushing in to see Emma as David pulled the car into the garage. It *was* a tight fit.

Over the next few weeks, Daphne gained driving experience and her confidence grew. She learned how to back the car out into the street and park downtown.

"I'm ready to take the driving test," she announced.

"When you get your license, I'll treat you to a dinner at a special restaurant in Birmingham," he countered.

A week later, Daphne walked over to David's office with her temporary driver's license. She reminded David of his promise to take her to a fancy restaurant.

"Can we go tomorrow night?" Daphne asked.

"Yes, I would enjoy that," he answered with a smile.

The next day, David dropped by the courthouse to see Madeline. He told her he would ask her daughter to marry him on their date that night. She approved, and gasped when she saw the diamond ring he planned to give to her.

At the dinner table in the best restaurant in Birmingham, David watched Daphne as she walked to the ladies room. The black dress she borrowed from Madeline outlined her slim figure. With her hair wound to the top of her head where it was pinned with a silver clasp, she looked elegant, a young woman any man would want. Other men in the room followed her with their eyes as she passed them. When she returned, they ordered and David took her hand. He placed the ring box in front of her.

"This is for you." She opened the box as the large diamond caught the light of the chandelier. "Will you marry me? I want to take care of you and Emma for the rest of my life. I want to adopt her and she shall always be my child and you will always be my wife." He knew he sounded corny but he couldn't help it.

She blinked back tears and said, "Yes, yes, I will marry you."

"I promise, you and Emma will never want for anything," David said as their food arrived.

Three weeks later, Daphne and David were married at the courthouse. The next day, David was sworn in as District Judge of Morgan County, Alabama.

CHAPTER 8

December 21, 1944

Skye found the rental house in town more than met her needs. She and Carrie adjusted quickly to the indoor bathroom and the modern kitchen. They turned on a spigot and, like magic, hot water flowed into the tub or sink in the kitchen. A refrigerator kept their food fresh and held two ice trays, a luxury that they'd never had before. The punishing poverty they had experienced on the mountain had evaporated with the move.

Skye, Carrie, and Ross went shopping the second day they lived in town. With two pairs of shoes for each of them, four changes of clothes, six changes of under garments, and three pairs of socks, they felt rich. They had their first beauty shop haircuts and a trip to the dime store resulted in make-up, nail polish, shampoo, and perfume for Skye and Carrie and a toy truck for Ross.

They bought food at the grocery store or from the peddler who sold fresh vegetables from the back of his truck. Rationing delegated their purchases but they ate well, hunger did not visit them in the cold months like it had before the move to town. T— old chores, milking the cow, processing the milk, c.

feeding the animals, planting the garden, cutting, and hauling firewood, had disappeared.

Carrie attended Decatur High School and had finished the first semester of her junior year. Out on Christmas break, she and Skye planned to bake twenty cakes to give as gifts and some to sell. The local grocery store wanted all they could supply.

They put up a Christmas tree last week, a small cedar that stood in the corner decorated with strings of popcorn and tinsel icicles. A package under the tree held a toy train for Ross and another one held three puzzles. Skye purchased a pink sweater for Carrie and wrapped it with a matching ribbon to wear in her hair. Another box for Carrie held a pair of gloves and a new slip.

Skye noticed a package for her and knew it was something Carrie made. Carrie had no money, except her lunch money and a dollar each week for keeping Ross after school. The two of them, partners in their new life in town, agreed to live on what Skye made each week. Her job at the meat packing plant kept her busy. The long hours on her feet and the frigid rooms took a toll on her body, but it was better than what she'd experienced on the farm. She pulled extra shifts when Carrie was free to watch Ross.

Carrie had made few friends at school. She had no desire to run with the crowd that gathered at the local drugstore after school to giggle and gossip. She studied, made good grades, walked to the baby sitter's from school and retrieved Ross, came home, and started supper. She did all of the laundry and housekeeping. Skye came home around six, exhausted.

Ross didn't look like he belonged to them with his fair skin, light blue eyes, and red hair. Smart and talkative, he kept them entertained and on their toes. Their biggest worries, that he'd run out into the street in front of a car or get polio or tuberculosis, kept him in the house under the vigilant eyes of Carrie and his mother.

Everything had gone well so far. Owen's body had not surfaced so Skye stuck to her story that Owen joined the Army after Pearl Harbor. Then Colin came back to Decatur on leave from the Army. The visit upset Carrie and she did not respond well to his questions about Owen. She told him Owen was dead then realized she shouldn't have said anything. Thankfully, before Colin demanded to know the details, Skye came home.

"I assume Owen is dead since I haven't heard from him the last three years," Skye told Colin, trying to redeem the story of his disappearance.

"That's not what Carrie said, she said he was dead and wouldn't be coming home from the war," Colin shouted. That prompted Colin to start a search of the Army records to find Owen. Skye had no idea records could be searched to find someone. That terrified her. He would never come home, and questions would be asked.

She wondered why Owen's body had not surfaced. It traveled down the river and disappeared, she had seen it bobbing around after they threw him in.

I saw him go down the river. I know some day he'll surface. The river was swift and out of its banks that day, maybe he washed all the way down to the dam. Maybe he landed in a slough and animals ate him. Skye turned over the possibilities in her brain.

Then there was the problem of a man Owen shot years ago, a revenuer who had been snooping around his still. Owen came home and bragged in front of the girls that he shot him between the eyes. He didn't bury the man deep enough. After a torrential rain, the man's body surfaced and the police came out to question her about him late one afternoon. Thankfully, Carrie and Ross were not home, they had gone to the grocery store. After they returned, Skye put supper on the table but didn't have much to say.

"What happened at work today? Something is bothering you. I can tell," Carrie asked her mother.

"Those detectives came back today. I'll tell you about it later." She motioned toward Ross who was engrossed in eating his spaghetti, slurping up a long piece with his mouth.

"Stop it, Ross. That's not how you eat spaghetti. Here, let me show you how." Carrie took her spoon and wrapped the spaghetti around in it with a fork then put it in her mouth. Ross continued to suck the long spaghetti, laughing when the end disappeared.

"I'll get Ross to bed," Carrie said, frustrated with her brother.

Methodically Skye scrubbed the dishes while Carrie bathed Ross. The possibility that the detectives would arrest her kept running through her mind. *They know Owen killed that man but they can't prove it. I lied. Is it a crime to lie about her husband killing someone?*

She was married to Owen and he'd have beaten her or killed her if she ratted on him. He could kill her as easily as he'd shot that man. Skye knew her only way to get out of her predicament was to disappear. She'd been thinking about leaving Alabama for months, before the war was over and soldiers came home. If they relocated now, she could buy a house in the new location.

Then there was the problem of Colin. He would be a man when he returned, and she wasn't sure she could handle his questions about Owen's absence. She couldn't take the chance he'd harm one of the children. If he had any of the tendencies of Owen he would be mean, violent and abusive.

I can't wait any longer. I hope Carrie agrees, that will make it easier. I need her to be on my side in this decision.

Carrie, now sixteen, had grown into a mature and beautiful young woman. She adored Ross and understood her mother's concerns. She had them, too. Every so often, she talked about Owen and what they did with his body, wondering if it was the right thing to do. She'd been in the room with her mother when the two detectives came the first time.

Carrie returned to the kitchen. "What happened?" she asked.

"Those detectives came back while you and Ross were at the store. They asked me about Owen, if I'd heard from him. They told me new evidence had surfaced about that man Owen killed. When Owen doesn't come home, they're going to be snooping around and I'm afraid I'm going to be arrested. I've been thinking about moving," Skye answered, wiping her hands on a dish cloth.

"We can get out of here tomorrow as far as I'm concerned. I haven't made any friends at school. All the girls are too snooty. The semester has ended for the Christmas holidays so this would be a good time for me to transfer to a new school, wherever it is. I'll start packing tonight," Carrie said as a tear escaped from her eye.

"Are you sure? I see a tear," Skye looked at her daughter.

"I'm sure, but I want Jenna to be with us. I miss her. What if she comes back? How will she find us? We don't know where she is, she could be on her way here right now," Carrie suggested.

"I hope she finds us, but I have to protect you and Ross. I cannot end up in jail. I have a feeling if Jenna wanted us to find her she would have returned or written by now. It's been three years. After we move, I'll write my sister and send her our address. Hopefully Jenna will think to ask her. She knows how to find my sister."

Skye spread out a map and pointed to California.

"People at work say California is a good place to live and we need to relocate a long way from Alabama. That's as far west as we can go," Skye suggested.

"Look, there's San Francisco. I'd love to go over the Golden Gate Bridge. Can we live where we can have horses again, somewhere in the country?" Carrie ran her finger around empty areas on the map outside of San Francisco.

"Yes, I have all the money from the sale of the place on the mountain, and I've saved another five hundred dollars from my job. We can buy a house with some land, if we go now, before the prices go up."

"What about our things, our furniture?"

"I'll leave Mr. Mayer a note at his office and tell him to sell everything. All we can take is our clothes and food for the trip on the train," Skye said as she folded the map.

"Let's go. I can come back some day and find Jenna," Carrie suggested.

"Okay, it's settled. I get paid on Saturday and we'll leave on the Sunday train. I'll buy our tickets for the trip west and two more suitcases. We will pack four; one each for our clothes, one for the new toy train and puzzles for Ross, and one for important documents. We're three days from boarding the train to California." Skye spoke with energy in her voice, buoyed by the decision.

On Saturday, they cleaned out the refrigerator and Skye baked a cake for Mr. Mayer. She put in inside a box and delivered it to his house, putting it on top of his car so he would find it. She left him a letter about what to do with her things. She'd already sent a letter to her sister to take the old furniture made by their ancestors. She told Mr. Mayer to sell everything else, including her old car. The last sentence was personal:

Thanks for all the support and all you have done for us over the years. I appreciate you, and hope you and Daphne have a great life. You deserve the best, Skye.

Sunday morning, December 24th, 1944, Skye, Carrie, and Ross boarded a train going west.

They celebrated Christmas Day on the way to California.

CHAPTER 9

August, 1946

Daphne and Emma moved into David's house the day after their wedding. The historic house, built in 1892, had four bedrooms upstairs but no closets or a bath on the second floor. Daphne suggested they take the middle bedroom and replace it with a large bathroom and closet, which they did.

David paid for all the renovations from his private stash of money, his "Anna accounts" as he dubbed the money. Daphne knew about the money Anna left, but she didn't know how much nor did she know about the envelopes in the trunk in the attic. He had not told her about those ghosts of the past. He still hoped someone from Anna's family would surface. The war had been over for a year, and people were emerging from the European front and out of Russia.

His salary as a judge was more than adequate for their needs. Daphne didn't want anything more than to be a wife and mother, and had dropped out of college after they married. They lived modestly. Their biggest expense was Daisy, but David insisted they keep her.

He felt he owed Daisy the job, she had been so faithful to take care of Anna and she needed the paycheck. Daisy did the laundry, most of the cooking, and planted a garden each year. They grew tomatoes, squash, turnip greens, onions, beans, and one year they grew gourds, running them up the trellis in the back.

Daphne's passive personality and patience gave inner peace to David. He had fallen in love with her more than he ever believed possible. She had also proven to be a good lover, coming to him at night with a need he never knew women had. He had been patient with her, not pushing her, considering her horrible sexual experience. A few weeks into their marriage, she relaxed and let herself enjoy their love making.

Daphne had never found the men that raped her. It was possible they went to war and didn't come back, or maybe they were transients who left the area. Except for Emma, who was the product of the rape, there were no reminders of the horrid incident.

David adopted Emma after they had been married a year, as per Alabama law required. He considered her his own child and his love for her grew each day. No one in town remembered seeing the child without David and she would never know she had a biological father different from him. David promised Daphne he would never tell her.

David checked his post office box every Monday where the statements from Anna's accounts and the rent from the New York flat were delivered. Once in his office, he opened the mail as he sipped on coffee. Gladys followed him to the courthouse to be his secretary and, even though she got on his nerves, he decided she should stay with him.

In the mail, he noticed a letter from a law firm in New York City, the one Anna used years ago. He opened it. The letter said someone named Eva Feldman had written to the firm, asking them to find Anna Mayer. The law firm attached the letter from Eva. She asked that they forward her letter to Anna Mayer who lived in Decatur, Alabama. In the envelope was another letter, sealed and addressed to Anna. The return address on the letters was from Baltimore, Maryland, postmarked June 3rd, 1946.

David opened the letter to Anna.

Dear Anna,

I'm now in Baltimore at a boarding house. I was advised to go here for an American contact when the war ended. It took me awhile to get out of the hospital. I was very ill after the starvation I suffered in the work camp. Then I was moved to a refugee camp and finally got permission to immigrate to America. I gave them your address but I no longer have it. I lost it on the ship when someone took my things. I arrived with some money and passport hidden in my clothes. I will be here until you send for me. I look forward to beginning my life in America after this horrible time. I fear mum and dad will not be found. They did not leave Poland in time. I'll tell you more of that story when I see you. I missed you so much and hope that you and David are both well. Your sister, Eva

David wrote a reply and sent it to the Baltimore address. He told Eva that Anna died years ago from tuberculosis. He told her about his marriage to Daphne and that they had a little girl. He assured her she would be welcomed to Alabama with open arms and that Anna left her a lot of money.

He thought about Eva and how hard it must have been for her. She would be thirty or thirty-one. He remembered the Eva he knew in Paris; young and carefree, smaller than Anna with lighter hair and gray eyes, but without Anna's pretty face. A talented piano player, she loved the Paris opera, as did Anna. They were friends with some of the performers.

Then he remembered Eva had Anna's complaining nature, both of them demanding to a fault, insisting on having their way. He wondered how that would work with Daphne but surely Eva didn't expect to live with them. His house wasn't that big and he didn't want to be reminded of Anna every day. If necessary, he would take the train to Baltimore to retrieve Eva but he hoped she could come on her own. He mailed the letter to her before he called Daphne and told her Eva had contacted him.

"I understand you need to do this. We'll welcome her and find her a place when she's ready, but at first she needs to live with us. She may be sick, starvation is not something you overcome quickly," Daphne suggested.

Three weeks later, Eva arrived. She looked nothing like David remembered. Searching for her in the crowd, he realized an old woman standing by three suitcases had to be her. Stooped and thin, with gray hair, sunken eyes and pallid skin, she had aged beyond her years. He greeted her with a hug, feeling bones through her clothes. Wobbly, she held onto him as she slid into the front seat of his car.

"This is a pretty town," she commented with a shaky voice as they drove down tree lined streets. Her English was thick with a French accent. It would be a surprise to Eva and a comfort to find that Daphne spoke fluent French.

"Yes, it's a pretty place. I like it here. In a few days, we'll drive out to the cemetery so you can see where I buried Anna," David said as they stopped at the red light.

"Let's wait awhile. I've had enough of dying and graves. I knew Anna wouldn't live to an old age. I'm glad she died a peaceful death. So many didn't, so many didn't..." her voice trailed off as Eva looked out the window, fidgeting with her purse.

When they arrived at David's house, Daisy opened the back door and waved them inside. She had been warned that Eva might be sick and fussed over her like she had Anna. Daisy had reverted back to a place she once held, being a caretaker for a dying woman.

"Miss Eva, your sister told me all about you. I'm so glad you survived the war. I wish Miss Anna could have seen you walk in that door," Daisy chatted as she took her purse and directed her to the table where she had food prepared for her.

"Were you with her in the end?" Eva asked.

"Yes ma'am, I was. She was very sick, very sick…uh, it was a sad day…" Daisy's voice stumbled.

"I know. I know," Eva cried.

"Eva, this is my wife Daphne, and our daughter Emma," David introduced them as they entered the kitchen.

"What a beautiful child," Eva stated as Emma ran to her and hugged her around the waist. Eva looked at David and smiled.

"Welcome Eva, we're going to get you back on your feet. We're going to take care of you," Daphne assured her.

A month later, Eva began to sleep less, walk more, and had gained weight with Daisy's good meals. Five weeks after her arrival, she put on lipstick and asked Daphne to take her shopping. She bought new clothes and shoes and asked David to find her a car and teach her to drive.

Eva thrived in the warm climate, tanned in the summer sun, dyed the gray out of her hair, and bought new glasses for her poor eyesight. Her cheeks filled and her eyes began to sparkle under the gold trimmed spectacles. She laughed at the antics of Emma, bonded with Daphne and their love of all things French. She considered Daisy her surrogate mother, David her brother, Daphne her sister. They were the only family she had. Everyone she left behind died in the work camps.

After six months, Eva announced she wanted to live in Huntsville. She had fallen in love with the quaint little town after David and Daphne took her for a drive to the area. They found her a house to rent and she began volunteering at the library in Huntsville. Later, she applied for a job at the university to teach French. It seemed David's fear of Eva's complaining nature had been unfounded.

David sensed Eva had not told them everything about her war experience. *I'll let her decide when she wants to tell us everything, if she ever does*, David thought to himself more than once.

He wasn't sure he wanted to know the details of her life during the war.

CHAPTER 10

October, 1949

Eva could not believe she lived in Huntsville, Alabama, a small southern town that she loved, one that enjoyed beautiful weather, low hung mountains, and a large river a few miles south of the town. The rolling hills, valleys, and mountains framed the picturesque downtown, dominated by a stately courthouse and historic buildings built around a square.

The oldest structure, the bank building constructed in 1830, rested on a solid cliff of limestone where fifty feet below a spring bubbled fresh water out to a pond that held swans, ducks, egrets, goldfish, and minnows. The remnant of a canal that had once led to the Tennessee River meandered to the water works station where the fresh water was processed to the citizens.

Eva didn't consider the town old. Compared to Warsaw and Paris, the town seemed new, pristine. She marveled at her fate for, as a young girl, America had never been a choice as a place to live. Her teachers in Poland and France presented America as a faraway country of cowboys, Indians, and uncivilized people who lived in filthy cities or on poor farms. Americans knew nothing about opera, wine, fashion, and manners. Their children, dirty, shoeless, and illiterate, were never portrayed as disciplined, educated, and refined.

America is populated by heathens, she heard more than once during her school years in Paris, the city considered the most modern and enlightened in the world. She and Anna were sent to school there to a Jewish high school where her parents had contacts in the jewelry business.

On each trip from Warsaw to Paris, they smuggled diamonds, jewelry, and money to contacts that deposited them in accounts and private storage places. Banks in New York held accounts for the family, the money sent with Jewish friends who took the steamer back and forth to move assets to the country with an excellent and trustworthy banking system. America was portrayed as an uncivilized country, yet the banking system was the most trusted in the world.

Eva had been among the elite, living life as a privileged school girl. She attended the opera on a regular basis, became friends with the performers, and helped Jewish families move their personal assets to safe places. That changed overnight when the Nazis overran Paris. Immediately she went into hiding with a family. When they feared retaliation, she fled underground to the countryside, hiding with a couple who passed her off as their daughter.

A few weeks later, she was involved with the French resistance spying on German troops, passing information to the men who blew up German trains. She helped them deflate the tires on the trucks, pour sugar in the gas tanks of the cars, poison the food, and steal ammunition and guns.

Then the Germans caught them. She bribed her way out of jail with money hidden in her clothes. She fled to the southern part of France where a family housed her. Living there for a month, she fled when the Nazis marched into town and shot a man and his wife who lived three blocks away. They had hidden a Jewish family in their cellar. The couple were hung in the town square, their bodies turning in the wind as they rotted.

Her next destination was a vineyard in Tenay, a village near the border of Switzerland, in the eastern part of France. She walked at night, along with a Jewish couple and their child, hiding in the woods during the day, one of them keeping watch as the others slept. Finally, they arrived at the vineyard, spread around an old house and several ancient buildings. The vineyard had not bottled wine since the war began. There was no one to harvest the grapes, trim the vines, and work the fields.

The family that lived there huddled in the old stone house or the warehouse where the huge wine casks lined the foot thick walls. The warehouse, built into a cave that wound under the foothills of the Alps, became a dormitory of sorts, a hidden place the townspeople knew about but the Nazis didn't.

At various times there were a dozen people sheltered at the vineyard, mostly men who were members of the resistance movement. They set up a radio in one of the rooms in the warehouse, inserting the antenna through a hole in the roof. During the day, some of them worked in the fields, planting potatoes, cabbages, pumpkins, squash, and beans. They picked the few grapes that survived and apples from a small orchard. Without that food, they would have starved.

The village, an outpost for the Germans, did not have a large population of soldiers roaming in the area, allowing them some freedom. That was their downfall. Ten of them were arrested setting explosives to blow up a troop train. Taken captive, the women were shipped to work camps, the men to prison. Eva was a few days from death when the camp was liberated by Americans.

After the war ended, she was sent to a refugee camp where the occupants were processed like cattle and given rations barely enough to keep them alive. A few months later, she was released and took the train to Paris, found the apartment where she had lived, retrieved papers hidden in the closet, including a bank statement from the New York bank that held Anna's accounts. She had also hidden some money and jewelry in the closet. Cleverly, she had placed them in a flat package and pasted wallpaper over it.

With these things in her hand, she applied for immigration, bribing the registrant to put her name to the top of the list. Loaded onto a ship that took her to New York City, then on to Baltimore on a bus, then south to Huntsville, Alabama, on the train, she hoped to find Anna alive in America. Instead, David and Daphne took her in and treated her like a lost sister.

Now on her way to see them, driving from her house in Huntsville to Decatur thirty miles away, Eva drove through flat farmland containing stubs of cotton plants stretching on her right and left as far as she could see. A field of pumpkins came into view, their round shapes like lanterns on the ground, the vines now brown and tangled. A gentle breeze moved fluffy clouds north, a line of ducks in a V pattern flew over the road in front of her, proceeding south to the back waters of the Tennessee River.

Eva loved her weekend visits with David and Daphne. She had hated to move away from their loving household, but she had to start a life for herself and Huntsville was the nearest town to them. Ironically, she moved there the same month that the Germans arrived in a caravan from New Mexico. They started the rocket building project that would be developed on Red Stone Arsenal.

She hated Germans, but they acted like the war was invisible in America. She'd run into them in the library, see them eating at restaurants, and several Germans attended the French class she taught at the University. None of them acted like her Jewishness bothered them. She had not seen any of the Germans mistreat or shun people, so she lived among them, wary and cautious, never trusting them.

She and David went back a few years. She met him in 1935, during the summer months when Paris budded with flowers, music, art, and love. Only eighteen, she had visions of her life, unrealistic visions that encompassed falling in love with a Frenchman and living in an apartment on the Seine. She had been picked by her parents to marry David, an American Jew who had left Poland as a child. The two families knew each other in the old days and had picked David from a Jewish list of available men in New York.

He came to Paris to meet her, but one look at him and she felt nothing. She wanted to marry a younger man, one without a limp, a robust man, tall and handsome. Anna, a few years older, sick with tuberculosis, and doubting she'd find a husband in her state, saw David as a chance for a better life. After a month of courtship, they married. Then the war took what was left of her family, shipped them off in cattle cars to Treblinka.

Often Eva wished she had married and had children but it had not happened, and now it was unlikely. The years of hardship put deep lines in her face. Her thin, brown hair hung straight to her chin and she'd dyed her locks to eliminate the gray streaks. She turned no heads when she entered a room, unlike Anna who had been a beauty. Her five-foot-three inch frame, stooped from brittle vertebrae from years of starvation, made her appear older. One thing she did was wear fashionable clothes, good leather shoes, and gold rimmed glasses. She had enough money to do that.

Eva knew she didn't have to work but it suited her to be in academia. She prized the interaction of the other teachers and had a social life of sorts, going to the movies with friends, to concerts, and plays on campus. She tried to let go of the past but her brain harbored memories of the night the Nazis caught them and shipped them to the work camps. Claude was injured that night, the man she admired, the leader of their resistance group, a cousin to the man that hid them at the vineyard. If he survived the war, he was somewhere in Europe with his wife and children.

Claude was the only man she had ever loved. Their forbidden love had been a flash of excitement for the times in which they lived, their love making a glorious event each time it happened. Was there another man out there like him, one that could make her heart spin, her insides ache for more, her body cry for the next climax? If such a man existed, she had not found him.

Eva pulled up to the entrance of the bridge and found herself behind several cars waiting on the draw bridge to lower the center part, raised to let barges and a tug boat pass. She rolled down the window and took a deep breath, inhaling a fishy smell and the dusty odors of fall. The sun hung low on the horizon, clouds slicing across the orange ball, the smoke of fireplaces throwing soot in the air, creating hues of red, orange, and lavender in the rays of the sun. She looked at her watch.

Daphne said we'd eat at five-thirty, I'll be there in time, she said to herself as the car in front inched forward. In five minutes she was over the bridge, thinking about the vegetables Daisy cooked: fried okra, green beans, stewed cabbage, fluffy mashed potatoes, and creamed corn.

I hope Daisy made meatloaf, Eva said to herself as she turned down the street.

Brilliant hues of fall, yellow maples, red oaks, orange elms and purple hawthorns, stood majestically beside dark green pines that lined the street. Goldenrods waved to the sky on an overgrown empty lot as black-eyed Susans surrounded a sumac bush, golden and stately with purple berries, ripe for the local population of birds.

A resident blue jay squawked as she pulled into the driveway of the house, a two-story brick structure David and Anna bought right after they married. It gave Eva a connection to Anna to know she had lived in the rooms, cooked in the kitchen, played the piano and, while she had not asked David in which room she took her last breath, she knew she had died in the house. That gave her peace. *She died at home.*

Daphne yelled out the kitchen window, "Come in, we're in the kitchen."

Emma ran to Eva and told her about school and her projects. After dinner, they settled into the living room to listen to the radio then Eva played the piano for a few minutes. When she finished, David went to the mantel and picked up a letter.

"This letter, addressed to you, came last week. It was in care of Anna and David Mayer," David said as he handed her the envelope.

It was from Claude, postmarked three months ago in Paris.

"Why don't you read it privately? The guest room upstairs is yours," Daphne suggested.

"Yes, I'll go up and unpack my things," Eva stated indifferently as she put the letter in her skirt pocket.

She took her bag upstairs, trying not to hurry. She closed the door and opened the envelope quickly. The handwritten letter was in French.

Eva, I am hopeful this letter will find you. I obtained your sister's address six months ago when an old contact found me living in Paris and gave me the records of the people that helped our cause. I was released from prison a month after the war ended then I was in the hospital for several months. When I returned to Paris, it took me a year to find out what happened to my wife. She was shot in the last days of the war, trying to steal food. The children were sent to an orphanage where they both contracted cholera. The oldest one died before I found them and the youngest died in my arms a month later. At least I got to be with her at the end. I was so despondent that I could not function for a long time. My health was ruined but slowly I have made a recovery. It has taken years.

Ironically, I obtained a position to rebuild the railroad that we blew up. I could not deal with the sick and dying and the confines of the hospital. I had enough of that while in prison so I have left the medical profession. I now live in a small apartment in Marseille.

I never forgot you and want to take a holiday. I believe America might be a good place to visit. Perhaps you could suggest a good time and maybe we could meet in

New York. I'll await making plans in hopes of hearing from
you. Since the Americans have been here, I now speak a
little English and think I can get myself around.

Best wishes, Claude

Eva couldn't believe Claude survived and had found her. She
read the letter again, unpacked a few things, and read it again. As
Eva dressed for bed, she cradled the letter close to her.

Claude, I am going to see you again, you and I together in
America. We will have another chance.

Over breakfast, she told David and Daphne about Claude.

"Will you ask him to come for a visit?" Daphne inquired.

"Yes, I will. I can meet him in New York. That would be a
great vacation for us. If he has the time, I will ask him to come
down here for a visit." Eva sounded buoyant as the words slipped
out.

She didn't tell them everything. Some things they didn't
need to know.

"Are we still going on our hike?" Emma interrupted.

"Yes, yes we are. Are you ready?"

"I will be in a few minutes. Are we going to the river walk?
That's my favorite place." Emma stated with excitement.

"That sounds good to me. Let's get ready, and I need to get
back in time to write a letter and get it into the mail," Eva replied.

David and Daphne knew who she was writing.

They looked at each other and smiled.

CHAPTER 11

June, 1950

David received a letter from the leasing manager of the building in New York City that housed his apartment. The flat had been vacant three months and the building inspector would not release it to be rented until it was up to code. The tenants had torn out the kitchen plumbing, the radiators no longer worked, the wiring had been eaten by rats and the floors had holes the size of a washboard, according to the landlord's report. If David did not bring it up to code, it would be surrendered to the city. The City of New York had cracked down on slum lords. David had a choice, remodel or lose his investment.

"We'll take the train and be gone three weeks to a month. I know a hotel across from Central Park so you and Emma will be able to get out of the hotel and walk around. Of course, you'll want to do some shopping and we'll see a couple of plays and eat at some good restaurants. I'll be working during the day to get the apartment up to code," he told Daphne after he advised the county clerk how long he'd be on vacation.

"Sounds wonderful. I can't wait." Daphne smiled at the news.

David, Daphne, and Emma boarded a train for New York City the first week of July, 1950. Once on the train, enthralled with the passengers, watching and listening to every person and sound, Emma didn't budge out of her seat. She sat between them reading her books then watched the landscape change as the train rolled north.

David had not been to New York since 1942. As the scenery along the eastern Appalachians unfolded, it was amazing how America had changed. New highways were under construction, houses were sprouting up in massive subdivisions and city skylines were reaching new heights as skyscrapers, built with steel girders, dominated downtowns. There was no stopping the post-war march of progress.

On the crowded train, all kinds of people were traveling. Young couples, some with small children, older people, business men, women traveling alone, elderly couples. David noticed a sense of pride in them, people were proud to be American and it showed. They won a war and defeated a horrible enemy.

Nothing was impossible and that attitude prevailed in everyone he met. New jobs in the post-war boom meant money and stability. Families were buying new cars, trucks, houses, and clothes. Farms were being plowed with modern tractors and fences were enclosing pastures as cattle fattened on new strains of grass.

Curious inventions had changed America. Food was beginning to be mass produced and recently David and Daphne had a cheeseburger at a restaurant that served it from a walk up window.

"I never thought of putting cheese on meat," Daphne remarked as she ate the sandwich.

"It's good," David agreed. "We'll have to tell Daisy about this, better yet, I'll buy her one and she can make this for us at home."

One invention David had purchased was a ball point pen. They were the new rage, replacing the ink well fountain pens that he found cumbersome. Filling one always resulted in ink stains on his shirts and now he could buy a pen with the ink built in. It was a simple but useful invention.

David bought a typewriter for home after Gladys had taught him the proper way to use the machine. With a typewriter in his house, he would be able to justify leaving early to work on documents. He liked typing his own opinions, leaving his spelling errors for Gladys to correct when she retyped them at the courthouse.

Lately he read about an underwater breathing apparatus, an aqua lung that made it possible to swim around for a long time, totally underwater, immersed like a fish. They called it a SCUBA machine. The article revealed how it worked but it made no sense to him. A man from France named Jacques Cousteau invented the machine. He wondered if he'd met him when he was in Paris, the name sounded familiar.

David gazed out the window when someone pointed to a line of cars at the railroad crossing. Several models of cars, new and old, waited patiently for the train to pass and in the back of the line a new Greyhound bus stood, the huge vehicle shiny and modern.

The war had caused America to mechanize and now that technology was paying off. People could afford to buy new products because wives had saved their allotments and worked in factories while men were away fighting. After the Depression emptied savings accounts, the war brought regular pay checks, money people needed for food, housing, and clothing.

Factories were reconfigured to make cars, trucks, tractors, refrigerators, lawn mowers, electric fans, and telephones. They were beating their swords into ploughshares, reinventing the old machines while developing new and better models.

People added bathrooms and installed electricity in their houses. Hot water heaters were the newest gadget, along with electric attic fans and phonographs. Telephones were being installed in record numbers as the lines stretched longer and further out into the country. In a few years, cities would be attached to other cities. It was mind boggling. Imagine being able to talk on the phone to someone in another state. That seemed impossible but it had happened.

A new gadget had entered homes in America, a gadget called a television. It was a strange thing and David had no clue how it worked. He had recently bought one and it sat in their living room but they didn't watch it, preferring to listen to the radio or sit on the front porch after supper.

One gadget David knew would change transportation was radar. It had been developed during the war and was being installed in airports. During the war, the Army used it to track airplanes. He read that large passenger planes were flying all the way across the Atlantic Ocean, from New York to Paris. That was hard to believe, and David doubted it would continue to happen. It took way too much fuel to go that far.

There were also a lot of advances in medicine. There was a readily available drug for the treatment of infections. Penicillin had been synthesized and could be used for the worst cases. If infections could be stopped, then gangrene wouldn't take limbs and lives.

A prediction that smallpox might be eliminated someday appeared in the paper last week. David knew an uncle of his died from smallpox in the old country. He remembered tales about how he suffered and how his mother would not go to see him for fear she would contract the disease. After he died, they took his bed to the back yard and burned it. Then his family left the house and opened the windows so the disease would be blown away. He understood that tactic. He had used it when Anna died of tuberculosis.

Hygiene had improved after the war. Since all soldiers were given toothbrushes and required to brush their teeth every day, most of them continued the practice when they went home. They bought toothbrushes for their wives and children and flavored toothpaste flew off the shelves. Suddenly it was fashionable to have cavities filled and it didn't hurt as much with the new anesthetic procedures. People began bathing more than once a month, especially in the southern part of the country where it wasn't so cold. Hot water heaters made it easier to have a warm bath, one a person could enjoy.

Vaccinations for some of the dreaded diseases, typhoid, diphtheria, and whooping cough, were offered free at clinics. People began to feel better and gain weight, they lived longer and stayed healthier to the end.

Clothing began to be mass produced after factories retooled from Army uniforms to make trousers, shirts, blouses, skirts, dresses, and pajamas. Clothes became affordable and people dressed better and changed clothes on a regular basis. Before the war it was common for a person to wear the same outfit for a week.

Now school children were required to wear shoes every day, eliminating stumped toes, infections, and parasites. New laws required children to attend school to age twelve and that helped them to get a better job when they entered the work force. Some of them taught their parents and grandparents to read. Illiteracy rates dropped and libraries opened and issued new cards.

Cities filled with people working in factories, living in apartments and sub-divisions. The increased population brought diseases that spread unmercifully. Polio and tuberculosis outbreaks were common. Word reached neighbors by telephone when a new case was diagnosed. A recent outbreak of polio this summer in Morgan County kept Daphne home with Emma. She would not take her to a place where large crowds gathered, not to the Catholic Church for mass, to the grocery store or to the public swimming pool. Emma stayed with Daisy, inside their house, where she would be safe.

There was a child who lived two blocks from them who had developed polio two weeks ago. Daphne knew the mother of the eight-year-old boy, and he and Emma attended the same Sunday school class at church. A day after swimming in a creek in Hartselle, his fever spiked to 105 degrees. He couldn't move his legs and had trouble talking. Three days ago, he was taken to the Crippled Children's hospital in Birmingham and put into an iron lung.

No one had an answer as to how polio spread. Even the doctors were stumped. Did the germs live in water, or milk, or did they live in dirt? Did polio spread by people or did mosquitoes spread it? Did it live in the air like TB? Everyone waited for someone to find a cure or create a vaccine. They kept Emma close to them on the train, not allowing her to visit with strangers or other children, for you never knew who carried the disease. She sat between them or next to the window.

David loved the three day voyage to New York. He remembered the last time he went, the spring after Anna died, a lonely man on a quest to find assets his wife had hidden from him.

102

Even that trip had been enjoyable in an odd sort of way, searching for a treasure with the allure of New York, mixed with the charisma of the train. There was something about being on a powerful machine that carried you to a destination. His euphoria and excitement for the trip was akin to a child on his first carnival ride. He felt anxious, then decided he would relax and enjoy this event.

His circumstances had changed dramatically. He had a young, healthy wife and a daughter. He had a job that paid well and gave him immense satisfaction. Being a judge, he felt responsibility, but in a good way. At first he was known as the "split the baby judge" around the courthouse, a compliment on his ability to be fair to both parties in a judgment. On the rare occasions when he'd have a criminal trial, he had no problem putting away a guilty criminal and he did, much to the satisfaction of the prosecutor and police.

After his appointment to the bench, he had to run for office to keep his job. Easily reelected, he had an opponent last election who dubbed him "a suitable judge for the South," which was meant to be an insult but the moniker stuck. Apparently, a suitable judge for the South was what the voting population of the district wanted, not a Yankee who recently relocated from New Jersey and knew nothing about Southern society. His opponent gave him a label that endeared him to the voters. A few months later, the opponent moved to Atlanta, running to a city that had enough business to make him successful.

David relaxed when Emma fell asleep in the seat, her head resting on Daphne. As he looked at them, a rush of love gushed through his heart. Never would he have believed he could love anyone like he loved them. Then he turned his mind to their home in Decatur, their safe haven from the outside world, their cocoon.

They had done their share to support the post-war spending frenzy. He had a two-car garage built to hold his 1938 Packard and his new car, a 1950 Ford. He bought a vacuum cleaner for Daisy to use and gave her his old radio when he bought their new one. He bought a phonograph and lately the television. Daisy didn't like the television and would stay out of the room when it was on. She vowed that if she could see those people in that machine they could look through it and see her. David laughed and tried to explain that people didn't have a window through the television into their living room, but he never convinced her.

David goaded Daisy about her age. She came to work for them in 1938 and thirteen years later she had more white hair and walked a little slower but she still cooked, cleaned, and fussed like she always had. Someday he'd figure out her age, or ask her husband to tell him. Then he'd surprise her on her birthday and buy her a cake with her age written on it.

She liked to fuss at him. That brought her immense satisfaction, but the lecture was to all of them in spite of picking him as her target. Her favorite complaint was people leaving dirty dishes on the table, a bad habit of David's.

"Why don't you put 'em in the sink? Then you could run a little water over them and that would keep down the flies. Them flies is driving me to the grave. I kill a hundred in this house every day," she'd say during the summer months.

"Now Daisy, you wouldn't exaggerate, would you?" David would ask.

"No, I'm going to save them dead flies one of these days and show you," she mumbled, and one day she did. She counted them out for him, all one hundred and five, claiming she swatted them all in one day.

"See, I told you, and it's because of your lazy ways, not putting your dishes in the sink. I didn't take you to raise. Your momma sure didn't teach you much."

"Now Daisy, you know my momma died when I was a boy and my daddy raised me."

"That's what's wrong. Men are slobbers," Daisy shook her finger at him as the lecture continued.

David came back to reality when the train passed a crossing and a loud horn blasted through the window. Daphne roused, looked at him, and smiled. He smiled back then closed his eyes and let his mind drift as the train progressed along its northern route. He reflected about life. Almost forty, it seemed time had stalled his aging process. He supposed he had Daphne and Emma to thank for that. They kept him young.

The train slowed and stopped at a small town to pick up passengers. A newsboy came aboard, selling papers and candy.

David bought the paper and a candy bar for each of them. The train jerked to leave and the paper boy ran to the door and leaped to the platform. Emma watched him and waved. He saw her and waved back.

"Did you see that, Daddy? A boy waved at me," she informed him. He wanted to tell her this was only a start.

After two days, the cities grew closer together, the buildings reached higher and the lawns grew smaller. Wooded hills, barns, scarecrows, and old farm machines surrounded truck farms where men in overalls hoed crops or drove their new tractors. Ribbons of gravel roads snaked to the railroad crossings, sometimes setting off bells that warned the cars of the approaching train.

When the train pulled into Grand Central Station, Daphne grabbed Emma's hand as David found their luggage and hailed a taxi. He pointed to the Chrysler Building, a thousand feet above Lexington Avenue. Then the boasting spires of the Woolworth Building and the Empire State Building came into view as the taxi wound through the tangled streets. Once they arrived at their hotel, a pre-war six-story building on 79th street, they stretched out for a nap then walked toward Central Park, a block away.

Once in the park, under trees where the air cooled and shadows softened the glare off the buildings, they found the boisterous aviary, which delighted Emma and Daphne. Then they strolled down Fifth Avenue, the magnificence of the buildings obvious to them. David pointed to the windows of his apartment, one with a pane missing.

106

"That's it, my apartment that will have to be remodeled or the city of New York will condemn it," he pointed as Emma watched pigeons fight over popcorn someone had thrown on the sidewalk.

David hired a contractor to oversee the remodeling of the apartment. Once the contractor started, they took the train to Niagara Falls, stayed there two days, then moved to a different hotel in New York, one at the tip of Manhattan. David took the subway to the flat while Daphne and Emma explored the shops, rode the ferry past the Statue of Liberty, staying outside, away from the crowd.

One night they dined at The Tavern on the Green and Emma fed the local pigeons popcorn, laughing at their antics. The next afternoon, David took them to see where he had lived and the shop where his father worked before he died.

When it was time to catch the train home, most of the work on the apartment had been completed. The supervisor of the building would oversee the rest and do the inspection. Then he would advertise the apartment for rent at triple the amount he had previously received. They vowed to come back during the Christmas season when the lights of New York would dazzle Emma and Rockefeller Center would be the center of the nation.

The hot summer dragged on as the polio epidemic raged in Morgan County. Emma started back to school the Tuesday after Labor Day and by the weekend a cold front blew in from the north, plunging the temperature into the forties. New cases of polio subsided and those with healthy children breathed a sigh of relief.

Around Thanksgiving, Daphne felt bad for a few days. She complained of nausea and threw up several mornings. Daisy insisted David take her to the doctor but the nausea abated and Daphne declared she felt wonderful. A week later the vomiting returned, and Daphne decided to see the doctor.

"You're pregnant," the doctor announced. A smile spread over her face.

"Wonderful! David is going to be thrilled," she declared to her mother, who had taken off work to take her.

"Why, I believe everyone in town will be thrilled, including me," Madeline laughed as she hugged her daughter while the doctor nodded his head.

"Everyone in town will know when David Mayer gets into the courthouse tomorrow. Oh no, he told me once that he'd had a child by his first wife and it was deformed. Were you the doctor for Anna?" Daphne asked the physician.

"Yes, I was, and that baby was probably deformed due to her having a case of the measles early in her pregnancy. It wasn't a genetic abnormality. We'll X-ray you later and find out if this baby is normal. We don't like to do that, but we will in your case. Stay away from sick people and limit your activities," the doctor advised.

"Don't worry, we'll all see to that," Madeline assured him.

During their marriage, David and Daphne had not used birth control. Daphne, a Catholic, did not believe in contraceptives so it had not been an issue with them. They decided whatever happened would happen. It had taken seven years, but finally a baby was on the way.

David told everyone in Decatur about the baby; all the people at the courthouse, all the attorneys in town, all the neighbors, the teachers at Emma's school, everyone. And Madeline had spread the word to those in her circle and Joseph, now home from the war and going to college, told everyone he knew. If there was anyone in Morgan County who didn't know Judge David Mayer and his wife were having a baby, they were hermits who hadn't come out of the mountains in years.

The doctor X-rayed Daphne in her seventh month and told her the baby had developed properly. There were two legs, two arms, and a perfectly shaped head inside her belly. In the early morning hours of April 20th, 1951, Daphne went into labor. David rushed her to the hospital. David, Daisy, Eva, and Madeline paced in the waiting room while Emma stayed with a neighbor. Five hours later, their little girl came into the world. The delivery room nurse had to dart through the hall to take the baby to the nursery to be bathed. David cornered her as she left the delivery room door.

"Is she normal? Does she have everything?" he asked the nurse holding her bundle.

Seeing tears on his face, the nurse gave him a knowing smile.

"She's a perfect little girl, and pretty big too. Now, let me by so I can get her into the nursery. I have work to do."

Glued to the nursery window, David watched as they bathed his newborn daughter. He could see her arms and legs dart outward as they handled her. Then they worked on her umbilical cord and sucked something out of her mouth. She was crying and her arms thrashed around. Finally, the nurse pinned a diaper on her and pulled a tiny white shirt over her head. Then she wrapped her in a pink blanket and put her in a crib, close to the widow. David pointed to the baby and the nurse knew what he wanted. She picked her up and held her close to the glass then uncovered her legs and tiny feet. All her toes were there and her feet were normal. *She was his child and she was normal. She did not inherit his club foot.*

Tears ran down David's cheeks as he swallowed the lump in his throat. He had the most beautiful and perfect baby in the world. She was his baby, *his*. He left the hospital sobbing, went outside, and walked around the block. A few minutes later, he went back to Daphne's room as they wheeled her in from the delivery room. The nurse ordered all of them out while they positioned her in the bed. He ran in when the nurse left.

"We have a beautiful little girl. She's perfect," David said, smiling at his wonderful wife.

"I'm so glad, now I want to sleep. They'll bring her in later. Don't forget to pick up Emma before you go home," Daphne mumbled in a drugged state.

110

"You can see her later this afternoon. We bring the babies to the mothers at three so come back then and you can hold your little girl," the nurse told David as she nodded to the women with him.

"Okay," they said in unison.

David went back to the nursery window but they had closed the curtains. He left the hospital and went to a nearby florist and purchased three dozen yellow roses to be delivered to Daphne's room. Then he went to his office in the courthouse and told everyone about his new daughter.

"She is beautiful and perfect. She has all her fingers and toes and a head full of blonde hair," he repeated to all the people who gathered around his chambers to hear his news.

Many of the attorneys, already gathered for court, slapped him on the back or shook his hand. He left to be at the hospital at three. When he held his daughter, a rush of love filled his heart. It was the happiest day of his life.

They named her Grace. The next few days spun by as Daisy got the house ready for them to come home. Daisy and Emma were in the kitchen when they arrived, Daisy with her arms outstretched. Once they were settled in, David stood over the crib waiting on the baby to wake up. When Grace opened her eyes he smiled in amazement. He stared at her, afraid to touch her.

"It's okay to hold her," Daphne assured him. She scooped the baby out of the crib and handed her to David.

Then he walked with her, all around the house, and told her about her nursery, her mother, and her big sister. Emma followed him, watching her little sister, waiting on her turn to hold her.

"My goodness, I never saw people act so foolish over a baby," Daisy said, clearing her throat.

"Oh, it's time to take you home. I guess I will relinquish the baby to her mother," David said as he handed the baby to Daphne.

David loved being a father to a newborn. He rushed home every day from the courthouse eager to hear Grace's soft cry, smell her baby powder, change her diaper, dress her in a little gown, and rock her to sleep. At night he would jump out of bed when the baby cried. He didn't want to miss anything and mentioned to Daphne that he wished he could be home all day. Daphne assured him he needed to go to work. She needed some time with her baby.

David vowed he'd do everything he could to make their happiness last. Nothing would come between him and his family.

Nothing.

CHAPTER 12

Late August, 1954

Gordon Walton, a detective for the Morgan County sheriff's department, had a commitment to himself. He wanted to solve all cases assigned to him, no matter how long it took, no matter how complicated or old the crime.

One case he hadn't solved involved Owen Campbell. The no good SOB had killed Morris Elliott, shot him between the eyes, and had gotten away with it. Owen disappeared in 1941. His wife said he left to join the Army right after Pearl Harbor, but now he wondered. There was no evidence he had joined the Army, and he had never returned.

Morris Elliott had been a friend of his, a mentor who attended the same church as his parents. Gordon opened the file once a month and kept it on his desk for a few days, a reminder that he would solve the murder and give Morris' parents the closure they deserved. Meanwhile, he had Colin Campbell, Owen's brother, in his sights. A kid of thirteen or fourteen when Morris died, Gordon figured Colin knew about the shooting but he'd not gotten a confession or any information out of him, not yet.

Colin returned from the war a grown man and opened Campbell Builders, located in Huntsville. He'd married a local girl and ran in the best social circles, due to his wife who came from an established and popular family. It puzzled Gordon that Colin had maneuvered himself into the elite crowd of Huntsville.

The Campbell brothers had been back woods ignorant most of their life, living in a one-room shack close to the river where Owen operated his moonshine still. Owen managed to marry Skye Ross, a widow with two girls, a woman who raised horses that were rumored to be the best in northern Alabama. She existed on a meager living until Owen joined the Army and left her stranded in a shack on top of Robinson Mountain with a newborn son.

Shortly after the war started, she sold her place and moved to town. That made it easier for Gordon to question her about Morris Elliott's disappearance. He knew she withheld information about Morris' death but he couldn't corner her. Then she and her kids disappeared. No one knew where they were, not even her sister who lived in Guntersville, a quaint town east of Decatur.

Gordon loved to take his kids to Guntersville State Park, a mountaintop adventure for them at the lodge on a cliff overlooking Guntersville Lake, one of the best fishing lakes in the South. Newly divorced after his wife decided she had enough of his long hours and weekend absences, he missed his two kids but made sure he spent quality time with them on his weekends.

Every other weekend, his eight-year-old daughter and seven-year-old son spent time with him, from Friday night until four p.m.

114

on Sundays. They ratted on their mother when he had them, how she had a boyfriend who worked at a bank and he drove a red car. Gordon didn't care who she dated as long as she was respectable for the kids. He wanted the best for them.

One thing he kept from his marriage was his saving account and a secure retirement from the county. She had been in a hurry to get the divorce so he gave her the house and five thousand dollars for a new start. The child support he paid her and her job as a school teacher gave her a decent lifestyle, and his kids would never want for anything. He'd see to that.

After the divorce, he found friendship with Judge Mayer and they spent time fishing when they could both take a break from work. Last year, they took a fishing trip down to the coast with two attorneys from the District Attorney's office and fell in love with the panhandle of Florida and the Alabama coast in Baldwin County, a raw, undeveloped marsh and saw grass swamp. Populated by shore birds, egrets, fish, oysters, clams, and scruffy fishermen who loved living on the coast, it was an unclaimed wilderness that caught their attention.

After a hurricane caused extensive damage in the area in 1950, people left and didn't rebuild. A motel that had stood on a dune on the Gulf side of the coastal highway had a "FOR SALE" sign on a pile of rubble close to the highway. The roof of the motel was gone, the concrete block walls had crumbled and the old sign leaned at a fifty degree angle. The phone number, almost erased by the wind was barely readable. They'd seen the sign on their last two trips. He and Judge Mayer bought the four acre property, on the Gulf of Mexico, for eight thousand dollars.

At the closing, the realtor advised them to buy a large parcel of Puma Island bordering the Alabama-Florida line. No one wanted the delicate island, prone to destruction by each hurricane that blew across the narrow strip of land into the inter-coastal waterway. No bridge linked the island to the main highway but they figured someday a bridge would be proposed.

The Alabama Gulf coast had some of the best beaches in the world, the pristine, sugar white sands stretching along the coast of Alabama and Florida. But the beach worshipers wanted to vacation on the Atlantic side of Florida where fancy hotels dotted the coast and they could be seen in their skimpy bikinis.

Families wanted to vacation in Miami and the Keys where modern swimming pools and air conditioned rooms provided comfort. The little town of Gulf Shores, Alabama, remained the quaint, sleepy place it had always been, where colorful clapboard houses lined the north side of the beach highway. A few concrete block houses stood in the sand on the Gulf side. A couple of cafes kept the highway travelers from starvation and fed the locals.

Several little bays along the coast brought the oyster diggers out at daybreak, their long poles jabbing the beds. Alligators silently slid into the brackish water to find food but most of them stayed in the fresh water rivers that emptied into the Gulf. They swam with the manatees, snakes, bass, perch, catfish and eels all the way up the rivers past Montgomery.

In the Alabama River Delta, black bears, ferrets, mink, possum, raccoons, bob cats, otters, coyotes and beavers lived uninterrupted. Golden eagles, vultures, egrets, herons, turkeys, sea gulls and song birds multiplied, played, lived, raised their young and died in places man had not seen. The flooded backwater kept men cautious, even the seasoned fishermen did not know where the true river bed flowed. Slow moving back water wound around cypress trees laden with moss where catfish as big as torpedoes swam in the water along with perch, bass, bream and cottonmouths.

Rumors of men disappearing, never to be seen again, made the rounds at the local bars in Mobile, and Gordon knew some were true. He'd seen the reports on the missing men.

Gordon and "the Judge," as David Mayer was now called by the populace of Morgan County, had their favorite places to eat in Gulf Shores. Over a meal of fried catfish, slaw, baked beans, hushpuppies and fried onion rings washed down by two beers, they decide to buy thirteen acres on Puma Island. Full of seafood and beer, they drove to the realtor's office and asked about the history of the sand bar.

"A man named John Golightly bought one-third of the island in 1945 when goats roamed the entire parcel. The name at that time was Goat Island. He cleaned the island of most of the animals, roasting them on an open fire, selling the meat to the area residents. Goat meat is sweet, very good," the realtor informed them.

"Now it's named Puma Island because someone saw a couple of pumas wandering around on the sand, probably from a bygone time when they hunted for baby goats. Someday people will build houses on that island. The island has some buffer from hurricanes and is on the intercostal waterway." The man pitched his sale with enthusiasm.

They paid five thousand dollars for thirteen acres of sand. On the way home, after the beer had escaped their body, they laughed at the stupidity of the purchase.

"I can't believe we bought several acres of sand. What were you thinking?" Gordon asked the Judge.

"Me? I bought it because you said it would be a good investment. We now own a piece of an island with no bridge to it, no sewage, no water, no electricity and no way to get supplies to it. We should have 'stupid' written on our foreheads," the Judge laughed as he pulled out a cigar and lit it.

Gordon liked David Mayer. He had the family life Gordon coveted, a warm home filled with love and admiration. He'd never heard him and his wife argue, but David assured him they had.

"But, in a good way. She says I spoil our kids and I say she's too hard on them. That's our biggest clash, the children," David said, flicking ashes from a cigar out the window.

They passed through Montgomery where the vacant countryside unfolded with rolling hills sporting tall pines, oaks, elms and pecan trees. Small farmhouses, surrounded by fields, marked the landscape where rusty farm equipment, ragged

118

scarecrows and an occasional new tractor guarded the patch of earth a man owned. It was his place where he raised his family, his spot to retire, his land to leave to the next generation.

On the way home, they discussed cases they shared, the detective and the Judge united to bring justice to the people they served, each guilty man getting his due, the innocent protected and freed. They put away criminals, separated men and women in domestic disputes, protected neglected children and solved border disputes between neighbors. In Alabama, a man would fight harder and longer over a ten foot strip of disputed land quicker than the threat of someone hurting his mother or running off with his wife.

They drove over Oak Mountain into a beautiful valley where Homewood and Vestavia Hills graced the southern slope of Red Mountain. The mountain, a tall and long blade of iron ore, coal and limestone, ran sideways toward Chattanooga where it joined Lookout Mountain a hundred miles to the northeast. The Appalachian Mountains began in Birmingham, running all the way to Maine.

Past Birmingham, they stopped for a pulled pork sandwich and discussed the upcoming fishing tournament on Lake Guntersville, the best fishing lake east of the Mississippi. Held on Labor Day weekend, several county Bar Associations sponsored the event when the shallow lake, warm from the August heat, harbored huge fish fattened during the summer months.

The lake, built by the TWA in the late 1930s, was surrounded by hills and mountains creating islands, small bays and hundreds of miles of shoreline. Dubbed the "Switzerland of the South," the lake was the third largest body of fresh water in the world when backed up behind Guntersville Dam. A part of the Cherokee Indian reservation and one of the loading docks used for the Trail of Tears were under the waters, the ghosts of the past silenced, their graves flooded, the foundations of their villages lost.

The Saturday before the tournament, Gordon and the Judge cased out the lake, finding the best fishing spot, cruising the inlets and around the islands. Excitement grew as the Judge registered them and paid the entrance fee. Gordon supplied the boat. This year, Gordon took his seventeen-year-old nephew and David brought Emma, now thirteen, barely eligible to be on the boat for the tournament.

The night before the tournament, they checked into a local hotel, each with their own room, Emma sleeping on a cot, listening to her father snore until the alarm clock sounded at four a.m. The four of them found the truck in the dark, fireflies sparkling in the blackness, the full moon setting. The owner of the motel handed them coffee and a biscuit as they slipped into the cab of the truck. They drove to the landing and slid the boat off the trailer, Emma helping the men.

When everyone was aboard, Gordon drove to the line-up. At five a.m. the horn sounded, and the boats sped off to their spots. Whoever got there first claimed the area. They had to return by four p.m. to weigh in. Daphne had packed them a lunch. Drinks, iced down in a cooler, kept them hydrated. Each person used his own fishing gear, and in no time Emma caught the first fish. She beamed with excitement.

When they weighed in, Emma claimed the largest fish and Kyle, Gordon's nephew, the most. They didn't win the tournament but had a great time, until they ran into Colin Campbell.

"Well now, how are my two favorite people from Decatur?" Colin asked as he waved at them.

"Hello, Colin. How are you doing?" David replied. Gordon didn't acknowledge him.

"Who is this pretty girl?" Colin asked as Emma helped unload the boat.

"Meet my daughter, Emma," David waved his hand toward her as they unloaded their gear and started toward David's car, where Daphne sat with Grace.

Daphne had driven over from Decatur for the weigh-in and to bring Emma fresh clothes to wear to the fish fry, held at the town center after the tournament. Everybody who was anybody attended the Labor Day fish fry at Guntersville. David waved at Daphne in the car. Emma ran over to her mother, gushing about the tournament.

"This was awesome. I loved it. I caught the biggest fish. Mom, what's wrong? You look funny." Emma saw the look on her mother's face.

David put his fishing rods and tackle box in the trunk then slid into the front seat behind the wheel. Daphne sat still then turned to David. The color had drained from her face and her eyes, wide with shock, watched Colin Campbell as he continued to talk to the men standing around, fussing over their gear, talking about the tournament.

"That's him. He's one of the men. That man, right there." She pointed to Colin.

"Uh, you mean that night long ago when you lived up on the mountain?" David inquired.

"Yes, that's one of them. I'm sure. I will never forget that face," Daphne said as she turned down the sun visor.

"Mom, what's wrong? What are you talking about? Who is one of them?" Emma asked from the backseat.

"Nothing, it's nothing. Okay, we're going home, your mother has a headache," David stated methodically.

"Yes, yes, I have a horrible headache," she cried.

Daphne saw Colin approach the car. Then Colin leaned down and began talking, leveling his eyes to David.

"David, don't you need some work done on your house? Your sister-in-law hired me to remodel her kitchen and put on a new roof. She bought one of those old homes up on Monte Santo, but you probably know that. Say, is that your little girl?" Grace stuck her head out the window.

"Yes, she's the little one."

"And is this your wife?" Colin looked past David.

"Yes, she has a headache. I need to get this bunch back to Decatur," David replied moving the car backwards a few inches.

"And miss the fish fry? It's always a good one," Colin took his hands off the car and backed away.

"Let's get out of here," David whispered as he turned the car around and found the road leading to the highway.

They drove home in silence. After they were in the house, David suggested Emma get her sister in the tub for a bath. When they emerged, David handed the girls a sandwich for supper. Daphne had retreated to their bedroom and closed the door.

"What's wrong with Mother?" Emma asked, noticing her absence.

"She has a bad headache. She'll be okay in the morning. You girls play in your room then go to bed. Let your mother sleep," David replied.

David wiped the crumbs off the table and put the milk away. He went straight to Daphne, who had curled into a fetal position on the bed.

"What if he recognized me? What if he puts it together?" Daphne asked.

"He's not going to put it together, but now that we know he was one of the men we will keep as far away from him as possible. Eva wanted to have a party when the remodeling is done but we won't go. She would invite him. You or I, or one of the girls will be sick and I'll tell her not to use him again. Calm down, no one is harmed by today. He'll probably never see you or Emma again," David tried to comfort his horrified wife.

"Okay, you're right. I can get through this. I can, and I will."
Daphne pulled the cover up to her chin.

That night, David dreamed about Emma. In the dream, Colin
grabbed her and took her away on a boat and threw her overboard.
David yelled for her to hang on then realized the sound came from
Daphne, who had shouted out in her sleep. Now awake, he crept to
the girls' room and looked at their faces. Both of them were asleep,
peaceful and safe in their beds, the soft light of the night revealing
their features. Their dog, a golden retriever, raised his head then
put it down and turned over. Everything was okay.

He went back to the bedroom and glanced at Daphne.
Moonlight danced across her face as the shadow of a tree swaying
in the wind interrupted the soft stream of light. He went to the
dining room, opened the liquor cabinet and poured two fingers of
Jack Daniels in a glass. He found one of the rocking chairs on the
front porch and settled into the seat. An owl hooted from its perch
in the hollow spot in the large oak and a flash of lightening danced
in the distance. Soft thunder followed a few seconds later.

He stayed on the porch, watched the storm approach, felt the
temperature drop then smelled the rain and dust in the wind. When
it passed, he went inside and slid into the bed by Daphne.

Why did he have a feeling the tranquility of his home would
not go on forever? He had no reason to believe that yet he knew.

*I love her so much. Nothing can ever happen to her or the
girls*, he said to himself as he watched streams of rain slide down
the window pane.

CHAPTER 13

1960 – 1970

The years flew by, folded over onto each other and wrapped around the seasons. The war had been over fifteen years, a new generation had been born and a young Senator, John F. Kennedy, became the thirty-fifth President of the United States. Voters in the South could not believe a Catholic sat in the White House, a travesty they felt would destroy the country. Daphne voted for Kennedy while David supported Nixon.

At the beginning of the new decade, Emma started college in Florence, Alabama, sixty miles away, far enough to be away from home and close enough to drive home on weekends. She wanted to be a school teacher and chose Florence State Teachers College, a smaller college than the University of Alabama, which had courted her with a partial scholarship.

For her first year, she had a new wardrobe, a monthly allowance and the friendship of several girlfriends who were on the same floor. They revealed their secrets, shared clothes, nail polish, lipstick and class notes. Emma made the Dean's list while two of her friends left after failing grades sent them home.

Emma strived for perfection in everything she did. She was valedictorian for her high school class and head cheerleader. A beauty, tall and poised, she turned heads when she entered a room. She kept her clothes arranged in her closet in colors, sorted into blouses, dresses, skirts and sweaters. She hated clutter and could not tolerate sloppy habits. She and Grace were exact opposites.

Grace, still a little girl at nine, spoiled and selfish, scraped by in school, had constant reprimands for excessive talking, played pranks on her friends, talked on the phone too long, threw her clothes on the floor and generally drove Daisy ragged. She could, and did, argue her way out of battles. David loved the amusement of the fights, her maneuvering and persuasions to get her way. Daphne, afraid the spoiled child would rebel in her teenage years, kept a vigilant eye on her and vowed she'd end up in prison or reform school.

"Grace will be the death of me," Daphne stated once a week.

"She's a survivor, she'll do fine," David assured her, but secretly he wondered.

Their nightly routine encompassed watching television, catching the news then *The Twilight Zone, Hogan's Heroes*, or *The Ed Sullivan Show*. Popular movie stars were Marilyn Monroe, Elizabeth Taylor, Clark Gable, Rock Hudson and Doris Day. Once a month they caught at movie at the Princess Theatre. Elvis Presley was the musical rage, but Daphne and David preferred Frank Sinatra, Dean Martin and Perry Como.

Emma came home for Christmas and hinted she could use a car to get back and forth from Florence instead of riding with friends.

"You can drive the Ford or the Packard, and I'll drive the other one," David offered.

"Oh, Daddy, why do I have to drive one of those old cars? Everyone else has a new car."

"I've been to parent's day at the college and everyone does not have a new car, so I wouldn't press my luck," David reminded her.

"Why do my parents have to be so old fashioned?" she remarked as she packed the 1950 Ford. "I guess this one will do. It's the newest."

Later that week, David bought a 1960 Buick. He kept the old Packard, it wasn't worth much and he liked the car. A few weeks before, it wouldn't crank, the battery had run down.

Unless it was raining, David walked the four blocks to the courthouse each day and Daphne only drove back and forth to Grace's school, the grocery store and around town. She had not ventured out of Morgan County since they bumped into Colin Campbell six years ago.

There had been no more encounters with Colin, but to satisfy Daphne they kept a low profile, not venturing to Huntsville. He and Gordon still did the fishing tournament each year, taking Emma when she could go. Kyle had grown up, and after college he joined the Army and was in Viet Nam.

Colin's popularity in Huntsville had suffered a setback. It seemed he had some trouble with one of his customers who accused him of fraud and theft. From the rumors around town he appeared to be guilty and the accuser, Alton Barber, a pillar of the community in Huntsville, might have a good case against Colin.

On August 12th, 1963, the body of a male surfaced on the banks of the Tennessee River in Limestone County. David received a call from Gordon that it looked like the body was Owen Campbell.

"We're pretty sure it's him. The body has red hair and a gold tooth. It matches Owen and had been in the ground a long time. Colin will be coming over to ID the body in the next couple of days. If this is him, I won't be able to close the file on Morris Elliott. I'd hoped to question Owen, but that doesn't look possible," Gordon told him.

A few days later, news of the body was in *The Decatur Daily* with a photograph of Owen Campbell. Daphne saw it and identified Owen as the other man that raped her.

"Thank God he's dead. Wasn't Owen married to Skye, that lady that baked those delicious cakes?" Daphne asked.

"Yes, and she was married to him when he raped you. They have a child, a boy," David informed her.

"So Emma has a half-brother? He would be her half-brother," she realized and shook her head.

"Emma's father might be Colin," David reminded her.

128

"Either way, her son would be related to Emma. I can't think about it, I won't think about it. You're Emma's father."

"That's right. Put it out of your mind and stay away from town until Colin buries his brother. He's all over the place, making arrangements and making accusations that he knew Skye and her girls killed Owen."

"I'm not leaving the house until you tell me that man is in his grave."

"It'll be over in a few days and things will go back to normal," David assured her.

On November 23rd, 1963, President Kennedy was shot in Dallas, Texas. Disbelief shrouded the country. Thanksgiving plans were shattered as the hearse carrying his body kept everyone glued to the television. As Christmas approached, Daphne put up a small tree, assisted by Grace who complained she had better things to do. Emma came home for Christmas and observed Grace during one of her tantrums.

"She's so spoiled and hateful. Why do you put up with this?" Emma asked her mother.

"I don't know what to do with her. She's out of control," Daphne replied.

On Christmas morning, they had a huge breakfast then everyone moved to the living room. When all the boxes were emptied and the wrapping paper in piles on the floor, Grace asked, "Where is the sweater I wanted, the red one I asked for?"

"They were sold out at the store and you know I don't drive to Huntsville to shop," Daphne replied.

"You could have made an exception and gotten that sweater for me. You would have done that for Emma," Grace screamed as she stormed out of the room, kicking wrapping paper out of her way.

Everyone in the room sat in stunned silence. Finally Emma spoke.

"I'm going back to college where the atmosphere is better. It stinks in here." Emma left the next day.

Two days after Grace turned thirteen, she and Daisy had an argument. Grace refused to eat the fried chicken Daisy prepared for supper.

"This chicken is too greasy. Look at the grease underneath it," Grace complained as she pushed the meat aside.

Then she raked the creamed potatoes off her plate, claiming they were lumpy and cold. She left the dining table in a huff. When David drove Daisy home that afternoon, she didn't speak a word. She turned her head toward the window. When he stopped to let her out, he noticed she had been crying. David watched her husband help her up the steps to their front porch and noticed she had lost weight, her hair seemed whiter and her deeply wrinkled face revealed years had passed that he had not noticed.

He drove away with a heavy heart. Grace had been rude and he and Daphne had let her get away with it. They should have stood up for Daisy, but they didn't. He felt awful. Daisy was not

130

only their maid, she was a close friend. He loved her and he had wronged her. He saw the hurt in her face.

As he drove home, he reminded himself that Daisy had never revealed her age to them. She remembered the change of the century and she talked about the sinking of the Titanic like it was yesterday, but she wouldn't tell them the year she was born.

"I don't have to tell you how old I am. That's none of your business," she replied once when he asked her. "I was born on March tenth and that's all you need to know. The year I was born is my secret."

After she told them the day she was born, they began to celebrate her birthday. Daphne baked a chocolate cake for her and David gave her an envelope with a fifty dollar bill inside. Daphne also bought her something from the department store, a new sweater, a pair of gloves, a new hat, a nightgown or a new appliance for her kitchen. She loved the electric mixer Daphne gave her.

"It sure makes baking cakes for the church easier," she told David on one of their talks when he drove her home. She liked that private time with him, their time to reminisce about Anna, Daphne or the girls. Sometimes she talked about her two daughters and four grandchildren, sometimes about her husband.

The first day of March, 1964, Daisy resigned. She handed David an official resignation letter when he took her home that afternoon. It was two weeks after the incident with Grace. He had no warning.

"No, no, you don't have to do this. If you want to work only one day a week you can and we can make it easier on you. I can't imagine my life without you. You've been with me a long time," David pleaded.

"I've been with you almost twenty-four years and now it's time for me and Willie to do some things we want to do. I've never seen the ocean and I want to do that before I go to heaven," Daisy informed him.

"Okay, why don't you take a few weeks off and we can talk about his later," he offered.

"No, I'm not coming back. I'm real tired and things hurt and I can't do stuff at home that I needs to do. You have been good to me but it's time for me to take care of Willie. He's real sick, real sick. Friday will be my last day," Daisy argued.

"Okay, but you can change your mind if you want to," David assured her.

When he returned with the letter Daphne cried then he handed the letter to Grace.

"Is she leaving because I'm mean to her? I've been mean to her and I know it. She tells me all the time that I'm spoiled and now she's leaving. I feel awful." Grace ran to her room.

"I don't want her to go, but we can't stop her. I can take care of things here. I'd already taken over doing the laundry and if we need to hire someone, we can hire a part-time girl," Daphne cleared the dishes off the table as she tried to hide her disappointment.

132

"I'll give her a good bonus," David replied.

"How much?"

"Two hundred. Do you think that's enough?"

"No, give her three hundred," Daphne countered.

"I guess you're right. She'd been with us a long time. I'll give it to her the last day when I take her home," David agreed.

Daisy didn't have much to say that Friday. Daphne hugged her when it was time to say goodbye. David started the drive to take Daisy home.

"I'll miss you. Thanks for all the years you've given us, and for being there for me and Anna. I couldn't have made it without you," David said, and he meant it.

"You are a good man, David Mayer, a good man. You have a good woman and a wonderful family. You have those girls to raise but love them like you do and everything will be alright. God won't give us more than we can bear," Daisy said as they turned down the street to her house.

David saw her husband and granddaughter waiting for her on the front porch. He handed her the envelope and told her not to open it until she went into the house.

"I know you put some money in there. We'll use it for our trip to the ocean. Come over to see us anytime you want," Daisy said as she exited the car.

Her granddaughter helped her up the front porch steps. David watched her go into the house then he turned toward the highway to go home. Tears ran down his face. He drove over the bridge then turned around a mile north of it and came back across, composing himself as he drove into his driveway.

Four days later, he received a call at his office. Daisy's granddaughter was on the line.

"Grandmother died sometime during the night. She complained of being tired yesterday and went to bed early. She was already cold when Grandpa found her this morning. She spent some of the money you gave her for a new hat to wear to church. I'll bury her in it," she said between sobs. "She didn't get to see the ocean," the granddaughter added.

"I wish I had known she wanted to go. I would have taken her and Willie," David commented.

"She should have told you," the granddaughter suggested, her voice trembling.

"How old was Daisy?" David asked.

"Eighty-three. She was born in 1881."

"What caused her death? I didn't think she was sick," David asked.

"She had some kind of blood ailment. The doctor said she didn't make enough blood and there was nothing they could do for the condition. He said it was common in people her age."

David, Daphne, and Grace went to the funeral. The minister talked about Daisy's family and her good works and how she'd have a home in heaven. The AME Methodist church, filled to capacity, contained young and old people, black and white. Her daughter wailed when they closed the casket and Daisy's husband stumbled when he followed it to the hearse.

Once they returned home, David pleaded he had work to do at the office. He went to his chambers at the courthouse, closed the door and sobbed. He felt like someone had reached into his chest and pulled out his heart.

The rest of the year flew by, the peach tree in the back yard yielded twelve peaches, the resident cardinal hatched two broods of babies, the horned owl that nested in the tall oak in the front yard hatched an owlet that flew away the day before Halloween.

Emma found love with Kyle Walton when he returned from his stint in Viet Nam. A week after he came home, he called David's house looking for her. Daphne gave him Emma's number at college and their romance progressed quickly. She graduated from college in May of 1964 and they married on the Sunday before Labor Day. The next day, they left for Tuscaloosa for Kyle to begin law school at the University of Alabama. They moved into a one-bedroom apartment in the quaint town built around the Warrior River. Emma found a job with the local school board, teaching fifth grade. They settled into married life and vowed to return to Decatur and start a family once he graduated.

Early in 1965, David came home with the current copy of *The Hollywood Star and News*, a tabloid magazine about movie stars. The magazine had made the rounds at the courthouse and Gladys saved it from the trash for David.

"You might want to look at this. It's about Skye Campbell's daughter," she said when she put it on his desk.

On the cover of the magazine was a photograph of Skye Campbell and her girls, taken in front of her house on Robinson Mountain. The article inside claimed Morgan Madison, a woman nominated for an Academy Award, and Jenna Ross, Skye's oldest daughter, were the same woman. Skye's daughter looked exactly like Skye at that age, a taller version, but her face was the same. David would have known her anywhere.

By the end of the month, Colin Campbell had reared his ugly head again. He called the Attorney General in Montgomery and brought to light the injustices and ineptness of the legal system in north Alabama who had failed to find his brother's body. He claimed the disappearance of his brother and Skye Campbell and her children were linked.

"My brother didn't throw himself into the river. Those 'women on the mountain' killed him and threw him in like a sack of potatoes," Colin claimed in an interview published in the local paper.

Gordon came by to see David after court with the latest about the Campbell brothers.

"This may be trouble for Morgan County. If Skye Campbell and her girls took his body down the path from their house to the river, he would have died in Morgan County. However, men digging the foundation for the new interstate bridge found him buried under twelve feet of clay in Limestone County. I'm pushing for jurisdiction on this case for Limestone County," Gordon argued.

"How did the body get to that grave? It probably floated down the river and where it was thrown in will be an issue. No one could bury a body in twelve feet of hard packed clay," David countered.

"That's a good point," Gordon replied. "Damn, I don't want this case. I don't want to deal with Colin Campbell. I believed I was finished with him. There will be an inquiry and guess who will do it? I'm the detective who will deal with this mess."

"I need to excuse myself if the matter comes to my court. I represented Skye Campbell years ago, so there's a conflict of interest," David advised.

"Lucky you, I wish I could get out of it," Gordon countered.

Colin Campbell caused more than an inquiry. He accused the Morgan County Sheriff's department of negligence in the death of his brother, claiming he had informed them years ago of Owen's disappearance and they did nothing. The Attorney General insisted the case go to Morgan County.

While they mulled over Owen's cause of death, Colin drove to Los Angeles where Morgan Madison had her real estate business. His girlfriend walked around with Morgan, pretending to be interested in purchasing a house. Colin called Gordon after they came home and announced he wanted Morgan questioned.

"There's no reason to question her. She's not charged with a crime. Moving out of Alabama and changing your name isn't a crime," Gordon replied, and hung up.

Then Colin found Carrie, Skye's youngest daughter who had moved back to Huntsville. He caused a scene with her and insisted Gordon question Carrie. The Attorney General also insisted. She would have been thirteen the night Owen died. During the interview, no new information surfaced but she did verify what they knew, Owen Campbell entered the Tennessee River a dead man in the early morning of December 7th, 1941.

The body of Owen was exhumed and a new autopsy performed. The medical examiner from Montgomery could not determine a cause of death and they could not prove foul play. The grand jury heard testimony of the facts and when they realized Skye was eight months pregnant when her husband died, they returned a no-bill in the case.

The Attorney General, furious about the way the media portrayed the Sheriff's department, called Gordon, demanding he investigate the matter further.

"Owen Campbell was a murderer. He killed a man, a federal agent who was investigating Owen Campbell's illegal moonshine operation. I won't waste any more time on the case," Gordon told him.

"Do you know the consequences of your refusal to cooperate?" the Attorney General asked.

"I'm not refusing to cooperate. There's nothing more to investigate. I'm busy with other matters. Whatever you want to do to make my life miserable, you are free to pursue. This matter is closed," Gordon replied.

"You'll regret this," the Attorney General countered.

"I doubt it. Are we finished here?" Gordon knew the Attorney General was bluffing. He had power but Gordon could make it to retirement and that was all he wanted, to stay employed until his thirty-year hire date.

The next day, Gordon pulled the file on Morris Elliott, the unsolved murder of the man he knew Owen Campbell shot. He looked again at the photos, the skull with a bullet hole between the eyes, the roots growing in the rib cage, the shoes he wore to his grave, his belt, his billfold. The worn file, handled by Gordon for twenty-four years, had never left his presence for more than a month. It was at the front of the cold case files, the only murder in Morgan County that had not been solved.

"I hate those sorry, no good Campbell brothers. Owen Campbell won't be missed and whoever put him in that river did the world a favor," Gordon whispered to the photo of Morris in the file. He closed it and put it back into the cabinet.

Colin Campbell kept the controversy going. He did interviews, demanded investigations and talked about his brothers demise to the press. With his new found notoriety, his good looks and flashy clothes, he found the women of the area who were on the make. Colin made the rounds, hitting the local bars and topless clubs over the line in Tennessee.

One girlfriend had more than tired of him. She followed Colin and his latest conquest to the woman's house on May 14th, 1966, and shot him twice, once in the abdomen then in the head. Then the woman left without a trace. Some called her a hero, some swore she was mad with jealousy, the people she worked with revealed she was smart and they'd never find her.

No one shed any tears over Colin, no one attended his funeral and no one but the workers at the cemetery watched his casket go into the grave beside his brother. David and Daphne silently celebrated. They felt immense relief.

A few days later, they had more good news. Emma and Kyle were expecting a baby. Daphne beamed and danced around their bedroom, scouting a place to put a crib.

"A grandchild, we're going to have a little one to love. Right there by the window, that would be a good place. But it might be too drafty," she argued with herself, as David retreated to the living room to answer the telephone.

"Mr. Mayer, this is Skye, Skye Campbell. I don't know if you remember me," she paused.

"Of course I remember you. I have some of your money and you bake the best cakes I have ever eaten. It's good to hear from you," David replied with enthusiasm.

"I'm calling from California. I know that the Campbell men are both dead so I can come out of hiding. I moved to California when we left Alabama. I need to talk to you about what happened to that man named Morris Elliott. Owen killed him. I lied to the authorities. I feel awful about the lie," Skye confessed.

"I don't want you to say anything more to me about the case. You need to talk to Gordon Walton who is still employed at the Sheriff's office. I'll give you his number so you can call him tomorrow. Meantime, catch me up on what you've been doing all these years," David said.

Skye told him about her life in Napa, that she had remarried and had another child. She told him about her husband's death and where the other children lived. David replied with his news.

"Daphne and I have two daughters. One was born in 1951, so we have children the same age," David revealed.

Skye invited him and his family to visit them in California and he invited her to come by and see them when she came back for a visit.

"I will, I have a daughter and two grandchildren who live in Huntsville. You may remember Carrie. She and her husband moved there a few years ago. Her husband is a surgeon and she's a nurse," Skye revealed.

A week later, David received a four-bottle crate of wine from Poschett Vineyards and he sent Skye the money he held for her. Occasionally, Skye would call and talk to Daphne about their children and grandchildren, photos were included in Christmas cards and promises of visits exchanged.

New Year's Day 1969 rode in on an Arctic blast. Winter entrenched the area with a foot of snow and below freezing temperatures. Ice covered ponds and part of the lake. Trees snapped and caused power outages but a week later the weather warmed, the snow melted and mud replaced the white blanket.

Spring arrived in April with warm winds from the south. Grace graduated from high school in May and Emma and Kyle brought Dawson, their little boy, to the graduation. David began to think about retirement and he and Gordon saw more of each other as their families bonded.

When they turned the calendar to 1970, Gordon announced he would retire when he reached thirty years with the force. He planned to move to the Alabama coast where he and David would develop the land that they jointly owned in Baldwin County on the island now named Ono Island. A bridge to the island had been proposed.

Later that week, David calculated when his thirty year anniversary as a Judge would occur. He called Kyle at his law office in Tuscaloosa. He caught him eating lunch at his desk.

"I've made a decision about retirement. Gordon is going to beat me to the thirty year mark, but I'll be right behind him. You need to run for my seat in the next election. I can stay on payroll as a visiting judge long enough to bridge me to thirty years. Think about it. You guys need to move back here so you can get rooted in," David suggested.

"And the family can see more of Dawson. You were reading my mind. Gordon and my dad had already suggested that. I guess you guys had thrown this around," Kyle replied.

"We had. We aren't getting any younger," David countered.

"Don't throw out a 'pitiful old man' case to me. You're as healthy as you were in your thirties. I'll discuss it with Emma and let you know," Kyle countered.

David called home to give Daphne the good news. She didn't answer. He tried again thirty minutes later and still no answer.

"I guess she's outside," he said to himself. At four he called again, no answer.

She couldn't have gone to the store, the car is at the shop getting new tires, he reminded himself. He walked home.

"Daphne, are you home?" he yelled.

No answer. He looked through the downstairs rooms then heard a moan from the back of the house. He ran outside. Daphne lay at the bottom of the stairs leading off the back porch. She had a gash on the side of her head. Ants made a trail across her face to the clotted blood.

"Daphne, can you hear me?" he shook her.

She moaned and moved her hand. He ran inside and called the fire department to send an ambulance.

CHAPTER 14

March, 1970

Carrie Patterson's birthday slipped by, unnoticed to everyone except her husband and mother, Skye Poschett who lived in Napa, California. Carrie had always been close to her mother, the two women bonding as they moved from Decatur to California when Carrie was sixteen. They had been there for each other during the early years, when her sister ran away and Ross came into the world. Carrie delivered him on the day Pearl Harbor was bombed.

Her mother's family continued to grow when her mother married Martin Poschett, the man who built a sprawling vineyard next door to their cottage in Napa. His daughter, Josephine, became her little sister and her mother had a late in life baby, a son she named Phillip.

When Martin died from lung cancer at sixty-three, Carrie had finished nursing school and worked in San Diego. A month after she began her job at the hospital, she met a young doctor. Six months later she married Dr. Steve Patterson and a year later their first child was born. Three years later, a son followed.

Steve's ambition was to return to the South where he grew up, so he accepted a position with a hospital in Huntsville. That suited Carrie, for she grew up thirty miles away. But the best surgery position in the country opened in Birmingham, Alabama, at the new hospital there, so they moved to Vestavia Hills, a suburb south of town.

With Steve, a wonderful man who grew up in Atlanta, a surgeon who shared her love of medicine, she had a life she never dreamed she could have. Often she let her mind drift back to the place she grew up, in a shack on top of a mountain near Decatur. The log cabin had no electricity, running water or source of heat other than a fireplace. She had milked their cow, churned butter, picked vegetables, gathered eggs, shoveled coal for the fireplace, cut firewood, cooked on a wood burning stove and run through the forests barefooted. All of that changed when her mother moved them to town after her second husband, Owen Campbell, died an unfortunate death that they didn't discuss.

The mysterious death of her stepfather resulted in Jenna, her older sister, running away from home. Jenna and Owen committed a terrible wrong against her mother, but no one talked about that night. Jenna had been persuaded by her stepfather to have sex with him, then he promised her they'd run away and get married. Jenna fell for the lies, and a confrontation one night in the barn cost Owen his life.

Jenna ran away the next day, but she came back into their lives twenty-four years later. She had changed her name to Morgan Madison and had a son the same age as Ross. Her son was fathered by Owen Campbell and was a half-brother to her mother's son by

Owen. Everyone in the family knew that, but Morgan never acknowledged the fact, continuing the guise that he was fathered by a soldier who died at Pearl Harbor.

Well, the past is the past. All those entanglements are for Morgan and mother to sort out. I'm not going to live in the past so I won't dwell on it, Carrie said to herself as she looked around in her closet for a pair of slacks.

My forty-second birthday just happened. People don't believe I am that old so I am aging okay, I'm still in the game, Carrie said to herself as she pulled a pair of navy slacks off a hanger.

Always attentive, Steve apologized for not taking her to her favorite Italian restaurant for her birthday. They decided a quiet night at home, a good bottle of wine and time for themselves behind a closed door made the perfect night. With their busy schedules and two children in the house, private time had become a rarity.

A woman is good in her forties, she said to herself as she continued to dress. She and Steve found time to make love often and she knew he adored her and the children. So many of their friends had already divorced, some of them the second time around. She treasured their state, one of mutual love and a comfortableness that she wanted to last.

Can I make the years suspend me in a perpetual state of being comfortable, energetic and on top of my game? she asked

146

herself as she sat down on the end of the bed and pulled on her socks.

The kids were gone to school and Steve left hours ago for the hospital. She had the house to herself and she loved that. Carrie slid her arms in a blouse then ran a brush through her wet hair. At the mirror, she surveyed a few wrinkles at the corner of her eyes. She ran her finger along the scars she sustained from a long ago car accident. Always red when her skin was warm, she looked like a jig saw puzzle put together. *Thank God for plastic surgery and make-up.*

"What I'm waiting on is the empty nest years," she said out loud to herself in the mirror. Then she looked at the floor of the closet and smiled.

Yep, that's the spot, right there on the floor. That is where we made love last night, my forbidden spot, the floor of the closet.

They had done that twice in the last six months. She told Steve about her fantasy place early in their marriage and he had his favorite spot too, on the beach with waves crashing over them. They made sure that happened every time they went to Gulf Shores or Panama City.

Their last session on the beach happened one night in late August in the Gulf, when the water was its warmest and the glow of millions of plankton created a phosphorescent wake. They saw the glow when their bodies disturbed the water. They made love where the surf crashed onto the beach, the sparkling turquoise and green light flowing over them. It was a night with a new moon in

147

the inky sky filled with stars and a lone airplane traversing east, its blinking lights winking at them, approving their antics.

Afterwards, they swam out a few yards, naked and exhilarated. They splashed the sparkling water, laughing and frolicking until they heard voices and saw the glow of a flashlight coming toward the spot where they left their suits. They decided that night that they would retire to a house on the beach, one close enough to walk to the ocean or a bay, one on the Gulf of Mexico where the warm water lapped at their front door.

That was a fun night, one of the best in my life, Carrie said to herself as slipped on her shoes.

After she dressed, she thought about her day. She loved Fridays, her day to work in the women's shelter, her day to get lost in the needs of others. She looked at a photo of her children on the dresser, made last year at Christmas.

"I can't wait for you two to run away from home or go off to college, whichever comes first. Then we can build our place on the coast," she remarked to the picture of her children.

They moved to Birmingham in January when the recently completed surgery wing of the University Hospital opened. Steve and three other surgeons were recruited by the hospital. Carrie's husband had coveted this position for years. Birmingham was a new city for both of them and so far they loved the area.

Birmingham, "The "Magic City" as it was called from the rapid population advance in the late 1890s, had morphed from the industry of making steel to health care. The city, split in half by a

148

rail road, sat in a saucer shaped valley adjacent to Red Mountain where a large statue of Vulcan stood, his naked rear end flashing the citizens of Homewood, one of the "over the mountain" prestigious places to live in the area.

The glow of Sloss Furnace, the small steel mill located less than a mile from downtown, still produced small amounts of steel, the coke ovens glowing after dark when molten steel was poured into ingots. The children liked to pass over the furnaces on the viaduct that sported a billboard of a puppy with a tail that wagged back and forth, his tongue lapping a bowl of the best pet food in the South.

Two stately television towers stood on the pinnacle of the mountain that jogged east and west. Old mine entrances peppered the rugged façade where coal had been mined, the entrances tempting to teenagers and cave explorers. Occasionally someone went in and never came out, the news of their demise making the second page of *The Birmingham News* or *The Post Herald.*

A highway cut through the mountain to the south, revealing the geological richness of the area. Iron ore, coal and other minerals were identified on the incision where the highway sliced open layers of rocks. Signs, arrows and labels identified the veins from a narrow pathway that allowed geology students to see the strata.

Birmingham had not enjoyed a pristine reputation. The Civil Rights demonstrations, fire hoses, police dogs and the bomb that killed four little girls one Sunday morning tarnished the city, rendering it uninhabitable for some Yankees and hippies who never looked below the media hyped sensationalism. In spite of the headlines, the populace of the area, black and white, adjusted and stayed.

"We don't want people to discover our beautiful city. Let's let the well-kept secret stay secret," Carrie heard more than once at church and at parties she and her husband felt obligated to attend.

The city integrated after the horrid headlines that made national news, the articles never revealing that blacks and whites lived side-by-side with less violence than northern cities. Most of the black population stayed in the area, working, having children, sending them to school and taking advantage of the educational opportunities the community colleges of Alabama offered.

"People vote with their feet," one politician noted. "If you don't like this part of America there are other places to live. We have a great state and I want to make it greater," he stated in his newspaper ad. The feet elected him.

Some blacks left and moved up north to work in the car assembly plants in Detroit, in the stockyards of Chicago, the steel mills of Pittsburg, the factories of New Jersey. They returned after a few years. They missed the South, the laid back ways, the food, the Southern manners, the mild weather. Many stated the discrimination in the north was cruel, with gangs and violence they never saw in Alabama. Their children were terrified to play outside, the hospitals refused to treat them unless they walked in the door with cash, the schools immediately shoved their children into special education classes, labeling them "a year behind" before they tested them, delegating them to a status they didn't deserve. Once they returned to Alabama they stayed, advising their friends not to make their mistakes.

University Hospital treated everyone who walked in their doors. They hired qualified employees, black or white. The hospital encompassed several structures, including the old hospital erected in 1910. The sprawling complex covered eight square blocks in the southern part of the city. As a teaching hospital, it connected to the medical school, where doctors, nurses, physical therapists, respiratory therapists, X-ray technicians, dental students, optometry majors and other medical disciplines were educated and did their clinical rotations.

The city housed many industries associated with medical care. A mix of languages could be heard in the ER on any given day, including Greek spoken by the Greek immigrants who dominated the restaurant business in the city, their establishments filled on weekends.

Carrie and Steve felt at home in Birmingham, but the children didn't want to leave Huntsville. She reminded them it wasn't that far away and allowed them to call a friend once a week. Carrie knew the old comrades would fade away once new friends replaced them. By the time they had been in the house three months, the calls ceased. The children were too busy with school, church and the activities in the area.

They bought a house in Vestavia Hills, an exclusive area. The professional citizens, the wealthy and elite, lived in little towns that bordered Birmingham to the south. The satellite towns ran their own school systems where the students were expected to attend college. The curriculum of Vestavia High School offered Latin, French, Spanish, calculus, advanced biology, anatomy, physiology and a plethora of sports.

Their residence, a one-story red brick structure, was an oasis in the city. Built on a several acre lot with a winding driveway snaking through massive oaks, ponderous pines, a weeping willow and several leggy dogwoods, the manicured lawn never saw full sunshine. Behind them a hill had been flattened enough for a back yard, then the wooded lot rose so steeply that they could not climb to the top to see what lay beyond.

The house, bordered by azaleas, ferns, roses, irises, day lilies and spruces, was too large for them, but the owners were desperate to sell and the price enticed them. The three-car garage contained a woodworking shop that beckoned Steve on weekends. He loved to measure the planks, match the veins, smooth the wood with sand paper and stain a new piece of furniture. It settled him after a long week of surgery. When Carrie heard the saw buzz in the shop, she knew Steve was unwinding.

Carrie worked at the surgery clinic three days a week as Steve's nurse. They put in long hours, Steve operating on Monday, Tuesday and Wednesday, while Carrie stayed in the office, prepping patients, counseling them on their upcoming procedures or taking out sutures. At five, Carrie made hospital rounds with him. On Thursday and Friday, another nurse took over for her, a matronly woman in her late fifties, experienced, dependable and dedicated.

They hired a housekeeper to take the children to school, cook their meals and keep the house in order. The housekeeper had Fridays and Saturdays off and half a day Sunday. On Saturday, everyone slept until ten or later, the phone going off the hook when Steve wasn't on call.

Every year, Carrie blocked off time around Christmas for their annual trek to Napa. Usually they drove, but the four day trip had become boring and repetitive. The last two years they flew, the children claiming the window seats while she read or slept during the flight. Sometimes Steve went, but she didn't mind if he stayed home.

Steve had parents, a sister and brother, all who lived in Atlanta. They reserved Thanksgiving for their time to visit them. When Steve didn't go to Napa for Christmas he'd drive over for a day then come home and vegetate. Carrie understood that need; she worked alongside him, knowing the stress of their profession rarely lifted. Every week it surrounded them, ate into their hearts and there was no place to hide from the angst. Retirement was their goal, their salvation and someday it would happen. First they had to get the kids educated and then they could rest.

Weekly phone calls kept her connected with the family in California. Usually Carrie called her mother, unless a newsworthy communication gave her a reason to call Josephine or Morgan. Her mother, the hub of information for the rest of the family, lived in Ocean View, where she had moved several years ago to her beach house.

Their brothers didn't share the ticker tape of trivial information. They didn't concern themselves with details about which child had a runny nose, the new outfit bought for a bargain but wouldn't fit until ten pounds came off, the flat on the highway, the latest book they read and the scissors happy hairdresser. Ross and Phillip relied on Carrie to convey any bulletin that would be life changing.

The women of the family loved getting all the updates on everyone and Carrie took notes in a notebook beside the phone. Most of them time she called her mother mid-day on Thursdays, before she made her weekly trip to the grocery store, cleaners, drugstore and the boutique she loved in Mountain Brook Village.

Carrie wasn't sure when she became the matriarch of the family, there was no specific date it happened, no tragedy, no revelation of a horrible disease, no ceremony to mark the occasion. She tried to rebel, she didn't want the position. Her mother passed the torch to her without fanfare.

"I'm not the oldest, you are. You're the head of the family," she argued with her mother.

"Doesn't matter, you're the strongest one in the family, the rock. You're the one everyone already looks to, so you're the head by default. I'm removed from office," her mother informed her.

154

At sixty-three, Skye Poschett was not a little old lady who couldn't take care of herself. Her dark hair had a few gray streaks, her waist had thickened and tiny wrinkles stretched out from her eyes that now needed glasses. Her posture was erect and straight and she walked with energy, still making the rounds to the little stone house where they used to live.

Skye drove over to the vineyard every Saturday. She spent time in Martin's office, sat in his chair and pulled his quilt around her. She looked over the sales reports stacked on the desk by Ross or Anders, the managers of the vineyard.

Before she left, she walked the perimeter of the old ranch, the twenty-five acre plot she bought when they moved to Napa in 1945. Now a part of the Poschett vineyard, the little stone house had once been their home.

The trek kept her fit, the hike flexed her legs as she stretched to climb the hills. Then she walked over to the big house. She visited with whomever was home, always bringing them one of her cakes. She stayed for an hour or two and left with six bottles of wine. Then she did her grocery shopping and surveyed any new stores in the area, looking for bargains and searching the book store for the latest novel.

Looking back, Carrie realized it was the death of Colin Campbell that began the change in her mother, or maybe it was the call to the detective in Decatur. That was the day her mother confessed her part in the cover up of the man Owen Campbell killed. After that confession, she collapsed into a state of regret, remorse and reflection. She curled up in bed and cried for three days, missing her visit to the vineyard. Ross found her in bed, depressed and despondent. She had traveled to another place, one only she could go

After the episode of depression, her mother called her. "I've made some bad decisions. I failed you and Morgan. It's my fault Morgan ran away. It's my fault we had to leave Alabama. I've already called Judge Mayer and talked to him. You're now the one everyone looks to."

"Looks to for what? You're capable of handling anything that comes along, and of making tough decisions. What is this, a ruse to get out of throwing your annual Christmas party?" Carrie had suggested two years ago that the party was too much for her.

"No, I would never do that. I look forward to Christmas more than any other time of the year. Josephine and Morgan are going to help me do the decorating and cooking from now on, and I'll have some of it catered. I need you to be there for me, for the family. I won't live forever and one of these days I'll be gone. I need that assurance." Her mother's voice had softened.

"Okay, I'll do what I can. Let me know what you need me to do."

"You'll know when you have to step in, when a crisis knocks on our door and it will, it will," her mother's voice trailed off with the last words.

Carrie assumed the role, not that it was a hardship or an earth shattering event. No one in the family was needy. The only concern her mother had was Phillip and his choice of where he wanted to live. He'd moved to New York City. It could have been on the other side of the earth for her mother. She had never been east of Alabama.

"I don't understand why Phillip wants to live in that crowded, dirty city," Skye said when he left for the five day drive, his car packed with boxes, books, clothes and a couple of costumes he thought he might need.

"Let him go mother. He has a right to his life, to do what he wants and to live where he wants. He wants to be a Broadway star and Broadway is in New York City. If it doesn't work out, he'll come back," Carrie assured her mother.

"But he might need me and I won't be there."

"You can hop on a plane and be there the next day," Carrie argued.

"I'm terrified of flying," her mother reminded her.

"You'll have to get over it. It's a great way to travel and the rest of us fly."

"Maybe I could fly back with you this Christmas and that would help."

"Great idea, plan on it."

It hadn't happened. Her mother always found an excuse to stay in California; Clark and Josephine's baby was due, it was harvest time and she was needed at the vineyard, Ross was returning from France. Once she said Anders needed her to approve some changes in the planting schedule, then the library

157

needed her to volunteer more or she needed to be home to visit a friend that had cancer.

Then the mare she rode for twenty-five years died and she lapsed into another episode of grief. Anders took her to the doctor who prescribed an antidepressant. That got her on her feet in time for the annual Christmas party, but she never completely bounced back, remarking often about the brevity of life, the fragile state of women over sixty, the challenges of growing old.

Carrie wanted to remind her mother that Morgan should have the honor of being the head of the family, her older sister by three years. But Morgan, as she was now named, had been absent from the family for twenty-four years. When she reemerged she was an unknown, almost an intruder. The bond she had once enjoyed had been fractured and the formative years of Ross were lost to her. He didn't know her at all. Only Carrie and her mother had shared time and a home with Morgan before she ran away the night their stepfather died.

Phillip, Ross and Josephine shared the early years in Napa with Carrie and Skye where they forged a new life. Martin, Josephine and his cousin Anders moved to Napa in 1947 to escape war torn Europe. They desired a new life in America and Martin built a vast vineyard surrounding Skye's acreage.

Josephine, a lost child with no mother, had needs that they recognized immediately. Small, sickly and frail, they challenged her demons and brought her to normalcy. She had seen her mother shot, been uprooted from her country and dragged to a new one.

She needed a mother, a sister and a side-kick to play with. They provided that.

Then Skye married Josephine's father and Phillip came along. Morgan reentered their lives by default; she wouldn't have searched for her lost family if they had not found her. She had a secret to hide and if she had not been on the cover of a magazine and recognized by Carrie, she would not be a part of their lives. That bothered Carrie, it bothered her a lot.

After Morgan came home, as her mother always phrased the reunion, her secret was obvious. Her son, Clark Madison, was Owen Campbell's child. Morgan had not told her son the truth. Her fear of being judged tainted her decision to keep the lie intact. In truth, she had never forgiven herself. Clark and Ross looked like twins and while no one said they were brothers, as men they probably guessed the truth.

The family had morphed into three sections. The "medical corps" included Carrie, a nurse; her husband Steve, a surgeon; Josephine, a plastic surgeon and Lillie Anne, Ander's wife, a midwife when they were in her native France. The "entertainers" included Morgan, the actress and investor; her husband Levi, the composer; Clark, her son the producer, director, investor and actor. Included in that group was Phillip, in New York City pursuing his dream to be a star on Broadway. Then there were the "wine makers," Skye, Ross and Juliet, Anders and Lillie Anne.

Carrie brought her mind back to the present when the rumble of thunder sounded through the window that looked out to the back yard. Rain fell in torrents as she surveyed her unruly hair. *No need to try to style my hair in this humidity, and I've done enough reminiscing,* Carrie decided. She picked up the telephone and dialed a familiar number. Her mother answered on the second ring.

"Hello."

"Hi Mom, it's me. How are 'ya?"

"Nothing new out here. The vines are sprouting and all the crates from last year have been shipped. Anders planted more Zinfandel grapes on the back slope. He swears they are the newest rage. The surf is up today, splashing onto the patio. I've got a cake in the oven. What are you up to?" Skye asked her daughter.

"Well, we have a new patient. Daphne Mayer is coming in for a consult. She fell last week and had a concussion. She was out about an hour before her husband found her. When they did the X-ray at the hospital a spot showed up in her brain that looks suspicious. They advised her to see a surgeon. The Judge remembered Steve, and they'll be in Wednesday afternoon."

"Keep me posted. I love that couple. They were so good to me in the old days, so good..." her voice trailed off.

"I'll let you know," Carrie said as they turned the conversation to boring reports on the grandchildren and their antics.

CHAPTER 15

April, 1970

The whole Mayer family was in the surgery waiting room at University Hospital when Dr. Patterson and Carrie came out to give them a progress report on Daphne's surgery.

"She's in recovery and is moving and moaning. That's a good sign. The surgery went well, the tumor was bigger than it showed on the X-ray," Dr. Patterson said as he raked off his surgery cap.

"Is it cancer?" David asked.

"We won't know for sure until the path report comes back in three days, but my gut reaction is that it is malignant. It had some irregular borders and a couple of long tentacles. That's how cancer grows."

"Will she be alright?" Grace asked.

"She's young and healthy, and if her brain doesn't swell and no infection gets in the surgery site, she'll make a good recovery. She'll need care, bed rest and therapy. I hope you have someone who can stay with her," Dr. Patterson said as he pushed his hands along the side of his head. He shifted his weight and looked at Carrie, his wife, nurse and a friend of the Mayer family.

"I'm going to let Carrie take over and give you progress reports the rest of the day. I have more surgery to do but I'll make rounds at five this afternoon. She won't know much for a few days."

Carrie looked into the worried faces of David Mayer, his two daughters and a woman they introduced as Eva.

"Okay, who has questions?" Carrie searched their faces, the oldest daughter spoke first.

"If it's cancer, what are her treatment options?"

"She'll need radiation. That cleans up any cells left behind," Carrie told her in a low voice.

Carrie knew there were cells left behind, Steve couldn't get to part of the tumor, it had embedded and wrapped around a blood vessel. He left a tiny portion shaped like a half-inch piece of yarn.

"What are the side effects of radiation?" David asked.

"She'll be pretty sick from it, including some burned areas on her skin where the radiation goes in. She'll have a lot of nausea and will lose some of her hair. Let's wait for the report to worry about what her treatment will be," Carrie tried to throw in hope with the bad news.

Three days later, the path report came in. Dr. Patterson delivered the news to David in the hall outside of Daphne's room.

"I can tell by the look on your face the news isn't good," David acknowledged.

"It was malignant. She'll need radiation."

Daphne took the news well. She cried a little, David hugged her and Carrie came in thirty minutes later with the name of the radiologist in Huntsville who would do her treatments. Carrie examined her incision and they chatted for a few minutes.

"You're making great progress and can go home next week," Carrie told her.

"Wonderful. I'm ready to get out of here. I miss my girls," Daphne said with a smile.

Everyone in the town of Decatur knew about Daphne's surgery. The gossip line had been busy, some people thought she wouldn't make it through surgery, some believed she was faking the symptoms, some cried, most prayed for her and David grieved. He would lose the love of his life if she died. He'd buried one wife, now he might lose another.

David drove her home a week after surgery. The Catholic church Daphne attended brought in food, the girls hovered over her and neighbors called, offering to sit with her when David was on the bench. While Grace sat with her the first Saturday Daphne was home, David retreated to his office and called Kyle and Emma.

"This seals it for me," David told him. "I'm going to retire so my seat will be vacant. You need to run for the position. I want to spend my time with Daphne. We haven't done all the things we want to do. I'll endorse you and you should run on the Republican ticket. This state is going Republican. You'll win if you get out there shake some hands. People like you."

"If I win, it will be on your coattails. You set the excellent reputation. I've decided to put my hat in the ring so I'll give my notice at the firm next week and we'll start packing," Kyle assured him.

Daphne slowly gained strength. David hired Molly, Daisy's granddaughter, to be Daphne's attendant and do light housekeeping and some of the cooking. Two weeks after she came home, Daphne dressed herself and Molly rewarded her with a drive.

"We drove all the way to Huntsville and I saw Eva today. We had lunch with her at a quaint little restaurant." Daphne beamed when David came home from work, waiting for him in the living room in her favorite chair. Molly left and David sat beside her.

"You look great today. Your hair's coming back. I like it short," he surveyed the top of her head where the long scar sliced her head in half.

David continued, "Grace called me at the office. She's doing better in school and is off the academic probation list. She's coming in this weekend and I thought we'd ask Emma, Kyle and Dawson to come. I will go by Big Daddys Bar-B Que and get take-out. Maybe Molly can bake a cake for us. One of those fruit cakes from Skye's recipe."

"Yes, I'd love that."

Four weeks after Daphne's surgery, they drove down for her post op doctor's visit. Dr. Patterson and Carrie examined her scar and did some cognitive tests.

"You're making good progress. I feel you're ready to begin radiation. You'll be well taken care of by the radiologist in Huntsville. I've worked with Dr. Raymond, and he's the best," Dr. Patterson said as they gave him their full attention.

"If the radiation works, will this be the end of the cancer?" Daphne asked.

"Radiation is designed to kill any remaining cells," he replied, avoiding the word "cure."

"If there are some cells still growing in my brain and the radiation doesn't work, how long will I have?" Daphne surveyed his face for an honest reply.

"If the tumor grows back we may be able to do more surgery. We may have new treatments available. There are a lot of strides being made in the treatment of cancer and you're in the best place to get those treatments," he replied.

"Can I travel once the treatments are finished?" Daphne asked. "I want to go to California and see my brother, and I want to go to Hawaii."

"My advice is to travel and do everything you want to do. You'll be able to travel by fall. That's a good time to plan your trip."

"Why don't the two of you plan on coming to Napa on your way back from Hawaii? Mother would be thrilled to have you for our Christmas bash. I know she's invited you and by late December you'll be back to your old self. It would be wonderful to have you there. Mother asks about you every time I talk to her," Carrie added.

"We might do that," David interjected.

On the way home, they didn't speak for thirty miles. Daphne looked out the side window then began to cry.

"Damn it, why did this happen to me? I have brain cancer. I could have died from a thousand different things and this is what is going to get me. I'm forty-six years old and I have brain cancer."

"You're not dying. You have many years left and you'll die of old age in your rocking chair alongside me on the front porch. Quit talking about dying and leaving me. I can't and won't acknowledge that I could lose you. You are my life. Besides, we have the girls to think about."

"Yes, yes we do. But, I'm serious, I want to go to California and see Joseph. I want to see Hawaii. Let's make the trip to correspond with Christmas like Carrie suggested. Skye has asked us several times to come out. Joseph lives fifty miles from Napa. The girls can do without us for one Christmas. Can we do this?"

"You bet we can. I'll buy a new car for us to drive. Would you like to invite Eva and Claude to go along and help me drive?" David suggested. Eva and Claude married six months after his visit to America.

"Where do you think I got the idea to fly to Hawaii from California? Sure, let's ask them. That would be fun," Daphne replied as she wiped the tears off her face.

"I'm hungry. Where are we going to eat supper?" she asked David a few miles later.

"How about stopping in Cullman at that place we like? They have that new salad dressing, that bleu cheese stuff you like. I wish we could buy it at the store," David suggested as he turned off the highway toward Cullman.

CHAPTER 16

June, 1970

Morgan Madison pulled a new sundress over her head as she dressed for a party. She'd bought it the week before at a boutique on Rodeo Drive. She didn't want to show too much skin. The frock had wide straps and a full skirt that ended at her ankles, right above her silver sandals. She turned once in the floor length mirror. No cleavage showed, well, not much. It was hard to cover her ample breasts.

"You look fabulous, not trashy as some of those young starlets will look. Class always wins and you have class," Levi stated when she came down the stairs.

The wrap party at Ben Ferguson's house, one of the producers of the movie, *Traveling to Zocar: A Space Adventure*, would be attended by the cast members and their dates. Composers did not usually attend wrap parties, the music came later when the editing had been completed, but Ben insisted they come and Levi wanted to please him. Clark had a long speaking part in the movie and Levi did a walk on as part of the crew on the space craft. Levi's real contribution would be the score he composed. Ben liked to put friends in his movies and he and Levi were pals.

The producer wanted a different sound for the space travel movie, one that gave a feeling of euphoria to the audience, a buoyant score that would last through the ages, one that would be associated with the movie every time someone heard it on the radio. Levi had composed music for two movies for Ben in the past and both scores sold well.

Being married to Levi had been a challenge. They tied the knot three weeks after Clark and Josephine had their wedding at the vineyard. After Clark married, Morgan deeded her house in Beverly Hills to them, her gift to her son and his bride. It was worth a fortune.

Then she moved to Levi's home in Malibu where Levi had converted one of his bedrooms to a music room and studio. Sound proof and filled with musical instruments, a piano, an organ and electronics that were constantly coming in and out of the house, the studio was off limits to everyone.

On the rare occasions when she was allowed to enter, to bring food or leave him a note, she found the room intimidating. In constant fear she would bump into something or trip over one of the wires that stretched across the floor, she honored the "no one allowed" sign.

The Malibu house had everything they needed: four bedrooms, three baths, a kitchen with a long dining table, a living room that overlooked the ocean and a deck that ran the length of the back of the house. On a wooded lot high on a cliff, private and away from the peering eyes of the paparazzi, the house was their perfect retreat.

Morgan had semi-retired from her business, which was selling and finding real estate for the Hollywood elite. She went into the office one day a week to make sure the manager had everything under control. The rest of the time she devoted to Levi, and that suited her. She had lived so long trying to escape her past that she'd not been close to anyone but Clark, her son. Now Levi was her priority.

She wanted to be close to her mother and sisters, but it was hard. They had not been in her life after she ran away from home at age seventeen. Regretting the way she left, she wanted to return and ask her mother for forgiveness but when she realized she was pregnant with her stepfather's child, she vowed to never go back, to never let her son know who his father was. Her brothers, Ross and Phillip, were born after she left. She did not meet them until she returned to the family.

When she returned by default, "discovered" on the cover of a magazine, everyone treated her like part of the family but in reality, she wasn't. All the formative years were lost to her and hers to them. She revealed her secret about Clark's father to her mother, but she would have known. The time frame of Clark's birth put her in the house with her stepfather when he was conceived. They were fathered by the same man, Owen Campbell, her mother's second husband.

As long as Clark doesn't find out, she thought, *I'll be happy.*

Levi's house in Malibu was an hour from Clark and Josephine, who stayed busy, Clark with his movie projects and Josephine with her surgery schedule and charity work. Now they had a baby, a little girl whom Morgan adored. A doting grandmother fit her need to be a mother again, a need that wasn't fulfilled. She'd always wanted another child but there was never a right time, a right man.

So I spend my time with Levi, a man I adore and love, Morgan reflected as she watched gulls fight over a crab trying to escape back into the ocean. The deck on the house had spectacular views of the beach. Levi joined her and they had a drink before they left for the party.

Everyone in the movie industry knew Levi had a mysterious gift of music. The music he composed was cutting edge and different. Morgan did not understand his genius but had witnessed it many times. He processed sounds coming into his brain as musical notes. When he lapsed into a musical trance he entered music. There was no other way to describe it.

When he entered music, it occupied his consciousness and surrounded him, creating a bubble that expelled everyone and everything near him. He lapsed into a dreamlike state for hours, sometimes days. He walked into the music, crested in its waves, reached for its ceiling, filtered it through his eyes then wrote what he heard with the touch of his fingers on a piano, or guitar, or the string of a violin.

When he shut the door to his studio, he would stay for days, composing, writing, sleeping on the couch, eating sandwiches Morgan slipped in with juice and coffee. He never saw her during those times, she and the world were invisible.

Then he would emerge, take a long shower, shave, dress and then they drove to his favorite hamburger joint where he'd consume two hamburgers and a large order of fries. Then he wanted to go for a long drive with the top down on the car, allowing the wind to blow away leftover cobwebs. Sometimes they'd walk on the beach or hike on a mountain trail.

Levi disliked crowds, parties, family gatherings, concerts, malls, even movie theatres. He would relent and go to the family Christmas parties at the vineyard, arriving late and leaving early. Morgan respected his needs and understood them.

After one of Levi's musical episodes he would be a normal man for a while. The normalcy might last a week, two weeks or a month. Then he would lapse into another stint of days in the studio. Music gave him peace, clarity and joy. It always started with the same question.

"Do you hear the music?" he would ask her. Then he'd point to the source of the sound; the chatter of a squirrel, the swish of wind through the trees or the thump of a car over uneven pavement. Once he heard a tune in the song of a mockingbird, the honk of geese, the sound of a typewriter, marching soldiers or the train coming toward them then passing. He loved the sound of raindrops dripping on the window, the screech of an owl, the buzz of a hummingbird's wings.

Then he would compose. One of his scores sounded exactly like a typewriter, one like a train whistle in a rain storm, one like a music box dancer, one like birds chattering.

During those sessions, Morgan went about her daily life and it was a good life. She had all the expensive clothes she desired, a professionally decorated house, two cars and a good relationship with her son. She and Levi traveled back and forth from Los Angeles to New York City every month for Levi to work on the score for a Broadway play, one that would feature her brother Phillip in a minor role. It was a start for Phillip, and Levi had a particular interest in helping people like him, a young man struggling to find his place in the world. He understood his craving for a life in New York and the theatre scene.

When they spent time in New York, it was a reprieve for them. Levi had no studio there and gave rapt attention to Morgan. They ate at the best restaurants, went to the latest shows and took side trips around the state. Of course, Morgan did some shopping, but mostly they doted on each other, making love often, the magnificent view of New York City visible beside their hotel bed.

"We need to buy our own apartment here. I wasn't interested until we married and now I want a place, our place. We can decorate it like you want, modern, French, Italian, I don't care," he told her on the last trip.

"I agree. I'll have my people search the multiple listings and see what they have. Where do you want it? What part of the city?"

"A place with a view and close to Central Park. I'll buy it and put it in your name," he suggested.

"I have money I can invest. We'll each pay half and put it in both our names," she countered.

Levi liked being part of the big family, as long as he could pick and choose when he wanted to be around them. He had no one else, as all of his family had perished during the war. His father had been a university professor in Berlin, successful and well-liked. When the Nazis took control, Jews were stripped of their jobs, their shops closed and they were sent to work camps. His parents disappeared with the rest of the Jewish population. He was the only one left because they had sent him to American when he was sixteen. He went to Chicago to live with Mrs. Liebaum, a cousin of his mother's.

Mrs. Liebaum sheltered Jewish children sent to America to escape the war. They usually arrived sick, half-starved, filthy with lice crawling in their hair and clothes. Some died, some cried for days as the workers in the house bathed them and hydrated their bodies. On the days the sick children arrived, Morgan remembered that Levi curled up in a corner, his eyes wide with fear, his body shaking.

Morgan worked at Mrs. Liebaum's when Levi was there. She was pregnant with Clark when she arrived and everyone called her Dixie in those days. She stayed until the war was over and left,

174

marrying and raising her child in California after her husband, Tony, died. That was all she ever told people about those years. There was more to the history of how she ended up in California, but she had put those years away, they were lost to the past and she did not want to explain them to anyone. She did not see Levi again for twenty-two years.

Before she married Levi, she hoped he would tell her what horrible thing happened to him in Berlin and he did, a week before they married.

"I believe in full disclosure. With you I can do this. I didn't with my first two wives and maybe that was my downfall. In any event, I want you to know how I ended up in Chicago, what happened to me to make my parents send me away," Levi paced the floor as he gathered courage to continue.

"You don't have to tell me. I have secrets, too, ones I'm not sure I'm ready to reveal," Morgan replied.

"You can keep your secrets. You're well-adjusted and a strong woman, a woman who can stand alone and is a success. That tells anyone that your secrets are minor. I have not been well-adjusted and sometimes I revert back to the disgusting set of events that sent me to America. What happened is a horror story," he looked away, like he was seeing a newsreel playing on the wall.

"I was thirteen when this happened, a budding boy in school, top of my class in the Jewish sector of Berlin. We lived in a well-to-do area of the city. I had no comprehension of the political undertones brewing in Germany, how the police would allow crimes against Jews to go unpunished," Levi paused and took a deep breath.

"In the fall of 1934, Jews in Berlin knew bad times were coming. I was forbidden to go out at night, told I had to stay inside, and we kept to ourselves in the back room of our apartment, lights down so they couldn't be seen from the street. We were careful to do our shopping in the Jewish sector of town because we didn't want to be noticed," Levi kept his eyes toward the wall, his voice soft, his hands trembling.

"I rebelled. I wanted to go to the cinema with my friends so I slipped out one night after my parents went to bed. My sister heard me leave but said nothing. I will never forget that she waved to me as I took the latch off the door and quietly exited our flat, taking the back stairs down to the alley. I met my friends at the cinema, we watched the movie then we began the walk home. Three soldiers cornered us and we scattered, me running to the street one block away from our house then I turned and ran past it, I didn't want them to see where I lived.

A man followed me and grabbed me. He tied my arms behind me and pulled me to a house a few blocks away. He put me in the basement, locked the door and left me there for two days. I could see the traffic on the sidewalk through a small window," Levi stopped and took a deep breath.

"On the third day he came back. I was filthy. I did not have use of my hands to put my pants down to urinate so you can imagine. He cursed me and put a gag in my mouth. Then he tied one of my hands to a pipe and brought down a wash pail and some food. He demanded I clean myself and brought me some of his pajamas. He kept me there for a week, feeding me bread, milk and rotten vegetables. Then he loosed me, tied me over a chair and raped me," Levi flinched on the last statement, his head jerking to one side.

"I'm sure my parents were frantically looking for me. I talked to the man, begging him to let me go, promising I wouldn't tell on him. He slapped me and fed me nothing for the next two days, raping me each night. By this time, I knew he planned to kill me. My body would never be found, there would be no trace of me. He called me his 'pretty Jew baby.' Then he made a mistake. He left a bread knife near me. I put it into my pocket and that night when he started to pull me to the chair I stabbed him in the neck. I must have hit an artery, blood spewed out in spurts and he slumped over. I ran out to the street, it was dark and there were no people around. I ran home, straight to my back door and banged on it for my parents to let me in. I had been gone three weeks. They had given up hope of finding me," Levi stopped and wiped his eyes.

"My mother was a broken woman. After that, I didn't leave the house for a year, fearful I would be found, my deed discovered, my face recognized. My parents never told anyone I returned, then they decided to send me to America to live with her first cousin, Mrs. Liebaum. I arrived at her house in the fall of 1937, a sickly, depressed boy of sixteen, afraid of everyone, everything. She took me in, taught me English, had me privately tutored and put me in front of her piano because she knew I was musically trained. She bought recordings for me to absorb, fed me well, took me to the doctor and we both wrote to my parents. We never heard from them again." Levi grew quiet, looked out the window and shook his head sideways.

"I have never been able to go into a basement again. I had a horrible time adjusting sexually. I felt dirty, used, half a person. Music became my refuge, the piano my lover, classical music the window to my soul. I could relate to music and I threw myself into it." Levi turned around.

"I recognize that the man was tainted, not me. However, after the time in that basement I began to have this remarkable ability to hear music in everything. It might be due to the silence I experienced after I escaped from him. I could not tell my parents what happened but they knew, they saw the blood on my pants, the bruises. I could not speak for six months. I had no voice, no way to communicate. I have had a lot of counseling and shock treatments. Medications for depression help but the cure for me is time in my studio. A woman like you, one who understands me, one who gives me space and is not selfish enough to demand I be at her beck and call is the only woman who can share my life. If you can accept that, I will be the best husband in the world, I promise you that." Tears ran down his face as he spoke the last sentence.

"I can be that woman. You're right, I am a stand-alone person. I have hidden secrets and had to work out my problems. I will give you all the space you need," Morgan answered.

Levi pulled her into his arms before he left to go home. The next day he called.

"Can I come over tonight? I have something special planned, a surprise."

Around seven p.m. he drove into Morgan's driveway. He had a box with him and a sack from an expensive boutique in Beverly Hills. He also had a bottle of Poschett wine.

"Okay, here's the deal. You go to the bathroom down the hall and put this on." He handed her the boutique sack. "Don't look, just put it on," Levi insisted.

Morgan did as she was told. She heard Levi go into her bedroom and peeked. He had the box with him. In the sack, wrapped in tissue paper was red, lace nightgown. Long, with cap sleeves, it wasn't skimpy, it was elegant. Silk and shiny, it felt wonderful. In a few minutes, he called her softly.

"Morgan, come into your bedroom."

When she came into the room he had lit aromatic candles on top of the dresser and had stretched a quilt from his house on the bed. Rose petals were sprinkled around the room. He'd placed two plates on the quilt, a loaf of French bread on one plate, cheese and olives on another plate. The candles cast a soft light in the room, the scent of roses and vanilla filled the air. Morgan couldn't believe what she was seeing.

"Won't you join me for a picnic?" he asked, waving her to the bed. He had on red silk shorts.

They sat on the quilt, the soft light of the candles flickering on their skin. Soft light found the corners in the room with long shadows of their bodies. Wine flowed to crystal stems as they toasted to their upcoming marriage. They ate cheese and olives with the bread, talked and laughed, revealing the activities of the day and their plans for the future.

Then Levi moved all the dishes off the quilt and turned on a tape recorder.

"This is the first part of the music I wrote for the new space movie. The orchestra recorded it last week. I wanted you to be the first person to hear it." He punched play and they stretched out on the quilt.

"Aren't you too warm in that gown? By the way, you look stunning," he whispered as he slipped off his shorts. Morgan slipped the red lace negligee over her head and curled around his back as the music started.

"Close your eyes. You are going on an adventure into outer space. Let the journey begin," Levi whispered.

A clear, low sound lasted for two seconds, like the blast of a horn, a trumpet sounding before a battle. Then the sound intensified and went up one note, the note holding two full measures then fading, simulating a launch into the void of space. Then your senses caught the rush and you were on top of the ship where space had no ceiling, no beginning or ending. A flash of fast high notes caught your brain unaware, questioning the sound, wondering which distant star twinkled, summoning you, directing you.

Then each half measure ascended slowly up the scale, note by note, simple, strong and solid. This lasted for five or more measures then it repeated. Clear, concise and beautiful, the music encircled them, wound around their bodies and turned the quilt to a magic carpet. Levi turned toward her, finding her lips, her ears, her breasts.

Then chords danced through several measures. Morgan felt she was skipping through a meadow of stars with no roots, no ending, no beginning. Then she was traveling in the void of darkness where a distant light lured her. Euphoric, she felt Levi's hand travel down the outside of her thigh then the inside. She wrapped her legs around him, felt his hardness.

Levi whispered, "I love you," as their bodies bonded. He entered her softy then they made love as the music drove them to the other reaches of space. They climaxed when a crescendo carried them to the brightest star, to ecstasy. Lying back on the quilt, they listened to the music fading away as it disappeared, leaving them behind.

"That was the most beautiful experience I've ever had," Morgan admitted.

"I wrote it with this night in my mind. But the people of the world will relate it to the path of a space ship starting its journey to an unknown world, then it encounters space rocks, thus the fast moving part where they dodge around trying not to hit one. Then the space ship moves into a vast nothingness and the crescendo happens when they see the world they are searching for. You and I will know another use for the music," Levi suggested.

"Yes. It's different, exhilarating. What will you name the piece?" Morgan asked.

"I'm not sure. I gave the producer the right to name the music. He paid me well to have that right. I hope he likes it," Levi slipped off the bed and started dressing.

"Why don't you stay?" Morgan asked.

"I have to work on some parts of this composition. Listening to it gave me some ideas and I have to make the changes while the music is fresh in my head. I'll be in the studio and on Saturday I'll be at the beach for the wedding. I'm glad only Clark, Josephine, your mother and the minister will be there. I couldn't bear a crowd. Then we leave for our surprise honeymoon. Pack for warm weather. Bring a bathing suit or two and leave your worries at home. You'll like where we're going. See you then. Love you." Levi was gone two minutes later.

They spent a week in Hawaii for their honeymoon. The marriage was a new start for her, the beginning of a partnership, one with a man who had extraordinary talent and made buckets of money. The royalties from his music had made him a millionaire and Morgan also had that distinction. From rags to riches, they had both done well.

Why did she have this nagging feeling about Levi? Why did she fear he would lapse into a state she couldn't handle or he would find out the truth about Clark's father and hate her? Why didn't she come clean with her secrets when he revealed his?

The questions nagged at her then she dismissed them.

Right now their life was perfect and she wanted that to last.

CHAPTER 17

Christmas week, 1971

Carrie had never seen her mother this excited. Judge Mayer, his wife Daphne and another couple were arriving late on Christmas Eve from Hawaii for a visit. Ross would meet them at the San Francisco airport where they would pick up their car and follow him to Napa for a three day visit that encompassed Christmas.

"They're coming, finally they're coming," her mother told her before Thanksgiving during their weekly session on the telephone.

"I know. We saw Daphne and the Judge a month ago at the clinic and they told us about the trip. They wanted to do this last year but Daphne was still struggling with her treatments and too weak. Now she's doing well, completely recovered from the surgery, the cancer hasn't resurfaced and the Judge retired, so they can travel."

"I have the special place for them to stay. We converted the wine tasting room in the little house to bedrooms last year. I plan on them staying over there," her mother said, going into detail about the color schemes in the rooms.

"The kids and I will arrive on the twentieth, so we can have a long visit. Can Anders retrieve us from the airport?" Carrie asked.

"Sure, call the vineyard and give him the time. He'll be there," her mother replied.

Once off the phone, Carrie dragged a couple of sweaters out of the closet, along with her blue jeans. She didn't wear jeans in Alabama, but they were the rage in California. She loved going early for Christmas, visiting with everyone, eating too much and tasting the private collection of wines held for the family and special guests.

Sometimes Steve would go, but this year he declined. He needed some time to himself and Carrie understood. He'd drive over to see his parents for Christmas then come home and resume his surgery schedule. He was in demand and although the workload at the hospital was low around Christmas, some emergency surgery was always needed.

Carrie had a special bond with Daphne and the Judge, stemming from the medical connection as well as the friendship of Judge Mayer from the old days. She remembered he brought that package of clothes for them when they moved into town when she was a girl of thirteen. He found them a rental house in town and her mother a car. Then he taught her mother how to drive. When they left Alabama, he was the only one her mother contacted. It seems he'd always been there for them, and now she wanted to be there for Daphne.

Finally the day arrived for Carrie's flight out of Birmingham to Dallas where they would connect to San Francisco. On the plane, Amanda and Dave wanted window seats. Amanda, now seventeen, was a mixture of herself and Steve. Dave, thirteen and still a little boy, looked forward to being with Anders and Ross.

Anders and Lillie Anne had arrived from France earlier in the month. They would inhabit one of the apartments over the garage. Phillip would fly in on the twenty-third from New York, and Ross and Juliet lived in the big house. Morgan would arrive Christmas Day and stay a few hours. Levi hadn't been mentioned. Carrie doubted he'd come for the event; the small children made him nervous, he was too busy, too tired, some excuse was always given.

Josephine and Clark planned to drive up from Los Angeles on Christmas Eve with Colette, their daughter. A delight with her bubbly personality and curly red hair, the child kept everyone amused. Poschett Vineyard was home to Josephine. She arrived in America with her father when she was eleven. For a year they'd lived in San Francisco while the big house and vineyard were under construction next door to Skye's little house.

She'd bonded quickly with Skye, Carrie and Ross, running to their house after school, riding horses, expanding her English, eating Skye's cooking. When the families merged, Ross and Carrie became her siblings. Phillip arrived later, a welcome addition to the family. Martin, Josephine's father died years ago, lung cancer claiming him at age sixty-three.

186

Carrie relaxed as the drive to Napa from San Francisco unfolded, the trek across the Golden Gate Bridge a highlight to the kids. Anders drove slowly over the span so they could see the ships in the harbor and Alcatraz. Next was Sausalito, where a distant view of the bay and the city made the perfect postcard. The highway led north through Mill Valley, then to San Rafael where they stopped to buy sodas for the kids. In Sonoma they turned right toward Napa.

Her mother, Ross and Juliet ran out to meet them. Hugs were exchanged and Anders took their luggage to two of the upstairs bedrooms. One of them had been hers and Josephine's room before she left for nursing school. Josephine and Clark had the next bedroom, with a youth bed in the room for Colette. Carrie's kids settled down the hall in a room with two sets of bunk beds.

The house was decorated to perfection. Three Christmas trees, one on the front porch, one in the living room and one in the dining room, each one draped with tinsel, colorful blinking lights and metallic ornaments, added to the festivities of the house. Beautifully wrapped presents rested under the main tree. Snow globes on the mantle tempted the children to pick up one and turn it over.

The buffet sideboard in the dining room, covered with a red velvet runner, would hold platters of home baked cookies and cupcakes after the spaghetti supper on Christmas Eve. Now a bowl of fruit and several bottles of Poschett wine claimed the area. Two sleeves of crackers were there, cheese made in the area would be added at two when people started to drop by. Crates of Poschett wine, stacked in the corner, would be distributed to the visitors, neighbors in the valley, people they knew in the community and the mayor.

Napa celebrated Christmas with fanfare, colored lights ran around the eaves of several houses, wreaths hung on entrances to the driveways, circling the name of vineyards or a business. Christmas trees stood on front porches overlooking the smoky valley that held the scent of burning wood, baking bread, sea salt and newly turned earth.

Highway 29, often called the St. Helena Highway, now paved and widened, led to Yountville from Napa. The valley held quaint homes, cottages and a few massive houses, one a Victorian mansion. Small stone warehouses holding old casks and weathered barrels flanked the houses. Well-traveled paths led from back doors to the structures then out to the garden and vineyard. Families worked hard, never complained and held on to their property, passing homesteads to the next generation.

Rows of trellises ran up hills and across the bottom land in the valley. Most of the vineyards had small orchards, some people grew vegetables, most had chicken coops filled with fat hens and a few had horses that grazed in fenced pastures where they fattened on native grass.

The busiest time was harvest, the crazy time when the grapes ripen and have to be picked quickly, each variety coming to maturity at a different time, vines on higher elevations lagging behind a day or two. It was a hectic week when no one got enough sleep, manual labor found muscles that rebelled and tempers flared.

Picking the grapes was the start of a long process. Sorting had to be completed quickly, before the grapes reached the optimum sugar level, within six to eight hours after picking. Everyone worked during the night, sleeping in short bursts. Anders or Ross tested the grapes for the degree brix, the sugar level. Rain on the day of harvest would make the sugar level drop, bright sunshine brought it up, the perfect condition but hard on the workers. It was a delicate balance, a critical time.

Anders hired a machine harvester three years ago which greatly reduced the need to hire seasonal workers. Since the Poschett Vineyard was one of the biggest in the valley, finding workers for the harvest had become competitive. Bickering with contractors for the labor force, bringing them in, housing them and feeding them was a challenge. It took a hundred people to harvest the grapes and they stayed a week, some of them longer.

Families followed the harvest trail, grandparents, parents and children working side by side, most of them migrant workers from Mexico. Few spoke English and most were muscular, deeply tanned with weathered skin from years of working in the sun. A child was taught which grapes were ripe by the time he was five, his hands pulling the fruit alongside his parents, adding to the weight in their baskets.

The laborers stopped for lunch, sandwiches and drinks were delivered to the end of a row and dirty hands reached out for the meal. A few grandmothers left the fields after eating, guiding the smaller children to a huge shade tree where they left a blanket or quilt. They stretched out with the children and napped.

When the harvest was finished, celebrations erupted, cash was counted and workers moved north to the next area, ending the season in Oregon or Washington. Then the grapes were squeezed and the fermenting began. Once the wine was in casks, or the ripe grapes sold to another vineyard, the harvest was considered completed.

Then the vines, dormant by mid-December, had to be managed. Winter months were spent pruning and training, replacing dead plants, planting new ones, inspecting for diseases, fungi and lice, testing the soil, making repairs to the buildings, patching casks and barrels that leaked, buying supplies, trapping the little foxes and plowing under row grasses. There was no time to completely rest, no perfect time to take a vacation. Christmas week was the only time the Poschett vineyard was considered closed. People who weren't in the business believed vineyards were dormant during the winter. *Not true*, any owner would tell you.

Two hundred years ago there were no grape vines, no wineries in Napa Valley. The long, narrow valley with a river meandering southward down to a gigantic bay was no more than five miles wide at any point. It stretched thirty miles beyond St.

190

Helena, which, at 4,343 feet, was the highest point in any direction for a hundred miles.

In the shadow of St. Helena and along the shores of the river, thousands of Native Americans had once lived in the shade of thousands of fir, redwood and oak trees. Then Europeans discovered the valley, coming across the hills from Sacramento Valley. A young Spanish priest, Father Jose Altamira, was the first white man to explore the area, his military escort riding over the hills along the present day Highway 29 into the area on July 1st, 1823.

He returned to the Sonoma Valley and started construction of the Mission San Francisco Solano. Then the Mexican government decreed that the missions be secularized and their lands and buildings were taken over by the government. A twenty-nine year old man, Lieutenant Vallejo, assumed control of the mission lands and hired George C. Yount, the first American who settled in the area, to make shingles for the roof of the mission. Yount settled in the valley in 1831 after arriving on foot, walking from Missouri, leaving his wife and their three children behind.

Yount received a grant of 11,814 acres in the heart of Napa Valley for helping Vallejo build his mission. Yount built a two-story blockhouse that served as a home and a bastion to ward off Indian attacks. In 1843, Colonel Chiles, an Indian fighter and guide, brought Yount's wife and children from Missouri. He received a grant called the Chiles Valley and returned east to guide more settlers across the mountains to California. He settled permanently in the valley with his family in 1852 and built a flour mill.

During the great migration west, before the railroad brought settlers to the Pacific Ocean, pioneers began drifting south off the Oregon Trail, some of them finding the fertile valley. By 1846, there was a population of non-natives in Napa of fifty souls. Two grist mills were built on the Napa River and one still stands in its original place on Highway 29. Skye, Carrie and Ross rode their horses down to the mill many times, photographing the area, picnicking when the weather allowed.

Napa was one of the original twenty-seven California counties created in September 1850. The first official census of 1850 counted the county population at 405 with the town of Napa containing 159. The main road through Napa and the valley was improved with gravel and oil in 1860. A telegraph line was strung between Vallejo and Napa seven years before the telegraph reached across America in 1865.

Then disaster struck Sonoma Valley. Lice that attack vine roots caused most vineyards there to wither and die between 1876 and 1879. Napa began to surpass Sonoma valley as wine production inched ahead. Then the lice migrated to Napa. In 1893, one-third of Napa County vineyard showed signs of the voracious louse. By the turn of the century, Napa growers pulled withered vines and planted fruit trees in their place. Fruit orchards, olive groves, dairying and the resort business, even mineral water bottling, became the prominent businesses in the little town.

Then in 1903, the invention of a machine that mass-produced glass bottles made bottles cheap and plentiful and wine production in Napa soared. Wineries could identify their product with labels, leading to brands that have survived to find their rightful place on many tables around the world.

Then Prohibition shut down wine production in the 1920s. Stagnant vineyards closed their doors and the population of Napa decreased. When the repeal came on December 7th, 1933, Napa celebrated along with the rest of the country.

The area slowly recovered and by the time Skye moved to Napa in January, 1945, investors had begun to notice the area but the war kept them occupied. She purchased twenty-five acres of the best land in the valley for a song. Martin Poschett, newly emigrated from France, built his vineyard around her ranch, moving to the area after the war ended.

During the 1950s, investors flooded to the area. United Vintners started the big vineyard approach, attracting big corporations to the existing wineries. They made tempting offers on the Poschett Vineyard but Martin Poschett held firm. It was the vineyard in France that he wanted to sell.

Most of the vines at Celine du Village, the original name for the vineyard in France, withered during the war. The buildings at the vineyard had fallen to a state of disrepair from years of neglect. The vineyard had been on and off the market several times, each listing resulting in offers but none were solid. Either the buyer did not have enough capital to invest or their offer fell short. Martin renamed it Poschett Vineyard and delegated the task of reviving it to Anders Rousseau, a cousin and his vineyard manager who had been with him since the war began.

Located in the village of Tenay, the nearest town for shopping was Lyon. The vineyard was established in the early 1800s by Martin Poschett's great grandfather. At various times over the years it had shut down, during the European wars, during down turns in the economy. Only fifty hectares, the vineyard sloped toward the Alps twenty miles away.

Martin inherited the vineyard from his father and worked there until he left to go to the university in Paris, where he met his wife. She became a professor and he a chemist, a degree that benefited his blending of grapes and fermentation processes. They shuttled back and forth from Paris to Tenay. Then the war changed everything.

Carrie knew little of why Martin Poschett left France, only that he came to California with Josephine, his daughter, to begin a new life and plant a vineyard. His wife did not survive the war and Martin never returned to his homeland. Anders ran the vineyard there, planting new vines, repairing the buildings and bottling the wine. He hired a manager to run the vineyard when he spent time in Napa.

The small stone house Skye bought when she moved to Napa was still there, now offices of the vineyard. In the back of the house was Martin's office and it had not changed. His glasses were still on the desk, his favorite novel nearby with pages turned down to his favorite passages. The little stone house, as the family called the structure, was photographed often by tourists, its light stone façade, brown shutters and dark roof highlighted by red paint on the trim and the front door. Flowering shrubbery, plants overflowing in pots and the old barn added to the charm.

Carrie marveled at her life, how she had escaped punishing poverty with her mother and Ross in Alabama when they moved to California. There she obtained a nursing degree and married Steve. Her trips back to Napa were filled with nostalgia, the trek to the vineyard every Christmas the highlight of her year. She liked to arrive in Napa several days before Christmas, leaving the day after the children were out of school. She wanted to spend time with her family, especially her mother.

Once there, she and her mother walked over to the little stone house then climbed the trail to the top of the hill where Skye's acreage ended. One day was reserved for Carrie to take the children to the beach where they ate seafood at a quaint café. Then they drove up the coastal highway, stopping at quaint shops and in Napa at the grocery store where Skye had once worked.

Every morning, Carrie and her mother drank coffee on the front porch, sitting in two rocking chairs, the same ones that had been on the porch for twenty years. They laughed and reminisced about the past, grateful for the good memories, avoiding the secrets that haunted both of them.

Each day someone arrived for Christmas and the house and apartments over the garage filled with laughter, suitcases, beds in disarray and conversation. After the traditional spaghetti dinner on Christmas Eve, everyone settled in the living room as Ross left for the airport to pick up Judge Mayer, Daphne and the couple traveling with them. A welcome addition this year, they would complete the arrivals.

"Save me a piece of the fruit cake," Ross pleaded as he walked through the kitchen and out the back door.

Arriving at the house around ten p.m., the Judge and Daphne came in the house first, followed by a middle-aged lady. Skye embraced Daphne then the other woman took her hand.

"Hello, I'm Eva, David's sister-in-law. My husband Claude is helping Ross retrieve the luggage," she said, pointing to the man who had walked in the door.

Then Anders came in from the kitchen. He shook the Judge's hand and introduced himself to Daphne. Then he stared at Eva. He looked her over and narrowed his eyes. When Claude turned to greet Anders he yelled something in French. It was a cry more than a greeting, a stabbing cry of shock. The two men obviously knew each other. Both men began to sob as they embraced each other.

"What happened?" Carrie asked.

Josephine said, "They're saying, 'Brother, brother, I believed you were dead.'"

The two men turned toward Eva, then Anders pointed to Josephine.

"That is Josephine, all grown up," Anders said in English.

"Josephine, everyone, this is my brother Claude Rousseau. I did not know he survived the war and we never found each other afterwards! Now we have! We found each other today in America," he said, his voice shaking.

They looked like brothers. The same height, both had gray eyes and thinning brown hair, the same nose and mouth. It was hard to tell who was the oldest.

"Come now," he waved to Claude and Eva. "We must catch up with all the years. Let's go to the kitchen and eat, we saved food for you." Claude and Eva followed Anders to the kitchen where the cook placed food on the table.

"I think I will see to the Judge and Daphne." Skye excused herself to the living room. Obvious that she was in the way, the three of them speaking in French, she understood their need to reconnect. She had experienced that when Morgan came back into her life.

Anders, Claude and Eva talked in the kitchen for an hour. Finally they emerged, and Anders announced he wanted to tell them what he'd learned from Claude. Carrie's children went to bed, not interested in the revelation. The other children in the house were already asleep.

Everyone settled in the living room, finding chairs or a place on the couches.

Anders began his story. "First of all, I am going to reveal to the family some secrets you do not know about the vineyard in France. Don't worry, it is nothing sinister but it is a sad story. One

Josephine especially needs to hear, for it involves her and I'm not sure you remember much about the war." Anders looked at her. She nodded, confirming his analysis.

"Claude was a doctor in those days, in Marseille, about two hundred kilometers away. I am the youngest and left school when the war began, working on several farms and vineyards after our parents died. I had studied to be a railroad worker but the war stopped that profession when the Germans took over France." Anders shifted his weight and tightened his mouth as he looked at Claude and Eva.

"Claude and I are related to Martin Poschett, being second cousins. I found him at his farm in the village of Tenay and asked for a job. He took me in and I realized the farm had once been a vineyard. Josephine was five years old when I arrived, her mother and Martin trying to get through the Occupation like everyone else. There was a particular reason for Caris, his wife, to be hidden. She was half-Jewish and most of the people in the town knew that. She could be shipped off at any time, turned in by a person in the village. Martin feared for her," Anders said as he paced in front the Christmas tree, the lights behind him twinkling.

"We lived there for two years before the incident happened. One day, Martin told Caris we were going to Chambery to the market. Caris had been inside so long she wanted to go, to take Josephine and show her the Fountain of the Elephants. When we got there, a couple told us the Germans had taken away two Jewish families. One man had been hanged and his body swayed from a

198

light post in the town. Caris joined in a demonstration around the fountain where the citizens were shouting at the Germans. Martin and I tried to stop her. I stayed with Josephine in the back and Martin pushed his way forward. Someone bumped into him, he fell and a man drove a cart over his leg, breaking it. He couldn't move. The Germans shot Caris and five other people. The crowd scattered, I grabbed Josephine and two men dragged Martin to a nearby house. I followed them." Anders stopped and wiped tears off his chin.

"That night, I went to retrieve Caris' body. Martin gave me money to buy a coffin and I put it in the man's wagon. The bodies were stacked at the back of the square. To get the body, you had to bribe the soldier, so I did. I found her and pulled her legs. She lifted her hand and moaned. She was alive, but the soldier didn't know that. I placed her in the coffin and took her back to the man's house. Martin sent for the doctor who set his leg. By that time, we had moved her to a bed. The doctor examined her and said she had lost too much blood and wouldn't live. We took her home to the vineyard the next day, carrying her in the coffin. Caris regained consciousness after we pushed wine down her throat, rubbing it to make her swallow. She asked for Josephine and we took her to her mother."

No one spoke. Josephine did not move, her eyes stared straight ahead. She was seeing the story unfold through the eyes of a seven-year-old, her age at the time. Anders continued.

"We knew Caris would die. She was out of her head and in pain. I sent for Claude in Marseille. He came. We got word that the Germans were searching houses and we moved her to the cave room where we stored wine in the coolness. We made a bed for her on a pile of hay. That night, other people from the village came to hide. They stayed for several days while the Germans searched the house, barn, warehouse and car. Two of the soldiers came back searching the warehouse again, helping themselves to bottles of wine." Anders turned to Claude and Eva at the last part of the story.

"Eva was there. She was one of the people we hid. No one was discovered and we felt the worst had passed. The next day Claude, Eva and I, and several others began a resistance movement. I knew how to derail trains, and that is what we did." Anders began to pace.

"Caris lived a week longer. Martin asked that we place her body in the coffin after she died and leave it in the cave room so he could bury her later. We pushed the cask in front of the small door that led into the room and bolted it. Then Claude, Eva and I left to blow up a train. We were caught and all three of us sent to work camps. Someone warned Martin. He carried Josephine to a neighbor and left her. They came for him that night and beat him. I am surprised he lived through the injuries, but he did. When the war was over, he found Josephine. She was safe."

No one moved. Claude joined his brother in front of the group and put his arm around him, wiping his eyes with a handkerchief.

"Is that when we left and moved to California?" Josephine asked.

"No, first everyone was sent to a refugee camp. A year later, you and your father left on the ship to America. He did not get a chance to return to the vineyard," Anders replied.

"So…what happened to Caris?" Skye asked the question everyone wanted to know.

"The vineyard stayed as it was. That room has not been opened since that night," Anders added.

"So…uh…is my mother's body in that cave room? Is she still in that coffin?" Josephine asked, stumbling over the words.

"Probably. I don't think the others would have gotten her out," Claude answered.

"The others?" someone asked.

"There were others in the room we sealed."

"My god," someone whispered.

"Who?" Ross asked.

"Seven other people. Two men who worked with us blowing up the railroad, and a Jewish family of five. A man, his wife and uh…three children," Claude took a deep breath after he finished the statement.

"Was the room bolted from the outside?" Phillip asked.

"Yes. They asked us to do that to keep anyone from crawling out right into the face of a German who might be there stealing wine. We planned on returning and letting them out when it was safe. We were not able to do that," Anders explained.

The Judge and Daphne shifted on the couch. Ross stood up and began to pace the room. Skye dropped her head, looking at her hands. Josephine stared straight ahead. Clark put his arm around her. Eva cried softly.

"Would they have smothered?" Carrie asked.

"No, there was ventilation under the door. It was not air tight," Anders answered.

"Starved, could they have starved?" someone asked.

"There was food in there, enough for a few days. If they didn't get out they would have," Anders answered.

"Could they have escaped?" Clark asked.

"There was another way out. The back of the room had a small opening where the cave led up the inside of the hill beyond the vineyard. Martin told us he had explored the cave as a young boy. It was a steep climb but it had an opening to the outside. If they left before they were too weak to climb, they may have made it out." Anders projected hope.

"Those children, those poor children. I knew them," Eva sobbed.

"There is only one way to find out. We have to open that room," Claude suggested.

"Is it behind that wooden wall where the old casks are? Those huge ones where three line the back wall?" Ross inquired.

"Yes."

"I will go back, cut up those casks and open the wall. Then we will know for sure who is back there," Ross announced.

"There is something more. When Eva came to hide at the vineyard she brought with her several boxes of envelopes. Those envelopes contain jewelry and money from people who asked her to keep them until the war was over. The contents of those envelopes were to be a new start for them. They are in that room," Claude divulged.

"I have a trunk of those in my attic. Anna did the same thing," the Judge said. "Anna was my first wife, she died years ago of TB. Eva and Anna were sisters."

"I see," Anders stated. "I wondered how Eva and Claude knew you. I supposed you were friends. Now I understand the connection. I will return with Ross and help him get to the cave. Claude and Eva will also go with us. We will give Caris the burial she deserves. We will find out what happened to the others."

"I will go with you. I want to see my mother. I want to look at her face, touch her, talk to her," Josephine cried, her shoulders shaking.

"But...uh...she is...well, she is," Phillip said.

"But... what? I know she will be bones. I don't care. I don't remember her and to see her bones is better than never remembering her. I am a doctor and I have seen skeletons before, cadavers, expired people. The person in that coffin is my mother. Those bones are hers. All of the memory of this time was erased until I was jerked back with this revelation. I now remember going to the bed of my mother, how I thought it was a big doll lying there because she did not move. I saw her covered up to her head with quilts, her long hair, her closed eyes and pale face. I remember living with those people. We were hungry and cold, then we moved to another town. Then my father came to get me and we were in a place with a lot of people. People cried at night and coughed and we were dirty. We lined up to get food, my father giving me most of his so I wouldn't starve. Somehow he put us on a large ship and we arrived at this big city then took the train across the vastness to California. I am going to that coffin to see my mother! No one can stop me!" Josephine cried.

"We will both go. You aren't going alone." Clark touched her hand.

"Is there anything else?" Skye asked.

"This is the reason Martin never returned to France. He wanted to sell the vineyard but he knew someone might tear down that wall and find skeletons behind it. The vineyard had too many terrible memories for him. Once the war was over, he cashed out his money and left. When he met you, his life turned around. He was happy with his new family. He made me promise I wouldn't open the room until he died. He couldn't bear living with the results if the others were still there. Now I have the courage to open it since Claude will be with me," Anders cried.

Skye stood up and announced. "Let's not talk about this again until we're finished with Christmas. Afterward, the ones who are going back to the cave can plan when you want to go. I will not be going. It's not something I can do."

"I have no reason to go," Phillip said quickly.

"Nor do I. Shall we mention this to Morgan when they arrive for Christmas?" Carrie asked.

"No, she's not involved in any way," Ross interjected.

"I agree. I'll tell her later, if it becomes an issue. Josephine and I will consider the trip to France a vacation. That's all she needs to know. I don't want her to worry about this and Levi doesn't need to get involved. He has enough problems of his own," Clark added.

One by one, they filtered out of the living room and went to bed.

Each person had his own demons to deal with.

CHAPTER 18

Christmas Day, 1971

Skye and Carrie were the first ones up Christmas morning. They retreated to the front porch with their coffee, settled in the rocking chairs and watched the sun rise slowly over the hill across the valley. A gentle breeze blew through the trees and several rabbits ran down the driveway, chased by the dog that lived across the street. A rooster announced it was time to get out of bed as the front door behind them opened and Ross joined them with hot biscuits.

"I hope you two got some sleep. Juliet and I didn't sleep more than a few hours. The revelation about Josephine's mother kept running through my mind. Juliet decided she'll stay here while I go back and we handle the situation in France."

"I agree, there's no need for her to go," Skye interjected.

"We've decided we don't want to live in France again. Although it's her home country and I love it there, we want our child to be an American and that won't happen unless he grows up here. We hope to have one more, but Juliet won't consider it unless we've made California our home," he said leaning on the rail of the porch.

"I understand. When this is finished, we may want to put the vineyard in France on the market again. Surely someone will want the place." Skye drained the last of the coffee from her mug.

"I agree. I think one reason it hasn't sold is the earlier appraisal. The vineyard was overpriced. The land lies on the slope of a long hill that leads to the Alps. The altitude is close to 3,700 feet where the land ends. The limestone soil at the top of the slope, which has been eroded over the years, is planted with Chardonnay grapes. Pinot Noir grapes are planted lower down on land that is reddened by iron oxide so those soils give unique flavors to the wines. All of the plantings struggle to survive, taxing the vines. Our wines are favorites of the locals but competition is stiff. France has thousands of small wineries that have pedigrees dating back hundreds of years. Once this mystery is solved we need to have a meeting of the board of directors and decide the best way to go. Either modernize or sell," Ross stated.

"I agree, since I'm a part owner. But I live in Alabama. It's going to be up to the vineyard side of the family to make these decisions," Carrie reminded him.

"I understand. The family has factions; the medical corps, the entertainers and the wine makers. I may be cynical but the dilemma from last night can be boiled down to a couple of sentences. Claude and Anders found each other, long lost brothers who believed the other was dead. They revealed the demise of Josephine's mother and other people who were sheltered at the vineyard," Ross summarized as he finished his coffee.

"I'm worried about Josephine returning and seeing her mother. I'm afraid this is going to be too traumatic for her. She has problems with depression," Skye added.

"She's going to do it and what we think isn't going to change that. You know, at first I thought it was gruesome, but I actually understand. Seeing her mother will give her closure and when she buries her, that will give her peace. She'll be alright. She's stronger than you think. Juliet and I spend time with them, and she is quite a woman. I admire her and her work," Ross added.

"Let's go in. I need more coffee," Carrie suggested.

They found the Judge, Eva and Daphne at the table, enjoying hot biscuits, scrambled eggs, bacon, coffee and juice. The cook had been busy and the house stirred with excitement. The children wandered down to search under the tree for their presents, unaware of the tension in the house.

Skye settled in a chair in the living room, allowing Carrie and Ross to take over. She wanted to watch everyone, to observe the grandchildren's reactions, to allow the raw emotions of the night before to heal. Presents found everyone, new sweaters, toys, gloves, slippers, ten dollar bills for the children and a crate of the reserved Poschett wine for each family.

Morgan called and said she and Levi would arrive around noon. Clark reminded everyone not to mention the trip to France. He and Josephine would tell her when the time was right and that would be their decision.

Skye owned fifty percent of the vineyards and Ross, Carrie, Phillip, Josephine and Anders each owned ten percent. They had a board of directors meeting every Christmas at eight p.m. after the children were in bed. At the meeting, they opened the best wines of the last year, discussed problems and projections, goals and aspirations, and each one of them received a check. Then Skye gave each of them a check from her, sharing her fifty percent, keeping enough for her to pad her savings account and to live on for the year.

After the revelations of last night, Eva withdrew in silence, staying close to Daphne and the Judge. Claude and Anders continued their conversations about their lost years. Daphne and the Judge asked for a tour of the warehouse and bottling process. They would do that at eleven a.m., before Morgan and Levi arrived. At two, dinner would be served and from the aroma in the house, it would be a feast.

Around ten a.m., Skye whispered to Carrie, "I'm going over to Martin's office to have some quiet time."

"I understand. I'll cover for you," Carrie assured her.

Skye walked the worn path to the little stone house and settled into Martin's oversized recliner in his old office, tucked his quilt around her and stared at the wall in front of her. Weary and tired, she thought about Josephine, her brave Josephine, the little girl she loved immediately when Martin introduced them to her. Memories of the first time she met her flooded into her brain, how Josephine crawled out of Martin's car, tiny and sick. How she and

Carrie wanted to take her and hug her, feed her and shower her with love. They got their chance to do that and Josephine was as much her daughter as her biological daughters.

"I love you, Martin, I love you still. I will always love you. How hard it must have been for you to lose your first wife and endure those hardships. I cannot imagine how you survived but I'm glad you did," she said to the photo of them on the wall. She fell asleep in the chair. Carrie found her there.

"Wake up, Mother. Morgan and Levi are here," Carrie shook her gently.

They walked back to the house. Morgan looked elegant, her nail color matched her sweater, her velvet slacks fit well, large diamonds decorated her ear lobes and a gold bracelet circled her wrist. Levi, handsome with streaks of grey in his thick hair, in a red sweater vest over a white shirt, dressed in grey corduroy slacks, greeted everyone with a smile and handshake. He seemed buoyant and talkative. Introductions were made, then Levi stalled when the Judge asked him a question.

"Did you say your last name is Shulman? My grandmother was a Shulman. She lived in Warsaw," he commented as he shook Levi's hand.

"Really, my grandfather's name was Frankel Shulman. He was born in France but they moved to Warsaw when he was a boy. What was your grandmother's name?" Levi asked.

"Tenny, her name was Tenny Louisa Shulman," the Judge replied.

210

"I'll be damned. I believe they were brother and sister. That makes us cousins. Imagine that, I found a cousin and you survived the war! How did you do it? Most Jews left Warsaw in cattle cars."

"My parents brought me to America in 1918 so I went through the war here. I wanted to serve in the military but this kept me stateside." David pointed to his foot.

The two men spent the next hour talking, revealing what they remembered about their ancestors, making sure they had the right connection.

At one-thirty, the crowd increased as the mayor of Napa and his wife came in and next door neighbors stopped by with gifts. Food began to appear on the buffet side board: salads, olives, cheeses, carrot sticks, sliced turkey, sliced ham, cornbread dressing, creamed potatoes, gravy, green beans, candied sweet potatoes, creamed corn, rolls, apple pies, pecan pies and Skye's fruit cake.

The children were called in to wash their hands and everyone joined in a circle as Ross delivered a short prayer. The older children filled their plates first, then the line snaked around the table and people found seats at the dining room table and a folding banquet table erected in the living room for the overflow.

Light conversations began and were interrupted by children begging to sample the deserts. The cook took empty dishes to the kitchen and refilled glasses of tea.

"Levi, what movie score are you doing?" Carrie asked.

"It is a Civil War movie; a family is torn by the war, the mother dies, the baby contracts cholera and people starve. It's a real tear jerker, but it will be a classic. The music will have some old fashioned flare to it, like excerpts from 'Dixie' and 'The Battle Hymn of the Republic.' I will also have a new arrangement of 'Amazing Grace' and an old marching tune I found for the scenes with the soldiers. Of course, I'll write some new tunes but that's about it. Morgan and I are flying to New York next week to meet with one of the producers."

"Where do you stay when you're there?" the Judge asked.

"We don't have a regular place. Wish we did. We'd love to buy something but we never stay long enough to look over the market," Morgan chimed in.

"I've been thinking about selling my apartment. It's empty right now, in a state of flux. It needs repairs and a face lift. I'm tired of dealing with it," the Judge revealed.

"Where is it located?"

"At Fifth Avenue and 79th. It's across the street from the museum, across from Central Park. I can call the manager to let you in and you can take a look at it," David suggested.

"Pre-war?" Morgan asked.

"Yes. I bought it during the war but it's been renovated twice. It has big rooms the new apartments don't have, wide plank hardwood floors, thick plaster walls, huge windows and high ceilings."

"We'd love to look at it. You may have sold your apartment to your cousin," Levi said as everyone around the table laughed.

Morgan and Levi left at five, taking two crates of wine with them. Ross and Phillip opened bottles from last year's harvest, pouring stems for everyone but the children. Compliments flowed as snacks appeared on the dining room table.

"I can't eat another bite," the Judge said. He and Daphne excused themselves to take a nap and Eva escaped to her bedroom a few minutes later. Claude and Anders left in the truck, driving toward town. Carrie took her children on a drive around the valley, Ross and Juliet retreated to their bedroom for a nap and Skye found her rocking chair on the front porch and pulled a quilt around her shoulders.

She watched the sun sink over the hills, as several deer grazed in the shadow of a tree across the road, a crow cawed loudly in the sycamore behind the house and a light fog began to roll in from the ocean and settle in the valley. Skye closed her eyes, took a deep breath and inhaled the scent of baking apples, cedar, wet earth and wood smoke. A gentle breeze circled the porch and vanished. The valley settled in for the night, lights coming on in houses, blinking lights of Christmas decorations soft in the hazy fog.

Then she saw a disturbance in the fog. In a whirlwind, the body of Owen Campbell rose up and laughed at her. Colin floated up behind him. They were standing by Colin's red convertible where she saw him the last time before he was killed by his girlfriend. Colin's head jerked from one side to the other, his eyes turned red and his hair flamed.

He yelled, "I'm coming back, I'm coming back."

Someone pulled into the driveway and the headlights hit Skye's face, jerking her back to reality, the fog dissipated, the images gone.

That night when she went to bed, she wondered what the vision meant. Was her brain playing tricks on her? Those ghosts of her past were dead, Owen and Colin Campbell were buried side by side in Alabama. What could they do to her now?

Would they ever leave her alone?

CHAPTER 19

Last week of December, 1971

David and Daphne, Claude and Eva left early on the morning of the 27th, their goodbyes said the night before. Only Skye was up to see them off in the new Cadillac the Judge bought for the trip.

"Drive carefully. It's not daylight yet. Watch for deer on the highway." She handed them a sack full of homemade cookies, made the night before.

"That is one sweet lady," Claude remarked as they started down the driveway.

Eva and Daphne slept in the back seat until the sun hit their faces. Streaming through the windshield the eastern sky revealed a bright yellow ball.

"I've got to stop for a bathroom," Daphne announced when they'd driven fifty miles.

"Me too," Eva joined in with the same request.

They ate breakfast at a café near the gas station where Daphne bought postcards and T-shirts for the girls.

"I'll be glad to get home. I enjoyed seeing Joseph, touring Hawaii and the time in Napa, but that session about the cave room was so sad. I feel for Josephine and for everyone involved," Daphne commented when they were back on the highway.

"Who would have ever believed I'd be on a vacation with my friends and find my brother that I believed to be dead? I never knew what happened to Martin Poschett. He was a good man," Claude replied.

"Yes, he was. His son Phillip looks like him," Eva added.

"From France to America to find Eva, then on to California where I find my brother, it is a…uh…fairy tale. Is that the term?" Claude couldn't find the right phrase.

"That expresses it pretty well. Life's full of surprises," the Judge added.

"When are you going over to open that cave?" Daphne asked Claude.

"We agreed to go the first of April. Josephine has to clear her schedule, she and Clark plan to stay a month and go on to Paris. They are taking their little girl, so they need a nanny to go with them. They have to find someone," Claude replied, his French accent still in his voice.

"We are thinking about going on a steamer and taking a long vacation. Claude wants to trace down some people he knew before the war. We also have a connection to an organization that has a list of Holocaust survivors. We might be able to get those envelopes to them and see if they can find the rightful owners," Eva added.

"Good. Don't forget I have that trunk of envelopes in the attic. If you find an organization that will find the owners, I will give the trunk to them. None of the envelopes belong to me," David reminded her.

It took them five days to drive home. In Arizona, they stopped for an hour to peer over the rim of the Grand Canyon. In Santa Fe they ate enchiladas and guacamole at a sidewalk café on the town square and spent the night in a downtown hotel with adobe walls. The next day, they drove to Amarillo where the men ate a huge steak for $3.95 at the Grand Slam Steakhouse while Eva and Daphne looked on with amazement. The restaurant advertised the dinner a hundred miles out and both men bragged they could eat the twenty ounce steak. They did.

They spent the night in Conway, a small town east of the restaurant, the men claiming they were too full to keep driving. The next morning, a dusting of snow covered the parking lot and the car. David wiped off the white powder and continued east, driving out of the snow a few miles later.

Along the highway they saw antelope, prairie dogs, deer, wild hogs, longhorn cattle, road runners, horses, cowboys and vast stretches of nothingness that led to the horizon and back. They passed red cliffs and blades of rock that created spikes and plateaus. Then the highway crossed gullies, dry except for puddles that revealed a swift current had recently cascaded through the small canyons.

Around a curve, a sign announced "Oklahoma, the Sooner State." Fifty feet past the sign, a dust devil followed the car for a hundred feet then crossed the highway and lifted. Tumbleweed rolled in front of them, some catching on the barbed wire fence where cattle grazed close by. Roadrunners darted in front of the car, barely escaping the front fender. Off in the distance, a circle of vultures intrigued them.

Traveling due east in Oklahoma, the vegetation increased as they drove into rolling hills and across rivers. They spent the night in Tulsa and the next night in West Memphis. Crossing over the Mississippi River the next morning, they noticed barges loaded with coal being pushed downstream in the swiftly moving, muddy water. The next day, they drove into Decatur.

After Claude and Eva left, David checked the mail and drove to the store for milk and bread. While he was gone, Daphne looked in the mirror. Her hair was a mess and she had dark circles under her eyes. She looked at her eyes again. The left one was still dilated. She'd noticed the uneven pupils while they were in Hawaii and Carrie noticed them on Christmas Day while they ate breakfast in Napa.

"You need to come in for a check-up when you get back to Alabama. Your headaches have come back, I can tell from the way you react to light and noise," Carrie whispered to her when no one was listening.

"Please don't tell my husband. He worries about me so much and I don't want to bother him with my silly headaches," Daphne replied.

"Wait a minute, let me look at your eyes," Carrie said as she looked at the right pupil then the left one. "They're uneven."

"I saw that last week. I felt it was my imagination, then the left one stayed dilated. What does it mean?" Daphne asked in a low voice.

"We need to check you out. I'll call you when I get home with an appointment time. We'll work you in," Carrie promised.

The Saturday after they returned from California, they had Christmas with the girls. Emma, now thirty, lived two streets over. They'd bought one of the historic houses north of the courthouse where her husband, Judge Kyle Walton, walked to work as David did when he was on the bench. Kyle ran on the Republican ticket and won in a landslide. They settled in with Dawson and joined the First Methodist Church where Kyle had been a member growing up in Decatur.

One of the social workers for the county, Emma stayed in a state of emotional turmoil most of the time. She was too involved with her clients. She kept a pantry full of canned food to distribute to the hungry, she took clothes to the girls who wanted to drop out of school because they couldn't dress as nice as the other girls, she bought tennis shoes for the boys who wanted to play basketball but couldn't afford the regulation shoes, she arranged appointments for dental work and vaccinations and check-ups for children she knew were malnourished, sick or had cavities. Sometimes she paid for the things herself, sometimes their church helped and she was a frequent visitor to the food pantry operated by the Baptist church.

Grace, twenty and still in college, had become a social butterfly at the University of Alabama in Birmingham. She partied most weekends, went to the basketball games, joined the tennis club, the bowling league, the acting group. She and a girlfriend lived in the dorm, where the room staying in a state of disarray, clothes on the floor, shoes strewn under beds and coat hangers scattered around the room.

Once they dropped by Grace's dorm unannounced and found the mess and a boy in the room with the roommate. At least the roommate claimed he was hers. They weren't sure. After that they called Grace before they took her out to lunch. Sometimes she answered, most of the time she didn't. She had been on academic probation a couple of semesters. When she came home for Christmas she declared her major.

"I'm going to be an accountant," she announced at the dinner table. Emma laughed, David's mouth dropped.

"Isn't that hard?" Daphne asked.

"I don't think so. Wayne says he likes the classes."

"So, you are declaring a major based on what your boyfriend is doing?" Emma said, rolling her eyes.

"I can do it. In spite of my grades, I can do the work," Grace countered with determination in her voice.

"Prove it," Emma challenged her sister as she took a bite of dressing.

"I will. I will," Grace tightened her mouth.

"How was your trip?" Kyle asked changing the subject, trying to keep peace between the sisters.

"Interesting," Daphne replied then told them about the coffin in the cave and the couples going back to open it and solve the mystery of what happened to the other people.

"Sounds like something out of a movie," Emma speculated as Dawson whined at the other end of the table.

"He's tired. We need to get him home for a nap."

"And I need to get back to Birmingham," Grace added.

In thirty minutes, the house was empty. Daphne cleared the dishes off the table and put the food in the refrigerator. She had a painful headache and when she turned to wipe off the table there were two of them.

I'm seeing double again. She held on to the wall to get to their bedroom. She crawled in the bed fully clothed and roused when David found her there.

"Help me undress. I'm tired, real tired," she whined.

"It's more than that. I'm getting you to the doctor Monday."

They worked her in, did an X-ray and admitted her to the hospital. The next morning, the neurologist did some testing. Daphne had to follow his finger from left to right then right to left. She had to stand up and turn around, touch her nose, touch her ears, stand on her tip toes. He left without saying a word. They did more X-rays, one of her chest, one of her spine. At five thirty, Carrie and Dr. Patterson came in for rounds.

"I'm afraid the tumor is back. It's bigger and lower in your brain. It's pressing on your optical nerve. We need to operate again. This isn't the news you wanted, but you're strong and healthy and we don't see signs that it has spread. I believe you'll do well," Dr. Patterson told her.

"I don't want to go through this again. How long do I have if I don't have surgery?" Daphne asked.

"Six months, maybe a year," he replied.

"She'll have the surgery," David insisted.

"The surgery may buy you a lot of years. Good years, time to be with your grandchildren, time to be with your husband," Carrie added.

"Okay. When?" A tear rolled down Daphne's cheek and stopped at her chin. She wiped it off and shook her head sideways.

"Monday morning. We moved you to first on the surgery schedule."

"I don't want to do this. Just so you know, I have lived a wonderful life with David and I'm ready to go if that is what happens," Daphne looked at each of them. No one spoke.

"I want to go home to get ready. We need to hire someone like we did last time and...uh...tell the girls." Daphne looked at Carrie. She knew Carrie understood.

"Be back at the hospital by noon on Sunday. Do not take any aspirin from this point on. It thins your blood and I don't want your blood thin. Stay close to home, drink plenty of fluids, no driving and no alcohol." Dr. Patterson wrote down the instructions and handed them to David.

"I'll discharge you in a few minutes. You can go home and I'll see you when I make rounds Sunday afternoon."

"Okay. I'll be good," Daphne laughed.

"Is there anything I can do?" Carrie asked.

"Say a prayer. I have a funny feeling about this," Daphne replied.

They drove home in silence. Daphne wasn't hungry and neither was David. He put her to bed then retreated to the living room and poured a glass half full of Jack Daniels. He built a fire in the fireplace and found a pillow and a quilt. He sipped on the whiskey and watched the flames curl around the wood, the crackling timber shooting sparks held back by a screen Daphne purchased. He thought about Anna, about Daisy and Caris in the coffin in that cave. A vision of his mother and little sister came to him, then his father. Then he thought about Daphne. *Why can't I go first, why is this happening to her, to us?*

He began to cry, his heart ached, his throat tightened. He poured more whiskey in the glass. He stared into the flames and wondered how the girls, his sweet Emma, his mischievous Grace, would survive without a mother. For the first time in years he thought about God. How could a righteous God allow this to happen to Daphne? How could he forsake her?

He went back to their room, showered and dressed for bed in the moonlight. He crawled in beside Daphne and watched a soft light dance across her face, the shadows made by a gardenia bush swaying in the wind outside the window. He heard the hoot of the old owl that lived in the oak tree out front and the deep horn of a barge going down the river a half mile away. He inhaled the fresh powder smell of Daphne and fell asleep.

Sunlight streamed through the window and hit David's eyelids. He heard noises, things banging. He turned over to reach for Daphne but she wasn't there. He smelled coffee, crawled out of bed and found her in the kitchen frying sausage. She had taken several frying pans out of the cabinet and stacked them on the counter.

"I'm hungry. We forgot to eat last night and why do I keep all these pans? They're in the way," she asked as she threw the oldest one in the trash, banging it on the side of the cabinet. She was energized by something.

"I don't know. Want me to get the eggs out of the refrigerator?"

"Yes. And we aren't telling the girls anything about this new surgery until an hour before we leave on Sunday. And I'll also call Joseph on Sunday. I want this week to be special with Emma and Dawson. Another thing, I don't want every Tom, Dick and Harry in this town to know about this. Last time, everyone knew when I pissed in the bedpan and grew a hair on top of my head. This is our private matter," she declared as she shook the spatula at David.

224

David stood in stunned silence. He had never seen her act like this.

"Grace is too busy to be concerned, and I'm glad. This is our battle, mine and yours. Well... mostly mine. I don't want a pity party, a sing-song of sad little Daphne circulating around this town. Do you hear me?"

"Yes ma'am, anything you want, I'm doing."

"And you are going to do that visiting Judge assignment and I want that vacation house we're going to build on the coast started. I want to decorate it before...uh...before I...get sick again, if that's what happens." She had the spatula aimed at his face. The popping in the skillet intensified as she slid the skillet off the burner.

The next few days Daphne had no symptoms, went grocery shopping, bought a new robe and slippers, new sheets for the bed and new pillows. They interviewed two ladies to be her aide and hired the one who went to college at night. David increased the amount he'd pay her when he found out she had to work every other semester to save money to pay her tuition.

David had been called to do a special case in Limestone County. Occasionally a judge had to excuse himself from a case, was sick or on vacation. Then the county would call in a retired judge and he'd accepted the job before they knew Daphne needed surgery. He would report to the case ten days after her surgery.

On Friday, Daphne and Emma went shopping in Huntsville. Daphne bought her two new outfits then they ate lunch at the only

French restaurant in town. On Sunday morning, they went to church with Emma, Kyle and Dawson then joined half of the congregation at Big Bob's Bar-B-Que. The population of Decatur loved the restaurant, its wonderful food and quick service. The coconut pie sold out if you didn't get there straight from church.

That's when they told Emma and Kyle they would leave at two to check into the hospital.

"That's not fair, Mother. You should have told me earlier. I have meetings at work tomorrow and Kyle has court," Emma said.

"That's why I did it this way. You can come down later when I'm over the surgery. I've been through this before. It's no big deal," Daphne assured her then added, "Well, we need to go home. I have to call Grace and my brother. I'll be back to the house by the end of the week. We have someone to help us and I don't want the entire town to fuss over me. I don't like that."

They were unable to get an answer in Grace's dorm room. Daphne called Joseph then they drove to Birmingham and checked Daphne into the hospital. The next morning, David paced in the surgery waiting room for Carrie and Dr. Patterson to emerge from the operating room. Four hours after he kissed Daphne's shaved head, Carrie came through the door.

"She's doing well, she's in recovery, moving her arms and legs. She's going to be in a lot of pain. The tumor was a mess. He couldn't get it all but he got most of it," Carrie shook her head, tears escaped from her eyes.

"What about radiation?"

"She's already had all her body can take the first time around," Carrie reminded him.

"Damn." David felt defeated.

"I'm glad you took her to Hawaii. I noticed her uneven pupils in Napa. You took her on her dream trip in the nick of time," Carrie said as she put her hand on his shoulder.

"Is she going to be in pain?"

"Not if she'll take her pain meds. We will make sure she has plenty."

"How long?"

"It's hard to say. A year, maybe longer. Tumors have a way of doing their own thing. Some grow fast, some stall and don't increase for years."

"Okay, I have a house to build on the coast and we have some more things to do."

"She'll be in recovery for an hour. Why don't you get some breakfast?"

"Okay, I think I'll try to find Grace," David answered. He left the waiting room behind Carrie.

He drove to the dorm, half a mile away from the hospital. He found Grace asleep and told her about her mother.

"No, no…I thought she was cured."

"So did I, but she's a fighter so maybe we'll have her longer than predicted." "Daddy, I want to move home. I want to be with her. I registered for this semester but classes haven't started so I can withdraw. I can transfer to Huntsville and drive over for classes. I broke it off with Wayne. He was too possessive," she cried.

"Then come home. Some rules will need to be honored," David added.

"I understand. I've grown up a lot, you'll see," Grace replied.

CHAPTER 20

April, 1972

The ones who would open the cave room agreed to meet at the Poschett Vineyard in France the first day of April. Anders and Lillie Anne arrived the first week of February, flying to Marseille where the manager picked them up at the airport.

In March, the weather was cold. Marseille was on the same latitude as Portland, Maine, yet people were fooled by the few palm trees that struggled to survive in the city due to the warm Mediterranean breezes. The travel brochures indicated a tropical climate but that was a misnomer. The village of Tenay was north of Marseille and the altitude added to the winter chill. Anders and Lillie Anne warned the coming visitors to bring warm clothes.

Once back at the French vineyard, Anders busied himself with inspections of the buildings, the condition of the vines and the sales reports. He found the vineyard had lost money again, there were cases of wine unsold, stored in the warehouse, the one where the wall in the back would be opened in a few days. The hundred-year-old casks stood there, empty and huge. It took three men to slide them.

He had an electric line installed to the back of the warehouse then wired two plugs and ceiling lights to the area in front of the casks. They had not seen a reason to have the lights before but now they would need the light. The warehouse, over a hundred years old, had been built of stone and backed up to a cave that made the perfect storage for wine. The stone and rock walls of the warehouse were solid, a foot thick in some places. The floor was hard packed dirt.

A new warehouse, built ten years ago, held the modern bottling line where the wine bottles were filled, corked, labeled and placed in crates. Built of lumber with a tin roof, there was a small office inside for the manager with bunk beds where two people could sleep.

The hundred-year-old stone house at the vineyard contained five rooms. Each room opened into the next one, the two bedrooms at the back revealing a spectacular view of the Alps. There were three other buildings, the old summer kitchen, a smokehouse and a well room. The old well was still used, the frigid water clean and pristine. A garden, chicken coop, a small
orchard and a lean-to for the cow completed the compound. Two cats kept the rodent population low and every day or two the oldest cat brought a mouse to the front door for their approval before she ate the morsel.

In front of the house, a road wound through the valley where the nearest house, small and quaint and surrounded by a rock fence, stood half a kilometer away, occupied by an elderly couple who worked at the vineyard when they needed extra hands. They kept sheep and goats, making excellent cheese from their milk.

Every time Ross and Juliet occupied the vineyard, they felt they were stepping back fifty years. Juliet had modernized the kitchen and toilet. Otherwise the house was the same, the walls thick, the furniture old and creaky, the rugs on the floor ancient, paintings in the parlor from a bygone era.

Anders and Lillie Anne didn't mind the lack of modern conveniences. They had grown up in similar houses and quickly adjusted to the culture shock when they occupied the vineyard. Lillie Anne had a sister close by and she stepped into her role of a midwife each time she returned, the profession not accepted in California where hospitals were used to birth babies.

The six of them who would be there when the room was opened, Anders, Claude, Eva, Ross, Josephine and Clark, agreed on the terms of the discovery, as the adventure was now called.

Lillie Anne and Eva agreed they would not be in involved. Along with the nanny, they would watch over Colette in the house and cook for the crowd. The rest of them would go into the cave room. Ross would remove the lid to the coffin, then Josephine would have time with her mother. Clark would stay with her, assuming the others had not taken her body with them, if they escaped.

Claude and Eva took the Royal Viking Star from New York to Marseille, arriving on the 28th of March. Anders picked them up at the port, the same port he, Martin and Josephine had sailed from in 1946. He deposited them at a room he rented for them in the village.

On March 30th, Josephine, Clark, Colette, their nanny and Ross arrived in Lyon by airplane. The next night, everyone gathered for a late dinner, Anders and Lillie Anne providing a meal of roast lamb, rice, cabbage, bread, cheese, baked apples and Poschett wine. A roaring fire in the living room warmed their spirits. There was no television. After dinner, they talked, drank wine, sampled cheeses, olives and dried fruit. At nine, everyone went to bed.

Ross and Anders agreed Clark could film the discovery, except the opening of the coffin and Josephine's time with her mother. If they discovered bodies other than Caris, the officials of the town would be notified and they would remove them. They agreed the boxes of envelopes would be brought to the house where they would deal with them later, not trusting the local police.

In the cave room, they expected to find wine bottles, a radio that had an antenna that ran out of the room and up through the roof of the warehouse. It had been used for the resistance movement and picked up a station in Switzerland that gave news of the Allied troop movements. There were coal oil lamps in the room, bottles of olive oil, cans of vegetables, maps, chairs, a table and a jar used for the toilet. Anders made the list of items from memory. He prided himself in his organizing skills. He kept things in order and he liked order. He wanted this discovery to go smoothly.

Anders tried to think of everything for the comfort of the guests. He had a cot for the nanny in the corner of the living room and he secured a burial site at the village cemetery so they could inter Caris. Lillie Anne put new linens on the bed in the spare bedroom where Clark, Josephine and Colette would sleep. There was plenty of food in the house; cheese, carrots, apples, olives, bread, cake, jam, butter, cream, juice.

Josephine had not been to her childhood home for twenty-six years. When she came into the house, she walked around and touched the furniture, the counters in the kitchen, the windows, the rugs and paintings on the wall.

"I remember this velvet couch and rocking chair. I remember my mother holding me when I hurt my foot, we sat in the chair, her soothing me with a glass of milk. I also remember going out to that old chicken coop and gathering the eggs in a basket, how we kept cats and a border collie that rounded up the cattle every night and guided them to the barn. Daddy told me the Germans burned the barn so no one could hide in it. They also took our cattle, goats and chickens," Josephine revealed.

She walked around the compound while Clark filmed the landscape, sweeping the valley slowly, the moving camera capturing the character of the area, the house and buildings. Then he photographed every room with a still camera, the out buildings, the road winding through the valley, the village, the Alps shining in the distance, the casks in the back of the old warehouse.

The morning of April 1st, a bright sun crept into the valley. Sheep across the road bayed to the cow that answered with her reply. Two roosters announced it was time to get out of bed. Anders was up first, followed quickly by Lillie Anne. Clark and Josephine finally pulled back the warm covers and slid out of the bed, vowing not to disturb Colette.

Claude and Eva arrived a few minutes later in a rented car. Everyone ate a breakfast of cheese, boiled eggs, olives and bread. Ross brought coffee from America and Lillie Anne made a pot of tea.

At nine, the men and Josephine walked to the old warehouse where the casks blocked the way to the cave room. A black and white cat jumped to the top of the cask in the corner and disappeared behind the wall where a plank left a small hole to the room beyond.

"She's been visiting that room for years," Anders laughed as they watched her tail disappear into the unknown.

Then Anders smashed the outermost plank on the middle cask and removed several from the metal ring. In thirty minutes, the men had the cask down and moved to the outside. A small door in the wooden plank wall, no more than three feet high and two feet wide, stood before them, its secrets intact behind the latched door.

Ross turned the latch and pushed the door. Hinges squeaked as the door slid a few inches. He took a flashlight and tried to push the opening wider.

"There is something piled behind this door," he said.

"It's dirt, a pile of dirt and a rock," he said reaching around the door. Finally it slid open and Ross pointed the flashlight through the door.

"What do you see?" Anders asked, Clark filming the process behind him.

"A coffin straight ahead and wait, I think I see a skeleton. I'm going in," Ross stated.

He disappeared into the room then emerged.

"We need lights in there. It's so dark you can't see anything. It's musty in there and cold, very cold," he said shaking and rubbing his arms.

Anders disappeared to the house and brought two lights and an extension cord.

"I'm back with the lights," he yelled to the crowd standing by the wall. Anders plugged in the cord then the men crawled through the door, pulling the lights with them.

"Okay, we can see," Josephine heard someone say.

"I'll be damned. Look at that. How in the world?" another voice said.

A hand of one of the men appeared at the door.

"Josephine, come on in. Watch your head," Clark said behind the wall, his hand waving.

The room had walls and a ceiling of solid rock. One wall was damp with dripping water hitting a small outcrop near the top where the water pooled then dispersed on its way to the hard packed, uneven dirt floor. The enclosure contained two chairs and a table with an ancient radio in the middle. A gas lamp sat next on the table beside two glasses, three empty bottles of wine, pencils, note paper and a pair of gold rimmed spectacles. Cobwebs, the remnants of insects and the skeleton of a rat were scattered on the table.

A coffin sat next to the back wall. Ander's cat sat on top of the coffin. There were no visible signs of mummified bodies or skeletons. There were signs that the occupants decided to find a way out. A stick made into an arrow pointed to a dark hole at the back of the room.

"Look at this," Claude said. "They left us a note."

"What does it say?" Ross asked.

Claude saw the fragile note on the table, anchored by one of the wine bottles. He brushed away cobwebs and dead insects as Anders pointed the flashlight to the paper.

"Don't pick it up, it will probably come apart if you do," Ross said.

"Right, I won't. It says: *After four days, we decide to escape to Switzerland if this cave has an opening. If not, we hope you come back.*

"We don't know if they made it. The only way to find out is to go to the end of the cave and see. If they didn't get out there will be…uh…skeletons," Claude stated.

"Okay, let's find out what's in the coffin," Ross stated as he moved the cat off the top.

He and Clark pried the lid off. A rancid smell escaped followed by fine dust. Ross moved the flashlight to the head area and turned it on.

"Wow, she is not in bad shape at all," He said and moved away.

"Come Josephine, look at your mother," Clark said with tears running down his face.

Everyone but the two of them left the room. They went to the house, where they were joined by Clark and Josephine thirty minutes later. Lillie Anne greeted them with hot tea and scones. They warmed up by the fireplace. Everyone waited for Josephine to reveal what she saw but she couldn't talk. Clark gave the details.

"For her body to have been in that room for twenty-six years she had not decomposed much. I guess it was due to the frigid temperatures, like she'd been preserved in a refrigerator. A rodent had eaten the tip of her fingers and part of her nose but I guess the cats kept down the rat population. She looked peaceful and serene. She had a yellow patch of mold on one cheek, a small patch on her forehead and some on the top of her hands, folded neatly on her chest. She had on a dark dress and her wedding ring was still on her finger. Her blonde hair, curly and long, was intact," he said softly.

"She was pretty and young. So young," Josephine added in a low voice as she stared into the fireplace.

"We will bury her tomorrow," Clark stated methodically.

Colette ran to her mother and Josephine held her a long time, crying softly. Eva and Lillie Anne surrounded her then they retreated to the bedroom. The men went outside.

"Josephine will be okay. She said her goodbyes. She wanted me to take some photos of her and I did. It was the right thing to do, letting her see her mother," Clark whispered as Anders handed him a bottle of brandy.

"Here, we are off to a good start, this will put some fire in our bellies," Anders passed the bottle around, each of them taking a swig.

"I've got the rope and a flashlight for each of us. I also have markers so if we start going in circles we can find our way out," Anders told them.

"What are the markers? Popcorn?" Claude laughed.

"No, rats would eat the popcorn if they are in there, but I didn't see any. Buttons, Lillie Anne gave me two jars full of old buttons. Some are metal so we can see them easily with the flashlight."

"Good idea. Did you say Lillie Anne has sandwiches for us and some juice? You know, in case there is a cave in and we are trapped," Ross asked.

"There won't be a cave in," Claude saw the look of concern on Clark's face.

"There may be. We have earthquakes and landslides in this area," Ross kept on.

"There won't be a cave in," Claude and Anders said in unison.

"Let's get started. I want to be at the end of this cave before nightfall. We don't want to spend the night high up in the mountain," Anders added quickly.

Claude and Ross each took a backpack. One had food and bottled juice, the other caving equipment and Anders had a hundred feet of rope wrapped around his shoulder. Clark had a flash camera, a flashlight and more rope.

They entered the cave at the end of the room. Anders led, followed by Claude, Ross and Clark. They crawled for ten feet, the cave no higher than four feet, sharp rocks tearing at their knees. At the end of the tunnel, Anders yelled.

"Come on, there is a large room beyond the tunnel," he yelled back to the line of men.

They looked around in the room. Bats hung from the ceiling, a couple dropping and flying over their heads. They stepped in slippery bat guano.

"Well these critters know a way out or they wouldn't be here," Claude stated.

"Oh...I see where they exit," Anders stated. He saw one disappear through a crack in the twenty foot high ceiling where a soft light no larger than the size of a pack of cigarettes revealed a way outside.

"Our friends wouldn't have been able to get through that hole," Ross surmised.

"Let's go, there is the trail," Anders said as he turned the flashlight toward the cave.

They walked a hundred feet or more, the floor of the cave uneven. In some places it was dry, some patches were wet from water oozing from the overhead rocks. Then the cave narrowed and was wide enough for them to get through sideways. Their heads touched the roof, the smell of dust, mold and decay surrounding them in the stagnant air.

"Wait, stop. There is a small place up ahead then the cave goes in three directions. Come on through if you can."

They crowded in the open space, but there was no room for Clark. He stopped in the narrow part, wedged in between the cave walls.

"Man, this is tight. Where to now?" Ross asked.

"We have to split up. One of us will go down the three branches and Clark you stay here. After you have gone fifty feet come back and let us know what is down your cave," Anders suggested.

"I'll take the right cave, Claude you take the one straight ahead and Ross, you go left."

The men left and Clark stepped into the opening. He put the flashlight down and urinated in the area behind him. Relieved, he picked up the flashlight and it blinked off. He was in the dark.

"No, no, come on you sorry piece of equipment," he said turning it on and off, shaking it and hitting it with his hand.

The flashlight did not come on. Afraid he would lose a battery if he took off the end he realized he didn't have any batteries, they were in the backpack.

He yelled. "Do you see anything? Hello, anyone there?"

He saw a light coming toward him. Claude returned and when his flashlight hit Clark's face, he knew the man was terrified.

"Why are you standing there in the dark? What happened? You look like you saw a ghost."

"This damn thing quit. Do you have batteries?"

"No, I have food. Want a sandwich?" Claude answered in a light tone.

"I'll wait till we get out of here."

"I smell urine. Did you piss in here?"

"Yes, my bladder was full. I aimed it backward so we wouldn't walk in it."

"Good idea, I'm doing the same."

They switched places and Claude relieved himself.

Ross came back, then Anders. Ross stayed in the entrance of his cave.

"My cave was a dead end," Anders said.

"Mine kept going around a ledge with a drop off twenty feet or more. I heard water below and could see a fast moving creek. I saw signs that they went that way, there is an arrow carved on the wall pointing ahead with initials and the date underneath. I turned around when I saw it," Claude revealed.

"That has to be it, my branch stopped cold," Ross said.

"My flashlight is dead. Who has the extra batteries?" Clark asked.

"They're in my backpack. Pass it over to me and I'll put some new batteries in it." Ross replied.

"Let's go," Anders started for the ledge, ten feet ahead around a sharp curve.

"Who is putting out the buttons? This is where we need them in case this is a dead end further up. We will need to know how to get back," Claude said.

"I'm dropping them," Ross admitted.

Anders entered the area, the ledge no wider than two feet. He inched along the trail, keeping his body close to the wall. Each man behind him did the same, the path wet from water running out of cracks in the rocks.

"Oh no," Anders said looking ahead.

"What is it?"

"There is a narrow spot ahead," he replied.

"Narrower than this?" Ross asked.

"Yes, it is very narrow. We need to tie off. If one of us slides we will have a mess," Anders suggested.

"And if one of us slides we will all go over if we tie off. Let's see if there are some hand holds, someone way to bridge the gap." Claude lifted his flashlight to the rocks above the gap.

"I see what we can do but first we have to get rid of these backpacks. They will cause us to be unbalanced." He took his off and dropped it over the edge.

"There goes our food," he said. They heard the backpack hit the water a few seconds later.

"It's a long way down to that water and who knows where it goes," Claude said.

"What about yours?" he asked Ross.

"I'm getting a couple of knives out and the extra batteries. Anything else we need? Maybe the compass?"

"Yes, take it out and put the stuff in your pockets," Claude advised.

"We may need this rope. I'm hanging on to it," Anders said as he looked to Claude. "What is your plan?" he asked.

"See that rock that sticks out? It is dry. Reach for it and turn your body facing the wall. Put your toes on the ledge and inch over with your hand anchoring you. You can do it," Claude suggested.

Anders reached for the dry rock, illuminated by two flashlights. The other one was aimed at his feet. He held on, but the rope caught on something.

"Damn this rope," he said as he wiggled and the rope loosened. He inched forward a few more feet then he was on solid land. The wedge opened into a three foot wide path.

"Come on, you can do it. It is dry over here and safe," he yelled, his flashlight shining back to the men.

Claude went next, then Ross. Clark hung back.

"Come on, Clark, you can do it," they coaxed him.

"Nothing doing. I'm turning around and going back. I'll fall, I know I will. You guys go ahead. I'll see you later. I can find my way back." He turned around and disappeared.

"If he was as terrified as he looked, he did the right thing. Come on, let's go," Anders stated.

They followed the cave for an hour, winding through large rooms, crawling under rock overhangs, jumping over a two foot wide crevice. Anders dropped a rock in the crevice. They never heard it hit bottom. Then they splashed through a shallow creek that flowed into a hole and disappeared. The cave wound down for a hundred feet, the walls closing in on them, the roof getting lower, the temperature colder. Then the cave turned left and went uphill. They climbed over sharp rocks and reached a dead end. They turned around and fifty feet back they found a small entrance to another room.

Each man crawled under a ledge to the next room where they crossed another crevice. They heard water running and found a small waterfall that flowed out of a slit in a rock then disappeared into the crevice. Ahead the cave room appeared to be blocked by large boulders but beyond the large outcropping of rocks they saw pale light. They wiggled through the rocks to a warmer and lighter room.

Bats were back, hanging on the ceiling. They walked through their droppings. The rancid smell overwhelmed them as the men looked up to a hole in the ceiling no more than six inches wide where soft light streamed sideways to the floor.

"I'm having trouble breathing," Claude admitted, panting.

"It's the ammonia from the bat urine and the guano. Keep moving and let's get out of here. Come on, I think we're getting close. I see light ahead." Anders picked up his pace, leaving the bats behind.

They came to a dead end with a large opening fifteen feet above them. Light cascaded down from the opening but they couldn't see the sky.

"Look, there is an old rope. This is the way they got out," Ross stated.

"And there, there is something. See it? It looks like a small skull, the skull of a child," Anders pointed to something round and pale in the dirt.

They looked at the object then Ross cleared dirt away from it. It was the detached head of a child's doll with dark hair attached, an arm of the doll a foot away. Beside it sat an empty bottle of wine, vintage 1942. Turning back to the opening, Claude looked at the rock walls on one side.

"I can climb it. I've done some rock climbing and this will be easy. I'll put the rope down for you two," Claude stated.

He tied the rope around his waist and two minutes later he disappeared through the opening. The rope came down, knotted in three foot segments.

Claude's head appeared. "Come on up, the view is spectacular."

They were a mile up on the mountain behind the vineyard, where deep snow glistened in the sun. The valley stretched out before them, the house in view, smoke rising from the chimney.

"Look at this," Claude pointed. "See this? There are seven lines and 1944 carved in the rock. They made it."

"Now I can rest in peace," Claude embraced his brother as the two men sobbed.

"Let's go home," Ross said as he started down the mountain.

Half way down the mountain, Claude pointed to two figures, two women searching the landscape. They waved, but Lillie Anne and Eva didn't see them. The sun was low on the horizon when they walked into the house. Anders gave the news that the others had escaped.

"Where is Clark?" Josephine asked looking past the men.

"He turned back. Isn't he here?" Anders asked.

"He was with you. He hasn't come back. Where is he?"

"Oh no…uh…he's still in that cave. Something must have happened." Ross bounded from his place in front of the roaring fire. "I'll find him," he said putting on his coat. He ran out the door.

"What if Clark is hurt? Why didn't he stick with you?" Josephine asked Anders with concern in her voice.

"He'll take care of him, he'll find him. After all, he is his brother. Brothers take care of each other," Anders stated.

Josephine jerked her head around.

"You know about that?"

"It's obvious, isn't it?

CHAPTER 21

April, 1972

Ross found Clark a hundred feet past the entrance of the cave, where the cave narrowed to the place it branched. He had slipped and fallen, cutting his hand on a sharp rock, scraping and cutting his knee. He could barely walk. Ross coached him through the narrow part then put his arm around him and the two of them hobbled to the tunnel.

"Damn this knee, I'm going to have to crawl on it to get through to the room," Clark stated as he bent down.

"Wait, I can tie my shirt around it and that will make it easier on your knee," Ross had already started unbuttoning his shirt.

They crawled out to the room, walked by the coffin, crawled through the door in the wall where the cask had blocked the way then stalled in the warehouse. Clark took a sip from Ross' thermos.

"Thanks, Ross. I guess I would have made it but Josephine would have been beside herself and this flashlight might not have made it long enough for me to see. I appreciate you more than you can know," Clark said, emotion evident in his voice.

"No problem. Let's get into the house. I'm freezing," Ross said pointing to his bare chest under his light weight coat.

Once inside, Josephine took over, examining the cut on his hand, washing the torn skin on his knee.

"You need a tetanus shot. This wound is dirty. What is that slippery dark stuff?" Josephine looked at the black smears on Clark's skin and pants.

"Bat guano," Clark stated.

"You could get a nasty infection from this," Josephine's voice cracked.

"I'll drive to town and find the doctor and tell him to bring the right medicine," Claude said as he grabbed his coat.

"Is there any food left? I'm starved," Clark asked once Josephine finished with his wounds.

"Me, too," Ross replied as he pulled a chair to the table.

Eva and Lillie Anne put food in front of the men while Josephine and Colette watched them eat. When Claude came back with the doctor, he examined Clark's wounds and gave him a tetanus shot.

"I don't think anything is broken. That knee and your hand will be sore for a few days. Watch for infection," he said to Clark, who told him Josephine was a doctor in California and Claude had once practiced medicine.

The doctor and Josephine talked in French about her plastic surgery practice in Los Angeles. Josephine invited him to come for a visit sometime and he nodded that he would.

The next day, the coffin with Caris inside was moved to the back of the truck and they carried her to the cemetery where the undertaker in town met them with a metal casket. A priest was called to do the service as two men hired by the undertaker dug the grave. They explained why they were burying her so long after she died and the priest understood. Bodies were still surfacing from the war, coming from unmarked graves and abandoned buildings. They buried her beside her sister, who died in infancy. Clark filmed the process as Colette watched in stunned silence. She did not understand what was happening but they would explain it to her later, when she was older.

With Clark's injuries and Josephine battling a cold, they decided to go home and skip Paris. They would do that on another trip. Anders took them to Marseille where they checked into a hotel.

Josephine, Colette, Clark and the nanny started their flight home on April 6th, exhausted and weary. With rolls of film in his pocket, Clark wondered if the images of Caris in the coffin would be disturbing to Josephine. He never wanted Colette to find the photos and they discussed that once Colette fell asleep on the plane.

"I will take the photos of my mother and hide them at work. She will never see them," Josephine assured him.

"Does it bother you, you know, what happened?" Clark asked.

"Yes, of course. I wish things had been different. I wish I remembered more about my mother but I can't turn back the clock. I have Skye, my sisters, you and my brothers. I have Colette. I found out that everyone knows Ross is your brother. When you were missing, Anders and Claude revealed that." Josephine watched for his reaction.

"I figured it out when I met Ross. He knows, too. It's mother who won't come around on that subject. My father was Owen Campbell, so we're half-brothers. I don't know if he raped her or if it was consensual. Not that it matters. She'll tell me someday and I'll wait for her to do that. I won't ask," Clark stated.

"She was young when you were born. She could have been persuaded by him. You have to forgive her for the lie," Josephine added.

"I already have. How can I not? She's my mother," Clark whispered as Colette stirred.

The attendant brought dinner, a small steak, mashed potatoes and English peas with a cold roll. They settled in for the night, a long overseas flight that would take them through Paris, where they would refuel, then on to Halifax where they connected to Philadelphia. They would spend the night there. The next day they would fly to Atlanta, then to Denver and on to San Francisco.

"No wonder Ross and Juliet want to live in California. To get back and forth to the vineyard is a nightmare," Clark commented as he searched his briefcase for paper.

"What are you looking for?" Josephine asked.

"Paper. I'm outlining two things. A documentary on how we will return those envelopes to the rightful owners, and a movie about the story of your mother's death and how you returned twenty-six years later to bury her. The story has been churning in my mind since Christmas when the cave room was revealed. The best part is the movie will state at the onset, *based on a true story*. I've already figured out who in the family can play some of the parts. And Levi will do the music. It'll be a hit, I'm sure of it," Clark revealed.

"Does your mind ever rest?" Josephine asked.

"No, never. Okay here it is; Mother can play the woman that lives in the house across the street from the vineyard, Anders and Claude can play the doctor and the man in town that grabbed Martin off the street. I think Phillip would be perfect to play Martin. Colette can be you at age seven, viewing your mother on the bed. Ross and I will be extras and you can be…"

"Oh no, you don't. I won't have a part in the movie. You know I won't do it and I'm not going to let Colette return to France. If you can film her in one day on a local set I will let her be in the movie, otherwise no. You'll have to find someone else," Josephine protested.

"I have to write the screen play first. The whole story is incredible, how your mother was shot, how they rescued her from a pile of bodies and took her home, how she ended up in that coffin in the room with the others and the room was sealed and the people captured and sent off to prison who were supposed to let them out…uh, oh…are you listening?" Clark asked.

"Yes, I'm listening," Josephine replied, stifling a yawn.

"How Claude and Anders were part of the resistance and then they were captured. How they didn't find each other after the war then your dad moved to California. Years later the brothers found each other in California and returned and opened the room. Then, the four men traversed to the cave. I will leave out the part of me turning back, it makes me look like a wimp. The final scene will be you burying your mother, standing there with your little girl. It will be a blockbuster. And the documentary will be filmed as we find someone to take those chests full of the envelopes. The two films will be masterpieces," Clark said as he scribbled on the paper.

He looked over at Josephine and Colette. They were sound asleep in the seat of the plane. He smiled and continued to write, the sky outside the plane full of stars, the dark ocean beneath them. A rush of love settled on his heart as he looked at his wife and daughter, their long blond hair hanging in ringlets around their angelic faces.

Then he thought about the man who was his biological father. How could any man do the things that man did? Clark decided he was glad he never knew him.

CHAPTER 22

June, 1973

Grace Mayer's college graduation was a big affair. When her name was called a whoop echoed through the auditorium. Her accounting degree in her hand, she marched off the stage with her head held high. David, Daphne, Emma and Kyle attended. Afterwards they went to a banquet at the Methodist church in Decatur were the graduates were honored.

The next morning, the Judge and Daphne left for the condo in Orange Beach. Built on the site where a motel once stood, the condos were completed six months from the day the first shovel of sand flew.

Daphne picked out the colors for theirs, the furniture, drapes and appliances. The complex stood on eight-foot tall concrete block foundations so a car could be parked underneath. A small utility room beside the stairs held a washer and dryer and the hot water heater. Stairs led to the first floor where the sixteen-foot wide condos contained a kitchen, living area and half bath. The second floor contained two bedrooms and a bath and the third floor held a crow's nest master suite with another bath.

Every condo had a deck and a view. There were ten units on each side, a pool in the middle and a hot tub. A paved path led from the property through a low dune to the pristine white sand where the warm waters of the Gulf of Mexico lapped at the shore.

The Judge and Gordon financed part of the construction and paid for the rest, Gordon from his savings and David from the sale of his apartment in New York to Levi and Morgan Shulman. When all the condos sold, their profit would be half a million. The monthly fees would be close to two thousand a month, more than enough to keep the outside painted, repair roofs, mow the grass and take care of the pool. Gordon held the contract for the maintenance.

The Judge kept the one nearest the beach and Gordon lived in one close to the highway. Half of the condos sold two weeks after the "FOR SALE" sign appeared on the highway, and three more were under contract.

Palm trees surrounded the pool along with hibiscus, bougainvillea and poinsettias. The short-clipped grass, laid down in rolls, was solid over a bed of foamy soil. Flower beds were mulched with cedar clippings and Gordon kept the complex pristine, never allowing a weed to take root, a cigarette butt to find the sidewalk or a shard of litter to lie overnight.

Sea gulls circled overhead, searching for a meal on the beach or from some tourist who catapulted bread into the air. Dolphins jumped off shore as sail boats traveled east or west for some unknown destination. Children ran along the beach looking for shells or chasing crabs as couples strolled along the tide line. Pelicans flew over the water in a row, their wings a few inches from the spray. They looked like ballet dancers as they lifted into the sky where a bright orange sun sank slowly into the water.

Sunset was David and Daphne's favorite time to be on the deck. When the sun sank low on the horizon, cool breezes brought the scent of flowers, sea spray and a hint of chlorine from the pool. Often Daphne made a pitcher of lemonade or sweet tea. They consumed it in their rockers, passing time until bedtime. Sometimes they opened a bottle of wine or David drank Jack Daniels over ice.

Daphne had done well after the last surgery, until a month ago when her face began to draw to one side. Her headaches returned and she had lost weight. They knew the cancer was growing again and there was no treatment, no remedy for the monster growing in her brain.

She knew the cancer would take her in a few months, probably before Christmas. She had pain medication to keep her comfortable and when her headaches started, she took the pills. Knowing what lay ahead, she got up each morning and stayed up as long as she could. They all watched her, David every day while they were at the condo. After they returned to Decatur, Emma came over every few days.

Grace lived with them, her time with her mother precious to her. She would start her job with a new company in Huntsville next month. Carrie had become Daphne's best friend in spite of the hundred miles that separated them. She called once a week, and so did Skye. They called on different days, each of them telling news of their children, the vineyard, the challenges of raising teenagers and the plans for the movie and documentary Clark was scripting.

Gordon and the Judge decided to wait to develop Ono Island where they owned thirteen acres. The new name for the Island was derived from a fight over the sand bar in the middle of Bayou St. John. Florida claimed the land then Alabama said, "Oh no, it's ours." Alabama won. A recently constructed bridge to the island led to a few houses on the long spit of land. A road cut down the middle where prime waterfront real estate on each side invited investors and people who wanted second homes on water.

Carrie and her husband bought the first lot Gordon offered for sale. Gordon kept one for himself and the Judge and Daphne kept one. Kyle and Emma bought the one beside Gordon and the rest of the lots would be placed on the market later. Gordon and the Judge knew that later meant that they'd wait until Daphne was no longer with them.

The condo fulfilled Daphne's dream of a vacation house on the beach. When there, they ate their fill of seafood, took trips to Florida, to Mobile and last November they went to the seafood festival in Apalachicola. The quality time meant a lot to them, their time after the children were gone, their empty nest years. It was supposed to last thirty years, but they knew the time was limited.

On Labor Day, they returned to Decatur. Carrie and Steve drove up the next Sunday and Steve examined her at home.

Daphne could no longer walk. Steve renewed her pain pill prescription and told David her time was near. David stayed by her side, feeding her, taking her to the bedside commode and bathing her in the bed.

Six days later, she lapsed into a coma. Emma, Grace and David took turns by her bed. The third day of the coma she woke up, smiled at David then moaned and turned her head. She tried to speak. David put his head down close to her. She whispered, "I love you," then her eyes closed. She took her last breath an hour later, her children and her husband by her side.

The funeral mass, two days later in the Catholic church, was conducted by the priest who had done the service for Daphne's mother. The church was filled to capacity, the long eulogy a blur to David. He felt like he was in a dark tunnel, suffocating and unable to breathe.

He felt Emma and Grace direct him to walk behind the casket to the side door of the church. He watched the casket slide into the back of the hearse then he realized he was in a car behind the hearse. He couldn't remember how he got into the car. At the cemetery, Emma and Grace directed him to the burial site, the one where Anna rested on one side with a space in the middle for him. Grace and Emma threw roses on the casket then they pulled his arms to move him away.

"Come on, Daddy, let's go home. You're exhausted. We need to get you to your chair at the house. You need sleep, deep sleep," Emma stated.

"I can't leave her, I can't," he cried and pulled away from her.

Grace followed him to the place where the casket had been lowered. He stood at the end, staring at the box that held his wife. Two men stood at the other end, shovels in their hands.

"Daddy, we have to leave. None of us wanted it to happen like this. I wanted her to hold my children, but God had other plans," Grace stated between sobs.

Emma and Grace surrounded him, pulled him toward the waiting car. Gordon helped him into the back seat. Dawson sat beside his grandfather.

"Grandpa, I know you want to stay but we can come back later," he said between sobs.

Back at the house a crowd gathered, but Emma pleaded that they had to put their dad to bed. Grace gave him two sleeping pills and led him to his bedroom. She sent him to the bathroom to strip down and put on his pajamas.

"Are you decent?" she asked through the door.

"I guess, I'm dizzy, damn it. I can't turn the handle. It won't budge," David replied.

"It's the pills and you haven't slept in days," Grace said through the door.

"Open it for me," David sobbed.

She opened the door and led her father to the bed, covered him with a quilt and turned out the light. He curled into a fetal position.

"I'll check on you in an hour. You'd better be asleep," Grace said as she closed the door.

CHAPTER 23

September, 1973

Claude and Eva decided to stay in France after the trip through the cave. They moved in with Anders and Lillie Anne, sharing the house while the weather warmed, the vines budded, several hens hatched broods of chicks, apple and peach trees bloomed and the valley turned green.

The summer brought sunshine as the vines wound around the wires, sporting clusters of grapes. The apple and peach trees produced bushels of fruit, the cat had three kittens and Eva made cheese from goat milk she bought from the couple across the road.

Claude interviewed the mayor of Tenay and citizens who were there when the Germans entered the area. He found names of people he remembered and searched the archives of newspapers in the library at Lyon. He and Anders traced people they had known, finding some doing well, finding the headstones of some in the cemeteries.

The two brothers and their wives took the mission of getting the envelopes kept by Eva and Anna to their rightful owners while they cultivated the grapes, planted a garden and repaired the buildings.

When the trunk arrived from America, shipped by David from his attic, they started the tedious task of photographing each envelope, compiling a list of the names and the messages on the front. There were three hundred seventy two envelopes to process between the two stockpiles. Some had loosened over the years. They taped them with clear tape and continued with the next one.

During the years immediately following the end of World War II, statistical departments of many agencies complied lists of survivors of the various work and concentration camps located around Europe. When Bergen Belsen, Buchenwald, Hillersleben, Turkheim, Dachau, Theresienstadt, Flossenbury and other camps were liberated, the Allies tried to list everyone who was alive to help in the relocation efforts.

The Allied armies hydrated the walking skeletons, feeding them a healing soup of shredded cabbage, salt, sugar and diced potatoes until they could digest solid food. Medics treated open sores, gave them soap to bathe and treated them for lice. Cholera and typhoid hit the camps and many died. When the survivors could walk, they were released. Most had no homes to return to but they wanted to find missing relatives in their home town. They left with a determination to regain their health and start their lives over.

Once they returned to their home towns, they voluntarily registered themselves. That data was forwarded to the statistical departments and compiled into card indexes. Lists began to emerge at displaced persons camps and refugee centers. The lists expanded over the years as various organizations added names. The Register of Jewish War Survivors I, II, III and IV provided survivors by country; Poland, Slovakia, France, Czestochowa, Bavaria, Lithuania, Sweden, Palestine, Germany Netherland, Sweden and various cities.

By the time Eva and Claude, Anders and Lillie Anne began their search, the heads of several agencies were interested in their project. They provided accurate lists of survivors and their next of kin, but it had been twenty-eight years since the end of the war. Sometimes they had accurate addresses, but often they did not. People relocated, many had died, some changed their names and women married and assumed different last names.

The Search Bureau for Missing Relatives of Poland, the Jewish Congress of the World and Refugee Lists of Europe provided a volunteer to help them. Once an envelope was matched to a survivor, the name or names were placed on the outside of a manila envelope and the old envelope, with its contents intact, was placed inside.

Clark filmed the process, documenting each step, providing dialogue for Claude and Anders who would do a press release once they were ready to contact the rightful owners. Clark shuttled back and forth from Los Angeles to Marseille, leaving Josephine and Colette behind, dreading the long and difficult trip each time he packed his bags and equipment.

Anders and Lillie Anne also had the responsibility of running the French vineyard. Eva and Claude pitched in with the planting, pruning and fermentation process. Eva designed several labels and she learned how to mix the blends. The two couples seemed inseparable.

Finally, it was time to distribute the envelopes to the owners or their survivors. Anders and Claude read from the compiled list as Clark photographed them holding up the manila envelope. The list was also published in newspapers of the capitals of each European country. Poland and France were the two cities with highest numbers on the list. The announcement was carried by the local television station with a news release.

In Warsaw, they set up a distribution center in the lobby of the Wilanow Palace Hotel. Persons claiming the envelopes had to provide ID, then the envelope was released. Many sat down in the nearest chair and opened the package, some sobbing when they viewed the contents. They were happy to see old photographs, a watch, a wedding ring, coins, paper money that had no value, deeds to land, keys, locks of hair, love letters, marriage licenses. Clark filmed people as they took the package, some of them thanking them in English for their efforts.

They did the same in Paris and Marseille. At the end of the project, only twenty three packages remained unclaimed. They donated the unclaimed packages to the Jewish agency that had plans for a Holocaust Museum in Poland.

Finished with their project, exhausted from the extra time spent while keeping the vineyard intact, Claude and Eva, Anders and Lillie Anne, Clark and his film crew celebrated in Monaco,

264

crashing in the best hotel, eating at a fancy restaurant and sleeping late. Clark picked up the tab and returned to Los Angeles to splice the film and compile it into a documentary. His working title, *Eva and Anna's Secret*, wouldn't do for the release, but it fit. He hadn't known Anna, but he felt he knew her. He admired David for his part in the process. He had kept the trunk in his attic all those years, waiting on the right moment to release the packages.

Clark had not had a lot of time to work on the film about Josephine's mother but he had written the script. With the documentary completed, he'd devote as much time as he could to the film. He started the long journey home.

Once there, he found his grandmother Skye in the hospital in Napa. She'd fallen at her house and broken her leg. While at the hospital, doctors discovered a cloudy spot on her right kidney.

He and Ross visited her at the hospital. She seemed old, frail. He wondered how long they would have her, the matriarch of the family.

CHAPTER 24

June, 1978

Skye celebrated her 70th birthday at the vineyard. The festive affair brought the family together and a professional photographer made family portraits of families grouped around the fireplace in the big house. A picnic around the pool in the back yard was enjoyed by all. Ross and Juliet had the pool installed two years ago.

Skye had aged in the last few years, a broken leg and diagnosis of a severe kidney infection affecting her health. The leg healed and the kidney returned to normal, but it took a year for her to return to the healthy person she had once been.

The years had begun to show on her face. More wrinkles outlined her face, her hair was now streaked with gray, her body stooped slightly, she had lost weight, walked slower and rested more but her mind continued to be sharp and alert. She no longer made the trek around her old property. The climb up the hill was too much, so she walked to paved driveway to the road and back.

"I don't need to fall again, my back hurts and I'm worried that my bones are brittle," she told Carrie when she arrived from Alabama for the party.

"I don't think you have osteoporosis, but you may. You need to be tested for that. It's a plague in women your age," Carrie advised.

The family seemed close in spite of the separation of miles. Morgan and Levi split their time between Los Angeles and New York City. Clark and Josephine lived in Beverly Hills in Morgan's old house and declared Colette would be their only child. Carrie and Steve lived in Birmingham. They owned a lot on Ono Island and planned to retire there.

Ross and Juliet lived full-time at the Napa vineyard with their two children. Phillip lived in New York City and last Christmas brought a friend home with him, a man ten years older than him. He announced they were partners, that they had a loving relationship. No one was surprised, as they had suspected for years that he was gay. Anders, Lillie Anne, Claude and Eva remained in France, remodeling the vineyard, improving the line of grapes, struggling to make a profit.

Skye finally flew to visit Carrie, who kept in touch with David Mayer and his daughters. Carrie promised Daphne she'd look after her girls after she died and she took that job literally. David sank into a deep depression after he lost Daphne, hiding from everyone and eating sporadically. Carrie reported that he skipped the fishing tournament on Guntersville Lake and hadn't been to his condo in Orange Beach since Daphne died.

"I have no interest in life. I don't understand why I'm alive and Daphne is gone. I don't want to live, I hate this house. I can't go into her room and it's been four years," he told Carrie.

Carrie called her mother with a suggestion a month after she returned from the birthday party in Napa

"David Mayer needs you to come for a visit. If he knows you're coming, he'll perk up and you two can plan a trip. He rescued you more than once, and you need to help him. I'll take you up to visit him then we can go by the old home place. You won't believe how the area has changed. Then we'll drive over to Guntersville to see your sister and her kids. You can suggest renting his condo at Orange Beach but tell him he has to come down and show you around."

"Okay, I'll do it. I'll fly in next week. I'll call David and tell him I'm coming." Skye called him the next day.

"David, Skye here. I'm coming to Alabama to see Carrie and the grandchildren. She's going to bring me up to Decatur for a visit and a drive around the area. We're going to come by and visit you. Then I want to rent a condo on the beach for a week. Will you will go down and show me the good places to eat and maybe we could drive over to Mobile? I won't take 'no' for an answer. I'll see you next Tuesday. I want to eat some catfish while I'm there. Be thinking of a place," she said quickly so he couldn't refuse.

"Uh, okay, uh…the place is a mess. I'm a mess, but I'll be ready for your visit. Actually, I need someone to talk to. I've been lonely," David replied.

"I know how it feels. We'll have a long visit and swap stories. See you next week," She had a lot of things to tell him. Clark had finished the movie, *The Daughter*. The script was true to the story of Caris and Josephine. Phillip played Martin, Colette played young Josephine. Ross, Claude, Anders, Eva and Lillie Anne played people in the village in France. Morgan played the woman who lived nearby and Clark played the German soldier that shot Caris. Levi played the doctor and wrote the score.

Levi used an unknown singer for the opening song and two others. She had been a roommate of Carrie's daughter at the University of Alabama, a talented music major with a voice that reminded him of his favorite opera singer in Warsaw. Levi liked to find new talent and help someone who needed a break. He knew this girl would go places and he was thrilled to have found her right under his nose.

Caris was played by a new actress, one with curly blonde hair who had been in some low budget films. Clark found an unknown to play Josephine as an adult. The young woman was someone Josephine had operated on, she had come in for plastic surgery for a deformed eye socket. Her aspiration was to be in a movie once her scars healed. Josephine moved her eye socket up an inch and an ophthalmic surgeon and a facial cranial surgeon centered her eye and aligned it so she had correct vision. She was eighteen years old and had been home schooled so she wouldn't have to go out in public. Her shyness fit the role of Josephine perfectly.

A film crew in France filmed the cave, vineyard and the valley on location. The village square where Caris was shot and the inside of the house were filmed on a set in Los Angeles. The California vineyard scenes were filmed at the Poschett Vineyard, except the vineyard was named Villastone Vineyard.

Maybe I'll invite David to come out and go to the opening night with me, Skye thought as she exited the airplane in Birmingham a few days later.

Carrie took off a week and they drove to David's house. He met them at the door with Emma, her husband and son, Grace and her boyfriend. They ate at Ole Whiskers Catfish Heaven for lunch. He seemed happy to see them and told them he would drive to the condo a day before they were scheduled to arrive. He had aged. His mostly white hair had thinned, his limp seemed more pronounced and his eyes had lost their luster.

After lunch, he, Carrie and Skye drove up the mountain to the old home place where the shack had once stood. Now a ranch house occupied the site, but the old barn was still there. Skye turned her head and asked Carrie to drive slowly to get a glimpse of the Tennessee River from the mountain. Carrie wondered if she wanted a view of the river or if the ghosts of the past had reared their ugly heads.

The road, now paved and widened, curved down the mountain, trees creating a tunnel over the road, the floor of the forest thick with decomposing leaves, pine straw, bushes of hackberries, honeysuckle and leggy dogwoods. The aroma of pine,

270

damp earth, skunk and dust flowed into the open windows as large drops of rain fell on the windshield. Crows pecked at carrion on the road, scattering quickly when the car approached.

"This road hasn't changed much," David commented.

"True, but the drive up to Decatur from Birmingham changed a lot," Skye added.

"Wait to you see Huntsville," David said with a lighter tone.

"We'll see it later today. We're spending the night with my sister in Guntersville. I've never done that, spent the night with her. Carrie arranged it and I can't wait to see her." Skye seemed buoyant.

"Is she younger or older?" David asked.

"I'm the oldest. I have a brother named Lance, one named Hunter and her name is Dawn. She is the baby, ten years younger than me. Guess you can tell my mother was Indian. But you knew that."

"There are a lot of the Cherokee nation still around, along with Creeks, Choctaws, Chickasaws and Seminoles. Some returned from Oklahoma, some never left and hid out when the Indians were deported to Oklahoma. The history of this area is rich with stories of the mistreatment of Indians and tales of their struggles." David's face lit up with the conversation.

"So true. I should write down my mother's story," Skye added.

They stayed two more hours, David serving them tea and cookies. He asked about the visit to the cave and talked about the past visit at Christmas in Napa. Then he mentioned Claude and Eva.

"I miss Eva but she and Claude made the right decision. I understand the four of them rent an apartment in Marseille for two weeks each winter for a holiday. I get letters from her with their news. Marseille turned into a great city, not like it was before the war when it was full of beggars, thieves and hoodlums," David said as Carrie and Skye stood to leave.

"Well, we're off to Guntersville. We'll see you around five or six at your condo on Wednesday night. Looking forward to it," Skye said as she hugged him.

"I'll be there. I've not been down since, well...uh..." David stuttered.

"It's okay, I understand. Do me a favor and have a pitcher of sangria ready for us," Carrie added.

"I will," David replied.

The days flew by. Carrie and Skye returned to Birmingham and packed for the trip to the beach. Steve had a full surgery schedule so it was the two of them, a mother and daughter spending time together.

They arrived in Gulf Shores on a beautiful day. Fluffy clouds skirted the horizon as they passed over the intercoastal waterway then the road dead ended into a highway that ran parallel to the coast. The Gulf Shores water tower stood thirty feet beyond the dead end. A quaint restaurant sat on one side of the junction, a beach outlet store on the opposite side. A fishy smell caught their senses, carried by a stiff offshore breeze.

Carrie drove around the water tower to a parking lot. The Gulf of Mexico, now at high tide, lapped at the two foot high seawall at the end of the pavement. The ocean, choppy from a recent storm with patches of seaweed floating on the turquoise water, seemed endless. A couple of sailboats, leaning in the wind, traveled east. Sea gulls flew overhead, watching for a handout.

"I love it here," Carrie stated as they sat on a bench.

Once back on the highway, they passed Lake Shelby on their left. Herons stood close to the lake's shore, dipping their large beaks in the water for small fish, their flexible necks curled like a soft hose. A reflection of fluffy clouds overhead was broken by a large fish jumping in the brackish water. Sand dunes held sea oats waving in the wind on the sea side of the highway, the dune splitting occasionally to allow beach access.

Colorful umbrellas, towels and beach chairs populated the coastline where families walked through the breaks in the dunes to the sugar white beaches. They arrived early to stake a claim for the day, their children picking up shells, running in the water and teasing the waves under the watchful eyes of their parents.

"This is different than the Pacific ocean," Skye commented.

"I know. The water is warm and there is nothing but white sand for hundreds of miles. No rocky cliffs, no large blades of rocks jutting out of the sand," Carrie said between gulps of a soda.

Two miles later, she turned into a condo complex where they recognized David's car. He was on the deck and waved to them. In shorts, a golf shirt and sandals, a huge smile spread across his face. He'd had his hair cut. He'd grilled hamburgers, had potato salad, baked beans and banana pudding ready to eat. A pitcher of sangria and margaritas waited on them.

"Here, let me take your things. I'm putting you two in the crow's nest, the bedroom on the third floor. It has two beds and the best view. I'm staying in a bedroom on the second floor. I hope that's okay," he said, grabbing their suitcases.

"Wow, this is beautiful," Skye said as she entered the condo.

"Yes, Daphne decorated it. She did a good job," David replied as he started up the stairs.

Carrie poured drinks for the three of them. They found chairs on the deck and watched people mill around the complex and relax in the pool. Chatter of children, adults and the distant sound of a ship's horn floated to the deck. They watched the sun set as they finished the margaritas, ate hamburgers and talked. Sea gulls circled overhead.

"Don't feed the gulls. If you do they'll find you again and bomb dive you. They are the rats of the beach," David laughed.

Carrie looked at her mother and gave her a thumbs up sign. They were glad to hear him laugh. Carrie left on Thursday morning to go home. David and Skye drove to Mobile that afternoon, visited the battleship *Alabama*, ate at Wintzell's, drove down to

Dauphin Island and took the ferry back. The next day, they drove to Pensacola and David showed her his lot on Ono Island.

"Carrie and Steve have a lot next to mine," he said, his eyes hiding behind dark sunglasses.

"I can see why Carrie loves this place. I know they are a few years away from retirement, but they'll make it. She talks about the beach a lot. I'm surprised it hasn't developed more," Skye added.

"Hurricanes are a big threat. We haven't had one in a while but we will. They hit every few years."

"Did you tell me that Gordon Walton is your partner on the condos? Isn't he the detective that I talked to way back?"

"Yes, the same. I've invited him and his girlfriend over for supper tonight. We're going to a place that has cheese grits and shrimp. I think you'll like it."

Gordon and his date left the condo at nine. The girlfriend had to be at work early the next morning.

"Well, it's time for me to pack for the trip home. I understand you're taking me back to Birmingham and dropping me off at Carrie's," Skye said as they finished the last of the bottle of Poschett wine she brought. "One thing before I turn in. Would you like to go with me to the opening of the movie my grandson directed and produced? I have a small part and a lot of the family are in the movie. Opening night is in San Francisco. Then I'll show you around the area, we can take a trip over to Yosemite and up to see the redwoods. I'd love for you to be my guest at my beach house," Skye asked.

"It's a deal. Let me know when I need to come," David replied with a gleam in his eye.

"One month from today you need to arrive at the San Francisco airport. I'll have someone pick you up and I'll come with them."

"I'll call you with my arrival time. Uh, would you like to take a stroll on the beach before we call it a night?"

"Right now?"

"The moon is full and I have a flashlight. It's beautiful down there this time of night, the waves lap at your feet and it's cooled off."

"That sounds wonderful," Skye replied with a bounce in her voice.

CHAPTER 25

Late fall, 1978

Opening night of Clark's movie, *The Daughter,* was a huge success. The leading lady who played Josephine walked in on Phillip's arm. Her royal blue chiffon dress, borrowed from Morgan, hugged her figure and accented her blue eyes. Her blonde hair outlined her face and heavy makeup hid scars near her eye socket. She blushed when a member of the press remarked that she was beautiful. In spite of her shyness, she handled herself well.

The starlet who played Caris brought her brother to the opening night, and Skye walked the red carpet with David. Skye wore a long dress of soft pink with long sleeves and a full skirt. David looked dapper in a navy blue suit. Morgan, Carrie and Josephine, with their glam makeup and jewelry, impressed the waiting crowd. Colette, on the arm of Clark, smiled as the flash bulbs captured her innocence.

Several times during the movie the crowd was reduced to tears, especially the part when Josephine talked to her mother in the coffin. Clark had secretly revealed to the family that he did not change the dialogue of what she actually said to her mother in the coffin. Josephine had blocked it out of her mind, it was too painful, but Clark recorded the one way conversation.

At the end of the movie, when the audience watched the coffin being lowered into the grave, Josephine holding the hand of her little girl, applause erupted as people wiped tears off their faces. Nothing but accolades for the movie and music were heard in the lobby as the crowd slowly left their seats. Several times, the term "Academy Award" was mentioned around the room and at the party that Clark and Levi hosted for the invitation-only patrons that included the press.

Clark and Josephine, along with Colette, were cornered for an interview. Colette smiled and spoke with poise beyond her age. She won the hearts of the press as Josephine retreated from the limelight, leaving Clark to handle the questions.

The movie hit number one three weeks after its release. The press loved that it was based on a true story, and it was no secret that it was Josephine Poschett who returned to bury her mother, found in a coffin in a cave room at a vineyard in France.

The Daughter was nominated for several Academy Awards in 1979, along with the documentary about the envelopes of the Holocaust victims finding the rightful heirs. Clark, Levi, Phillip and the actress who played Josephine were in the spotlight, in the press and on television.

It had been fourteen years since Morgan was nominated for her Academy Award. She pulled out the dress from the back of her closet that she wore in 1965 to walk down the aisle with Levi. It wouldn't zip across her waist.

At fifty-four, Morgan had aged well. Her chin length auburn hair held no gray due to an excellent hair dresser. Fine lines at the corner of her eyes and loose skin on her neck revealed she was past fifty, but heads still turned when she entered a room. In spite of her weight gain, her figure remained solid and toned.

They had all aged well. Carrie kept her thin figure. Josephine, the youngest of the girls, the tallest and only blonde, kept in shape by running two miles a day. Ross and Clark, in their late thirties, kept their red hair short. Their tanned faces and muscular bodies revealed their outdoor lifestyles.

The old scars from Morgan's brush with the press long ago forgotten, she and Levi were fodder for the paparazzi. Levi's score for the cave room scene evoked emotions that equaled the theme he did for the space movie years ago. His music played in every corner of the world. He had composed scores for Broadway and written pieces for several operas. Everywhere he went, he was recognized. He couldn't keep up with the demand for his work.

Phillip, now twenty-seven, had established himself as a Broadway actor and his role as Martin in *The Daughter* catapulted him to stardom in Hollywood. Within a few weeks of the movie's opening, he was on the cover of several magazines, his handsome face broadcast along with the title of most eligible bachelor in New York City. Phillip had not revealed to the public that he was gay.

Phillip and Levi had become close, their mutual love of New York, Broadway, movies, music and the city lifestyle bonding them. Phillip and his partner lived in an apartment in New York, four blocks from Morgan and Levi's condo on Fifth Avenue, the one David bought during the war. The singer Levi hired for his composition boarded with Phillip when she wasn't on tour.

One part of the agreement when David sold the apartment was he would always have a place to stay when he came to New York. Morgan and Levi honored that, furnishing one bedroom for David who advertised that anyone else in the family could use it at their discretion. The doorman had a list of who could occupy the suite.

David and Skye developed a special relationship. They were both lonely and alone, two people who needed a friend to enjoy, to travel with and share stories. Their fondness for each other showed in the way they looked at each other, the knowing nods, the smiles of endearment, the conversations about their past and their late spouses who were dear to them. They loved to play Spades, Hearts and Pinochle with Gordon Walton and his friend in Gulf Shores.

David sold his house in Decatur. The continued occupancy of the house where Daphne and Anna died pulled at his heart, along with the memories of Daisy. He moved to Gulf Shores, to the condo Daphne decorated. He wanted to be close to Gordon, his best friend who shared the grandfather responsibilities for Dawson, Emma's and Kyle's son.

Gordon's children lived in Seattle, following their mother and third husband to the area. Dawson was Gordon's grandson as much as he was David's. Gordon took him fishing, and Dawson spent a month with him each summer where he learned to fish off the pier, to cast nets for shrimp, set the crab baskets. He loved cruising on Gordon's boat. Dawson's grandfather, Gordon's brother, died of heart attack at age fifty-five, so Gordon filled a special place in Dawson's life.

After David sold his house, he traveled to California to visit Skye at her beach house. He bunked in her spare bedroom and they visited the vineyards, sampling wines of the area, taking side trips to places in California and driving to the Columbia River valley in Oregon. In turn, she spent a month at a condo next to his, one she rented.

On Christmas Eve, 1978, Grace married an accountant at the firm where she worked. Emma was her matron of honor and David walked her down the aisle.

"I wish Mother could have lived to see me get married, to be the one to zip up my wedding dress, to watch over me," Grace said to her father as they stood in the lobby of the church, waiting on the bridesmaids to finish their trek down the aisle.

David felt tears escape as he walked her down the aisle, tears shed for Emma and Grace who missed Daphne as much as he did. When the wedding was over, he felt relief and sadness. No longer were his girls his responsibility, but they were also no longer *his* in an odd sense. Married to good men, David felt he had fulfilled a promise to Daphne and now a new stage of his life had begun. A stage he couldn't explain, one of an elderly, widowed man, living alone on the coast with few friends.

Skye… oh my, how she has helped me, he said in his mind. She lost her beloved husband long ago and understood his needs. She comforted him more than anyone. He found himself thinking of her every day, wondering where she was, if she was okay, if she took her vitamins, if her back hurt from that old kidney infection.

The months flew by, heat waves rose off the sand and the pavement on the highway. The breezes off the Gulf were less intense and the water warmed so fast seaweed grew at alarming rates. The local news announced the water temperature had soared to eighty five degrees at Gulf Shores as a hurricane rolled toward the United States from the African coast.

On September 9th, 1979, Hurricane Frederick passed over western Cuba then turned north-northwest with increasing speed for the next sixty hours. The eye passed over Dauphin Island, Alabama, on September 13th as winds reached 120 mph with gusts to 145 mph. Storm tides of twelve feet were recorded on the island, in Mobile Bay and at Gulf Shores.

"I'm anxious to see how our condos made it," David said as he and Gordon watched the news on television in a motel room in Decatur.

"We're on the beach. You know they're gone. Those little sand dunes are incapable of holding back a storm surge of that magnitude," Gordon suggested.

David and Gordon had retreated to Decatur to ride out the hurricane. David had not been to Decatur for a year and it had been two years since Gordon visited. The day after they checked into the motel, they invited Emma, Kyle, Dawson, Grace and her husband to meet them at Big Bob's Bar-B-Que. When Emma and Kyle walked into the restaurant, Emma stumbled over a rain mat on the floor then jerked her body sideways as she righted herself. During the meal she stumbled over several words. Then she reached up and pulled her arm over her head and jerked her head sideways. The movement was awkward, unnecessary. It seemed she did it involuntarily.

"Are you okay?" David asked, concern in his voice.

"Surrrree. It issy nothingly," she answered, jutting out her jaw.

Out of the corner of David's eye he noticed Kyle and Grace shake their heads.

The next day David visited Kyle at the courthouse.

"She's having some neurological problems. The doctor here is sending her to a neurologist in Birmingham next week, one Carrie recommended. My opinion is that she's overly tired. She works too much, spends too much time on her clients and gets too involved," Kyle volunteered.

Two days later, David drove to Emma and Kyle's house late in the day. Dawson answered the door. David had been invited for supper.

"Mom's in bed. She fell this morning, hurt her leg and Daddy told me to stay home and keep an eye on her. He has a trial and is tied up. I've fixed us some sandwiches for supper," Dawson told his grandfather.

David found Emma in bed, sitting up with paper work and files strewn over the covers.

"There is nothing wongs ith me. I fell but its noth... nothing. I need to get out of here and check, cheek on the Ridings children. Uh...Kyle took my car keys. The Ridings kids are in danger, they fath, gother is a no good SOB. He uh...abuses his girls and beats wife," Emma stated, struggling with the words, her head twitching sideways.

"Emma you need to slow down until the doctor finds out what is wrong with you. Your coordination is off. You speech is slurred. I'm worried about you," David tried to hide the concern in his voice.

"I know but...uh, they done X-rays and uh...nothing showed in them. I dots have a tumor. Nothing is pressing."

David noticed her eyes darting from side to side. Kyle came home and they ate sandwiches around Emma's bed. She fell asleep with a file in her hand. Dawson, Kyle and David retreated to the living room.

"What's wrong with her?" David asked as Dawson went to his room.

"We are getting to the bottom of this next week. She has an appointment with that doctor. What about the storm? Did it do much damage?" Kyle asked.

"I'm afraid Frederick did a number on the condos. Gordon returned to assess the damage. He'll call me and let me know what he finds." David left thirty minutes later and drove to the motel.

The next afternoon, David spent some time with Emma. They looked through old photos of Daphne and the family when the kids were little. Dawson came home from school.

"What would you like for supper? I'm buying," David asked.

"Pizza," Dawson replied.

"Pizza it is," David said, and called in an order.

After the pizza boxes were in the garbage, Kyle and David settled in the living room. Kyle built a fire in the fireplace and fixed both of them a Jack Daniels over ice.

"I'm very worried about Emma. This is more than stress or a woman going through the change," David's concerned voice sounded over the popping of the fire.

"None of the doctors here can find anything. Nine months ago, she developed this twitch in her head and neck. Then a few weeks later, she began to have body jerks and a wobbly walk. She says she can't control it. It seems to happen more when she is tired. She also has times when her speech is slurred and her eyes dart from side to side, then she'll be normal for a few days, sometimes a week. The doctor told me to keep notes about her movements for the doctor in Birmingham. Her x-rays didn't show a tumor in her brain, so they are thinking Parkinson's. I called Carrie and her husband recommended she visit a neurologist. The one she's seeing is one of the best in the country."

"So her symptoms started nine months ago?"

"That's when she had a minor car accident, one we didn't bother to tell you about. When the officer arrived, he believed she was drunk but Emma doesn't drink. That was the first time I saw her so disoriented. In a few days she was fine, she went back to work and a few weeks later she had an incident at work where she got several cases confused. That night, she walked around in the house screaming and throwing things. Not rational behavior for her."

"Why didn't you tell me?" David asked.

"Emma wouldn't let me. The doctor couldn't find any disease to fit her symptoms. First he said it was stress then a hormonal imbalance. Then he suggested she'd had a stroke. He ruled that out, gave her valium to calm her down, and mentioned it could be a nervous breakdown. Still no symptoms fit anything. She's stubborn and dedicated to her job. She doesn't want anyone there to know about the doctor's visit to Birmingham so she can work on her cases. We are taking a day of vacation to drive down. Dawson will be in school," Kyle defended.

"Is she depressed?"

"She has mood swings. Sometimes she can't remember things, important things. She forgot Dawson one day at ball practice, left him there and never returned. He called me at the office to come get him. When I asked her about it she said she didn't hear the phone ring but Dawson said she did, she'd picked up the phone then hung up."

"I'd like to go with you to the doctor."

"I can tell you now she won't let you. You know how she is and she'll want this to be a private thing between us and the doctor. Don't worry, I'll keep you posted," Kyle assured him.

"Okay, I'll head back to the coast tomorrow if you promise me you'll tell me what he says."

David left for the trip south the next morning. The drive revealed fall had started its march toward winter. Patches of yellow, orange and red leaves hit the tops of the trees, like a fairy had sprinkled 'fall dust' on them. Goldenrods waved in the open fields and beside the highway. Flocks of geese flew overhead, south to their winter destination.

David loved this time on the coast when the fish hit the bait after a summer of gorging, when the oysters were prime, the mullet runs pushed thousands close to the shore and sailors unfurled their cloth to the stiffening winds.

Frederick had traveled inland as well as thrashing the coast. He left his mark a hundred miles above Mobile Bay. Tall trees were snapped and down, power poles leaned, roofs of houses were missing and stagnant water stood beside the highway. He met Gordon in Foley at a café that was open.

"The condos are gone, the pillars are the only things standing," Gordon informed him as they ate a sandwich.

There was no hot food anywhere in the area. All electric lines were down; crews from Alabama Power Company had already arrived, as well as ones from Florida, Georgia and Mississippi. Ice was in short supply so they drank room temperature sodas.

Gordon had friends in high places with the police force and National Guard. Once a policeman always a policeman, so his badge opened doors and access to restricted areas.

"We're homeless," Gordon remarked when they drove to the place the condos had once stood.

"I see. There's nothing but rubble and not a lot of that. Guess everything was pretty much washed out to sea. I want to shuffle through the stuff and see if I can find anything I recognize," David replied.

"Can't do that, they're still in rescue mode. In a few days they'll let us go in, but right now it's off limits. Good thing we have insurance. We're fully covered and so are the other condo owners. I made sure of that," Gordon informed him.

"Good, but I'm already hearing they won't allow us to rebuild. You think that will happen?"

"I heard that, too. Building codes will change. We won't be able to build what we once had on this site. Rumor has it they are going to require all structures to be concrete and the foundations will have to go down twenty feet. We still have the land. Meanwhile we have to find you a place to live. I rented a small house in Fairhope when I saw the hurricane would pass over Cuba.

I had a hunch about this. Well, actually some of the old timers told me it would turn and hit us. I listened. Want to bunk with me?"

"Well, I really would prefer a better looking cell mate, but you'll do," David laughed.

They drove to Fairhope where Gordon had already furnished the rental house. A bed and chest occupied David's bedroom, the bed made up military style with sheets, a thin blanket and a wimpy pillow. In the small closet, coat hangers lined up on one end and an ironing board occupied the other end.

"This is fine," David remarked as he sat his suitcase on the bed. "Is there a store where I can buy some clothes around here? What's in this suitcase is all I have."

"We'll drive over to Pensacola and find a place to get clothes and supplies. Mobile is shut down. No one will be buying anything in Mobile."

By the end of November, the two men knew the habits and idiosyncrasies of each other. They shared the chores of the house, mowing the slow growing winter grass and doing small repairs. David did the cooking one week while Gordon cleaned up, then they reversed the pattern. David had a phone line installed and Gordon bought a television. David had received two reports on Emma, both from Kyle.

"They don't have a conclusive diagnosis. The doctor says it is an autosomal disorder but he seems puzzled. He did a family work-up and stated the problem might be inherited but he didn't give the disease a name. Meanwhile, she is taking tranquilizers and an antipsychotic drug," Kyle said as Dawson yelled "Hello, Grandpa!" in the background.

"Maybe you should get a second opinion," David suggested.

"Actually, he suggested that. He has a friend in Atlanta who's agreed to examine her. We're going over the twentieth of December. That's the earliest he can see her. It's the day after Dawson gets out of school for the Christmas break. A friend is keeping him a couple of days."

"Did you hear the news about Grace?" David asked.

"That she's pregnant? Yes, I did. We're thrilled. She called and wants to go with us to Atlanta. She says she'll keep Emma occupied in the car while I drive."

"I'm going, too. You and I can be in the front seat and the two girls in the back. I'll be up on the nineteenth. I want to be with the family and I'd come up for Christmas anyway. Guess I'm lonely." David sounded melancholy.

"Aren't you going to Napa for Christmas?" Kyle reminded him.

"I was, but after this storm and with Emma sick, I changed my mind. Eva and Claude, Anders and Lillie Anne will be there from France. I can fly out after Christmas if I want."

By December 12th, the site where the condos sat was a pile of sand. A drive for hay bales to be deposited along the beach gained momentum and Gordon bought two hundred from a rancher in Montgomery. He hauled them to their beach lot and he and David placed them fifty feet behind the high tide line. Five days later a sand dune started to form and they figured in a few months it would be high enough for some protection.

Gordon made his plans for Christmas. He flew to Seattle to see his kids and David packed his car for the trip to Decatur. He didn't own a decent suit, so he planned to stop in Birmingham and do some shopping. Frederick took everything, including his box of photographs of his years with Anna. Thankfully he'd left the photos of his years with Daphne in the care of Emma, so they were safe.

He arrived in Decatur on the afternoon of December 19th. Kyle ordered food from Big Daddy's Bar-B-Que and they ate at home. When he saw Emma, he understood why they didn't go out. She was worse, her movements more erratic, her depression obvious and she had lost weight.

"She seems worse to me," David remarked to Kyle after Emma and Dawson were in bed.

"I guess I've gotten used to her symptoms," Kyle replied.

"She isn't still working is she?"

"She goes in some mornings. She has an assistant of sorts. They know she's sick so they hired a new graduate for Emma to train. She comes by and takes her to the office on her good days then the rest of the time they work off the dining room table. If they have to make a visit, the trainee drives. The doctor in Birmingham wants to put her on medical leave but without a concrete diagnosis, he hasn't written out the order."

"Well, tomorrow we may get to the bottom of this," David said, and went to bed.

Grace arrived at the house the next morning at six a.m. She hugged her father and the glow in her cheeks, the thickening of her waist and her fuller breasts confirmed that a baby was on the way.

"When are you due?" David asked.

"The middle of June. I'm so excited. We don't care if it is a boy or a girl as long as the baby is healthy. When are we leaving? I'm famished," Grace eyed some cinnamon rolls on the counter. One disappeared into her mouth.

The drive to Atlanta would take four hours. They would make the one-thirty appointment if there were no traffic delays. Emma and Grace occupied the back seat, sharing motherhood secrets, feeding shortcuts, laundry increases, sleepless night blues and helpless husbands.

Bare trees stood beside green pines and cedars that grew close to the highway. Small towns built around a courthouse square impeded their speed. In a few years a new interstate would replace the two lane highway, one that would speed the traffic quickly around towns that relied on travelers to fill their restaurants and buy gasoline from their stations.

Kyle drove while David sat in the front with him. At first Emma's speech was normal then she lapsed into erratic slurring. Both girls begged for a bathroom. They found a gas station and Emma exited the station with a bag of potato chips and a candy bar.

"Hey, woman, you didn't pay for that," a man yelled at her.

"I will," Kyle handed him a bill and looked at David. His eyes said, *she doesn't remember she has to pay.*

They arrived at the office of Dr. Jerome Vaughn, the neurologist. A nurse showed them to a conference room on the second floor. A few minutes later, Dr. Vaughn entered the room and told Kyle, David and Grace they could stay with Emma while he did the physical part of the exam, if they remained quiet.

"It helps to have family in the room with her. That way she's not frightened," he revealed.

He showed them to a large room where the nurse had Emma sit in a lounge chair. There was a stair climber in the room, a chalkboard, two kinds of wooden chairs, a stable bicycle and a cot. They sat in chairs lined up by the wall. Emma managed a little wave before the doctor started.

"Emma, are you ready?" he asked her.

"Yesss, I am," she replied and gave him a crooked smile.

He asked her to walk the length of the room then turn around and walk back to him and touch him on his right shoulder. She struggled to get out of the chair then walked with a rocky gait to the end of the room and turned around. She touched the top of his head.

Then he asked her to bend over and pick up a nickel he put on the floor. She fumbled with the coin then pushed it with her foot. Finally she managed to pick it up. She held it up and tried to hand it to him but dropped the coin. She laughed and jerked her head sideways.

"It's okay. You don't have to get it again," the doctor said as he smiled at her.

Then he asked her to touch her nose, follow his fingers with her eyes, stand on her tip toes, walk backwards, hop on her right leg, hop on her left leg, tip toe for five feet and sit down in the wood chair then rise out of it. Then he asked her to pedal the bicycle.

She couldn't do most of the tasks. She couldn't figure out how to get on the bicycle. Frustrated, she began to cry.

"It's okay. A lot of my patients can't ride a bicycle. Did you ride one when you were a little girl?" he asked.

"Yesss, I did. Way vee back when I was a girlee," she replied.

"Good, now I want you to read this sentence." He wrote something on the chalkboard.

"Tic, tokay, tic, tock, the cow jammed over the, the mooney," Emma stuttered.

Then Dr. Vaughn asked his nurse. "Caroline, bring Mrs. Walton some juice."

The nurse brought in a half-full glass of juice. Emma had trouble swallowing the liquid. She spit it out and then tried again, getting it down on the second try.

"Okay, good. Emma, you stay here with Caroline. She'll do the rest of the work up on you, take your blood pressure, weigh you and measure your height. She'll also do some cognitive tests on you. I'll be back in a few minutes."

He motioned for Kyle, David and Grace to follow him. They settled in chairs behind the desk in his office.

"I'm going to get right to the point. In my opinion, she has Huntington's Disease. Often you will hear it called HD. I have examined her films and there's no sign of a tumor. She does not have Parkinson's. I need to ask some questions. Huntington's is transmitted by a faulty gene. There has to be a family history of this. Spontaneous cases of Huntington's do not exist." The doctor searched their eyes for questions.

"What does this mean? Is it a type of cancer?" Kyle asked.

"No, it's not. It results from degeneration of nerve cells in certain areas of the brain. It's a familial disease, passed from parent to child through a mutation on a normal gene. Huntington's is acquired when the patient has the dominant gene, meaning that only one of the paired chromosomes is required to produce the disease. Each child of an HD parent has a fifty-fifty chance of inheriting the gene. Early signs of the disease vary from person to person. She is thirty-nine. Symptoms begin to appear around thirty-five or forty, so she is right on target. I need to ask some questions about her family. I understand you are her father," he said, looking at David.

"Yes, yes, I am," David replied.

"Tell me about her mother. I understand she died a few years ago. Did she have these same symptoms?"

"No, she had a cancerous tumor of the brain. She had painful headaches and would see double. She had none of the symptoms that Emma is experiencing," David replied.

"Well, it is obvious you do not have any symptoms. May I ask your age?" Dr. Vaughn was all business.

"I'm 68," David replied.

"Rarely does a person develop Huntington's that late in life, but it's not impossible," the doctor added.

"So you are saying I might get this disease?" David asked.

"Someone passed the gene to her. It's possible that her mother did and also had the brain tumor. How old was she when she died?"

"Forty-nine," Grace answered.

Dr. Vaughn wrote the age down in the chart.

David swallowed hard and adjusted his weight in the chair.

"Are you sure she had none of these symptoms?" Dr. Vaughn leveled his eyes to David's.

"I'm sure," David answered. Kyle hung on every word.

"What about her mother's parents? Tell me how they died."

"Her father died from lung cancer in his fifties. He was a heavy smoker. Her mother died from a stroke in her sixties."

"And your parents?"

"There's no need to go further on this search into my background. I'm not Emma's biological father," David revealed.

"What? She never told me that." Kyle looked at David, his eyes open with shock.

"Daddy, that's not true. You're our father," Grace whined.

"I'm *your* biological father but I adopted Emma. Daphne had Emma before I met her. Daphne never wanted Emma to find out she was adopted," David revealed, looking at Dr. Vaughn.

"Do you know her biological father?" the doctor asked.

"Her biological father is dead," David answered.

No one in the room moved, no one spoke. Dr. Vaughn stared into a space between the two men. David broke the silence.

"What is the treatment for this disease?"

"There is no treatment. No cure. We will keep her comfortable as the disease progresses. It's not a pretty picture. She already has the early symptoms; mood swings, uncharacteristically irritable, apathetic, passive, depressed or angry. Huntington's also affects the person's judgment, memory and intellectual abilities. She will continue to experience uncontrolled movements in the hands, feet, face and trunk. As the brain dies, she'll experience problems with balance, have trouble walking and will experience falls. Then the disease will cause problems with speech and vital functions, twitching, rigidity, problems swallowing, eating. She already has problems swallowing and some of the other symptoms."

"Did you say shell go insane?" Kyle asked.

"No, that is not what will happen. Her brain is *dying*. There's a big difference," Dr. Vaughn looked at him with a stoic face.

Kyle stood up and paced in the small room.

"Tell me again how she got this. Who gave it to her?" David asked.

"Probably her biological father, since her mother didn't have it. She inherited it. We don't know what causes Huntington's but someday we will. There's a lot of research going on in this field. She may live another ten or fifteen years. Slowly, she will go into a vegetative state. I'm sorry, I wish I had better news." Dr. Vaughn's voice had softened.

"Will our son inherit this? He's twelve," Kyle asked, standing behind David.

"He has a fifty-fifty chance of inheriting HD. We need to do a family workup. You need to reveal this diagnosis to the biological family of the father. There may be other people with the same problem."

"Can you test Dawson and find out if he has it?" Kyle asked.

"There is no test. There is no treatment. You'll have to wait until he has symptoms to know if he has HD or escaped. Sometimes symptoms begin in the juvenile years but the sad cases are the one where the victims already have children and passed the gene to them. That's the case here. Emma may have passed the Huntington's gene to her son. Someday, we'll have a test, someday we will know the gene that carries this, but science hasn't gotten that far. Not yet." Dr. Vaughn looked from one set of concerned eyes to the other.

"Will I get this? Will my child inherit it?" Grace asked between sobs.

"If Emma's biological father is the one who passed the gene, then you won't have the disease therefore you won't pass it to your children. Your father obviously doesn't have HD and it appears neither did your mother," the doctor assured her.

"Who was her father?" Kyle asked, now back into his chair. He turned to David for the answer.

"Two men raped Daphne during her last year of high school. They were brothers and are both deceased. Either Owen Campbell or Colin Campbell is the father of Emma. She's the child of one of them," David answered.

"What did you say? Repeat that statement," Kyle looked at David in disbelief.

Dr. Vaughn cleared his throat. "Uh…I'll leave the family secrets to you to discuss while I get back to Emma and the cognitive tests. I will send my opinion to her neurologist in Birmingham who will be helping her. Meanwhile, I'll give you some sedatives to help you get her home."

Dr. Vaughn left the room. Kyle continued to stare at David. Grace watched both of them.

"Now tell me how Emma became the child of one of those men," Kyle asked.

"In February of 1941, Owen and Colin Campbell raped Daphne at her house when she was in her senior year of high school. Owen abducted her coming out of the outhouse. Emma was born nine months later. Daphne identified Colin in person to me and Owen from his photo in the paper when they found his body."

"I remember meeting Colin once but didn't you know them? Did either one of them have any of these symptoms?"

"Owen died in his thirties. He was a mean and hateful man, full of violence, but I only saw him a few times in town. His brother Colin was shot by a woman when he was forty-two. I saw him a few times that year. He was irrational, hateful and didn't make good decisions. I often thought he was drunk and would smell whiskey on his breath. There's no way to know, they're both dead." David felt the words hang in his throat.

The doctor came back into the small room. Brisk and business like, he stood behind his desk.

"She'll be ready to go in about ten minutes. I'm going to advise you to let her let her work as long as she can work from home. She told me she's doing that. I understand you've already taken away her car keys. Good, do not let her drive under any circumstances. At some point she will need to know what is wrong with her but let's find the source of the disease first. When the time is right, the neurologist in Birmingham can break the news to her. You may take her home and I'll prescribe some medication to help her sleep. Her intellect is still intact, so once she finds out she has Huntington's you will need to watch her for suicide. Many patients take that route, especially if they saw one of their parents die from the disease."

"Thanks, we'll need to get her treated in Birmingham. It's too far to drive all the way over here," Kyle said as Dr. Vaughn left the room. Kyle turned back to David.

"So that sorry assed SOB Colin or Owen Campbell is the father of Emma. I can't believe it. Those two men are still leaving their mark on the world. The devil in them is creeping around destroying lives. One of them is the biological *grandfather* of Dawson. This is going to tear Uncle Gordon and my mother to pieces, not even counting what it does to us." Kyle put his head in his hands.

"That's not the end of it. Owen has a son named Ross, and he has children. Remember, he was married to Skye and they had a son born that same year. It seems Owen got around even though he was married," David remarked.

"I'll leave it to you to tell those other children," Kyle stated as the nurse led them down a hall where Emma exited the ladies room. They stalled while Grace used the facilities.

"Ready to go home?" Kyle asked Emma when they were outside in the sunshine.

"Yep, I'm reddee. Can we get some food? I'm hangry," Emma said as her face twitched to one side.

"Of course, we'll find a place to eat. Let's get out of this Atlanta traffic before rush hour. I saw a place on the highway that advertised fried chicken. How does that sound?" David said as he directed her to the car.

Idle chatter in the car kept Emma occupied until they found the restaurant. After they ate, she wanted to sleep. Grace let her lean on her shoulder as the medication took effect. Kyle drove while David sat in silence beside him in the front seat. No one spoke, each one had his demons to deal with, dreams of the future to rearrange, hopes for Dawson questioned and aching hearts to appease.

Near the Alabama line, they stopped for gasoline and an ice cream cone. Back in the car, Emma hummed in the back seat as they watched the sun set in front of the car. The orange sphere drifted below the horizon then dusk swept over the landscape. Kyle drove methodically, his eyes staring straight ahead as the miles slipped away. Once they left Birmingham and turned north, David noticed Emma and Grace were both asleep.

"When we get home I'll make some phone calls to California. I'll wait until after Christmas so I won't spoil the holiday for Skye's family. Carrie's there, and I'll talk to her. I've decided I'm going back to the coast tomorrow. I have to have some time alone. I'll leave the presents I have for everyone," David said in a voice little more than a whisper.

He looked out the side window as he spoke, he didn't want Kyle to see the tears running down his face.

"I understand," Kyle stated as he swerved to miss a buck that ran across the highway.

"This is going to be a challenge for all of us. For several families."

CHAPTER 26

December 27, 1979

Christmas at Napa was the biggest affair in the history of the family. With Eva and Claude, Anders and Lillie Anne in from France, Phillip, Carrie and her two children, Morgan, Levi, Josephine, Clark and Colette, Ross, Juliet and their two children, the house overflowed with laughter, food, slammed doors, roaring fires in the fireplace, ornate decorations and presents for everyone. Skye, now seventy-one, held the honor of queen of the family.

"This is all smoke and mirrors," she said when she took her place at the head of the table on Christmas Eve for the traditional spaghetti dinner.

Dressed in a pair of red velvet slacks, a sweater with a Christmas tree on the front and sparkling earrings that caught the light from the chandelier, Skye looked regal. She sat at the head of the dining room table, the aroma of baking apples, cinnamon, cedar and burning wood floating through the rooms as Christmas dinner was served by the cook.

Moist wind from the valley found its way inside each time a door opened. The crackling fireplace, constant chatter from the children, the Ross's two Dachshunds barking and soft music playing in the house created a sound of chaos and pandemonium that Skye loved.

"It's the sound of a happy house," she said when someone begged for some quiet time. Skye's love for her family was genuine. She was the grateful grandmother, mother and friend, loved and cherished by everyone. Her eyes glittered as she greeted friends who stopped by Poschett Vineyard to share the holiday. Photos were taken, food graced the buffet table and anyone in the town of Napa who wanted to drop by and pick up a bottle of Poschett wine were welcomed personally by her.

During Christmas Day, the sun filtered through clouds on the thirsty hills and fertile land. By the time the sun sank behind the trees, the chaos of the house settled as lethargic, sleep deprived bodies, full of food and ready for an early bedtime, lounged around, conversations ebbing, children surrendering to their rooms. At eight, the adults gathered in the living room for the annual and official board of directors' meeting and report of the vineyards. Anders started with his report about the vineyard in France.

"It is still losing money. In spite of everything we are doing, it isn't making a profit. The loss for 1979 will be close to eighty thousand. That is not considering my salary. I recommend we sell it. It has been eight years since Claude and I reconnected and during that time we have made many improvements. Also, the skeletons of the past are eliminated," Anders said as he stood by the large Christmas tree where he'd given his report of Josephine's mother years ago.

"I agree," Carrie added as others mumbled their approval.

"Mom, you own fifty percent. What are your thoughts?" Ross asked.

"Have it appraised and put it on the market. When it sells, it will be a blessing as far as I'm concerned," Skye added.

"Lillie Anne and I would like to return to Napa and Claude and Eva are moving back to the United States. They say the taxes are too high in France and it is leaning toward socialism. They tell me there is a lake in Alabama where they want to live, one that reminds them of Switzerland. I do not know of this place," Anders replied.

"Guntersville Lake," Skye, Carrie and Eva said in unison.

"We have a broker looking for a house for us," Claude chimed in.

Ross passed out checks to the owners. Skye had already given envelopes with checks earlier in the day, Christmas gifts from her were checks from her ownership share of fifty-percent. After the meeting, everyone went to bed. Skye slept on a pull out bed in the living room rather than drive home to her beach house.

The next morning, the phone rang precisely at nine. Skye answered. It was David.

"We missed you. When are you coming this way?" Skye asked him.

"I'm not sure. Emma is sick and I'm going to be needed here. I need to talk to Carrie about her diagnosis." Skye motioned for Carrie to pick up an extension of the phone.

"So, what did the doctor in Atlanta say?" Carrie asked when she picked up the receiver.

"He is sure it is Huntington's Chorea."

"What? Did you say Huntington's?"

"Yes."

"Huntington's is inherited. You don't have it and neither did Daphne. It's impossible."

"It's not impossible because I am not Emma's biological father. Daphne already had her when we met, but she didn't want Emma to find out she was adopted. For a long time, Daphne didn't know who Emma's father was because she was raped. Emma was the result of that rape," David said, choking on the words.

"Did the man who raped her have Huntington's?"

"We don't know. The two men that raped her were Owen and Colin Campbell," David revealed.

"Owen raped Daphne?" Skye asked on the other line.

"Mother, I didn't know you were still listening," Carrie said quickly.

"I wanted to hear about Emma. I know David's concerned about her," Skye defended herself.

"Yes, they raped her in February of 1941. Emma was the result. I met Daphne the same day I came up the mountain to help you sell your place when Ross was two weeks old. Emma was two months old," David said in a stressed voice.

"Mother, I'll explain this to you later. Right now I need to talk to David alone. Okay?"

306

"Okay, but you'd better tell me about this when you get off the phone," Skye said in a stern voice.

"I will. I'll tell you the whole story." They heard Skye hang up.

"Do you understand what this means? Anyone in the direct line of Colin and Owen Campbell could inherit this disease, and it's not a pretty one," Carrie cautioned in a low voice.

"That's why I am calling you. The doctor in Atlanta told us to inform the descendants of Owen and Colin. I hate to...uh...give you this horrible news." David stumbled on the words.

"I'll be flying home tomorrow, and Saturday I'll drive up to Decatur and we'll get to the bottom of this. Meanwhile, see if you can find any of their remaining family. They had an older brother and he had children. Surely some of them are around."

"Their older brother died years ago. He was a half-brother, but I'll see if I can find his children. I'm in south Alabama right now. I couldn't bear to be there with Emma for Christmas. She doesn't know. We'll put off telling her as long as we can."

"How is Kyle holding up?"

"He's taking it hard, real hard. As you know, this may affect Dawson."

And it will affect Ross and his children, and Clark and his child, Carrie knew.

"He has a fifty-fifty chance of inheriting it. Let's hope he doesn't. I'll be in Decatur on Saturday morning. Meet me at Kyle and Emma's around ten."

"Okay," David replied and hung up the phone.

He stared at the phone for a few seconds then walked outside to the fresh air of the tiny town of Fairhope. The house Gordon rented was small and David had to get away from the walls that were closing in. He was still alone in the house, Gordon would not return from Seattle for a few days. He walked three blocks to the town square on a sidewalk cracked by the roots of a huge water oak dripping with moss. He smelled coffee a block before the local café came into view.

Each street in Fairhope could be in a Norman Rockwell painting. Decorated for Christmas, poinsettias, wreaths and magnolia branches were tied to lamp posts that sported a top of artificial snow. Christmas music drifted to the sidewalks from stores. Tony Bennett, Perry Como, Dean Martin and Elvis shared the honors. Cloves, cinnamon and orange slices were simmering in potpourri pots inside shops where festive clothes, tableware, decorations, paintings, miniature Christmas villages, cakes and children's toys graced the store front windows. New signs stating "50% off Christmas Items" had been taped to some of the store fronts.

David knew he should feel festive, but he couldn't. He had a daughter dying a slow death and a grandson who might face the same malady.

"Good morning, Judge Mayer. The usual for breakfast?" the waitress asked as he entered the café on the corner.

"Yes," David replied, finding a booth. The smiling waitress brought him a cup of coffee. A plate of scrambled eggs, cheese grits and two biscuits followed.

David thought about Gordon and how he'd take the news. David had to tell him. He was Dawson's uncle and his surrogate grandfather. Gordon hated Owen and Colin Campbell, and this would not be welcome news.

So many families, David realized as he ate in silence, then started the walk back to the empty house. He pulled his suitcase from the top of the closet and threw some clothes inside. Leaving the suitcase at the front door, he walked toward the bay on the cracked sidewalk then down the cedar stairs that led to the city pier. He settled on a bench. A few people were milling around.

David stared at the water and watched the gulls and ducks swimming close to the pier, waiting on a handout. He turned up the collar on his jacket and watched a young man play with his beagle. He felt tears escape, his heart ached, he felt a tightness in his chest, a ringing in his ears and he rubbed his jaw where he'd cut himself shaving. Then a light rain began to fall. He climbed the stairs up the bluff to the street where the empty house waited. He packed his shaving kit, his raincoat and two more pairs of socks.

Then he thought about Dawson. *How in the world will Kyle tell him? He's a smart kid. Once he's older, he'll research the disease and find out he may inherit it. We need to shelter him from the truth if we can.* David poured three fingers of whiskey in a glass. He added two ice cubes and watched an old movie, falling asleep in the chair.

The next morning, he drove to Decatur and checked into a motel. He called Kyle.

"Carrie and I will arrive at your house in the morning by ten. We're going to find any remaining part of Owen and Colin's family. How's Emma?"

"She's sedated, so she's better. We had a good Christmas. She isn't asking any questions. Not yet," Kyle replied.

Around two, David walked into the records room at the courthouse. Several people from the old days greeted him. He stopped to talk to the clerk then searched the records for any property ownership, car tags and business listings of anyone with the last name of Hanson, the last name of Colin and Owen's older brother. Then he went to *The Decatur Daily* archives and found the obituary on their mother. She was forty-eight when she died.

He went to the health department and pulled a copy of her death certificate. It stated she died of kidney failure. She might be the carrier and could have been sick by the time she died from something else. Her husband was not revealed on the certificate.

Then David remembered that Harold's daughter came through his court a couple of years after Colin died. She was getting a divorce. He went back to the courthouse and asked for the records on the case. The file would contain an address for her. The address was an apartment. He drove to the apartment office and the manager said she didn't live there anymore.

310

Next, he drove to the cemetery and found Owen's and Colin's graves. A simple stone at their heads revealed their birth dates and the date of their deaths. Wilted lilies between the two graves rested in a mud puddle. Someone had been there or the wind had carried them from another spot in the cemetery.

David walked around the grounds and found the grave of Harold Hanson and realized that his sons were beside him. Both of them died in their late forties, Harold at age fifty-six. A stately headstone marked their burial plot with a place reserved for Carol, his wife. A basket of plastic poinsettias stood at Harold's head, the red petals creating little cups holding remnants of the last rain.

Could Carol Hanson still be alive?

Then a picture of Harold, his wife and children flooded into his memory. They attended the Methodist Church and David remembered that Harold had worked at the bank. A good man, he didn't share any of the violence and mean streaks of Owen or Colin.

David walked over to the plot where Anna and Daphne were buried and noticed a fresh vase of yellow roses, ones he had delivered for Christmas. They were in a vase on top of the headstone that had "Mayer" carved in a Roman Script. He didn't linger in the cold wind, he couldn't think about the empty grave between them.

David drove to the First Methodist Church, entered through the basement and knocked on the office door.

"He's not here. Go by to see him at the parsonage across the street," a man mopping the floor stated as David turned to leave.

The pastor answered the door at the house across the street. David stated his purpose.

"In the Methodist church, we change pastors every four years or so. I haven't been here that long. Let's go over to the office and I'll look in the records and see who was here when the Hanson family attended."

The janitor waved as the two men entered the office that contained two file cabinets. The pastor pulled out a drawer, then some files.

"Okay, here it is. In 1954 to 1958, Reverend Joshua McCoy was pastor. From 1959 to 1963, Reverend Carson Stone was pastor. Both of them are deceased, but Dr. Simpson Monroe was pastor from 1964 to 1968 and he is still alive. He lives in Atlanta and I have his address. He's in Southern Acres Methodist Retirement Center, so you can call him and get some information." The pastor wrote down the numbers.

David went back to his motel and called Dr. Monroe. He answered on the third ring.

"Yes, I remember Harold and his family. He was sick by the time I was a pastor there. They didn't attend much. I visited him a couple of times in the nursing home. He didn't know me or his wife. He lay there jerking, his mouth open, his mind gone. He was almost a skeleton. Then I got a call that he died. So sad, he was a good man from the reports from the congregation," the former pastor revealed.

"Do you know what happened to his wife and children?"

"I'd guess his wife is dead. She'd be pretty old by now. He had three children, two boys and a girl. They lived on Wilson Street about halfway down the block where it intersects the railroad. It was a two-story house painted green with a porch off the second floor and a row of windows on the left side. His daughter went to college to be a school teacher. I don't know about his boys."

"Thanks for your help," David said, and hung up.

David found the house on Wilson Street that Dr. Monroe described. He walked up a stone sidewalk under stately trees. A mockingbird hiding in the shrubbery flew out and squawked at him. Smoke billowed from a chimney on the side of the house. David pulled his coat around him as the evening sun sank behind the trees. He rang the doorbell.

A cold front is moving in, he realized as a middle-aged woman opened the door.

"I'm looking for the people who lived here years ago. The Hanson family. Do you know what happened to them?" David asked.

"Aren't you the Judge who used to be here? I remember you from a case you did years ago. Come on in out of the cold," the lady said.

David entered a living room decorated with early American furniture. A roaring fire in a large fireplace popped and crackled. The lady motioned to a plaid couch.

"Would you like something to drink? I have some sweet tea and some coffee," the lady asked.

"I'd love some tea," David answered as he settled into the couch. When the lady appeared with a glass of iced tea, David took a long swallow.

"I didn't personally know the Hanson's but Carol Hanson lived here until ten years ago. She was a friend of my mother's. They were in a quilting circle, back when that was popular," the woman revealed.

"What happened to Carol and her daughter?" David finished the tea.

"After Carol fell and broke her hip, she moved to Guntersville to live with her daughter. The daughter came into some money and she married an older man, then they divorced a few years later. She moved to Guntersville where she got a job teaching school. I don't remember her married name. I'm sorry."

"How old would she be?" David asked.

"Carol, or the daughter?"

"I guess either one."

"Carol would be in her late seventies or early eighties. Rebecca, the daughter, would be in her fifties. She was born before the war."

"Thanks, you've been a lot of help."

314

David drove to Kyle's office as dusk settled over the town. He saw his old car parked in front of the courthouse. The 1938 Packard, newly painted and in pristine condition, stood there like a ghost of the past. He'd given the car to Kyle when he sold the house. He'd kept a few things when the house sold, the chest Anna had when they left Paris, the bookcase that had once held his law books, a rug from the old country. His mother lugged it from Poland, the moth-eaten wool rug hooked by her mother.

The Packard had been in the garage when he left it to Kyle, and had not been moved in twenty-five years. A couple of raccoons once resided in the trunk, coming and going from a rusty hole under the tail pipe. The tires, rotten and flat were no longer available at the tire store and the windshield had cracks where someone had thrown pebbles at the passenger side.

Now, it warmed his heart to see the old car as it had once been. A reminder of the past, it was a thing he could touch that had held Daphne and Anna. He walked over to it and rubbed his hand down the side.

"Looks good, doesn't it?" a stranger stated as he walked by.

"Sure does," David remarked and went inside to find Kyle. He saw the light on in his chambers from the street. He found him in his office and told him what he'd found.

"Good, maybe we can get to the bottom of who has the faulty gene. Not that it will do Emma any good, but I'm sure the other children would like to know who the carrier was," Kyle stated.

"That's why we're tracing the family. There are other people involved," David replied.

"I'm doing blueberry pancakes for breakfast in the morning. Be there by eight-thirty or Dawson will have eaten all of them. That kid is an eating machine. I won't try to save any for Carrie. I'm so glad she's coming to help you trace down the clues."

"Me too. She's a great friend. Did Dawson like my Christmas present?" David asked, changing the subject. He'd given him an expensive fishing rod with one of those new reels, one that would hold up to a fishing expedition off the coast.

"He loves it and will be down this summer to spend a month with you and Gordon. He'll want to go deep sea fishing. By the way, I'm not telling him he has a chance of inheriting this disease. I'll tell him someday, but right now I can't," Kyle replied.

"I understand. I'm turning in, it's been a long day," David said as weariness crept over him.

On the drive to the motel he pondered over what he'd uncovered. The early deaths of Harold and his sons were evidence Huntington's may be the culprit. In that case, the disease had to come through the mother of Harold, Owen and Colin. Their father was a different man.

David showered then curled around a pillow on the bed. He drifted off to sleep and dreamed that Colin and Owen had Daphne between them. Owen pulled her from one arm and Colin from the other. Then she stretched out to a long string as they laughed. He woke up with sweat running off his face.

It was a nightmare. David turned on the TV to a low volume and watched a War World II movie until he drifted back to sleep.

At seven a.m., a wake-up call jerked him to consciousness.

CHAPTER 27

December 29, 1979

Carrie arrived at Kyle and Emma's promptly at ten. She spent thirty minutes with Emma then pleaded she wanted to drive over to Huntsville and do some shopping.

"You know I used to live in Huntsville. I love the stores over there," Carrie lied.

Five minutes later, she and David were driving east toward Huntsville. Once they topped Monte Santo Mountain, a quaint valley began on the other side, populated with farms, old and new houses, several orchards and a barn with a roof that advertised "See Rock City." Ragged scarecrows guarded fallow crops as bales of hay were stacked six higher than a man's head. "I love this drive. It's spectacular," Carrie noted as they passed the sign that pointed toward Guntersville Dam.

"We used to take the kids over to the dam and watch the barges and tug boats go through the locks," she said as David continued east, portions of Guntersville Lake coming into view. "My mother has a sister in the area. We went by to see her years ago. She is younger than my mother and in great shape," Carrie stated, then realized David had not said a word for miles. "I know why you are so quiet. I'm as terrified as you are about Huntington's being in the family. I'm concerned for Ross and Clark. If Owen Campbell passed this defective gene, then Ross and Clark could develop HD. I can't believe this. Oh my God. How will I ever tell them and Mother?"

"Clark is Morgan's son so how…uh…how could he inherit it?"

"Haven't you noticed Clark's resemblance to Ross? Owen Campbell is Clark's father. Seems Owen fathered three children within months of each other. The SOB left his mark."

"He was a sorry man. Any man who cheats on his wife like that is no good. Maybe there will soon be a cure," David suggested.

"I've seen Huntington's patients. They die a long and slow death. It's a horrible disease, wrecking the lives of the patient, their families. Hopefully we'll know more by the end of today. I feel like I'm doing something to solve the puzzle, thanks to you," Carrie stated as David continued to drive east.

Five miles later, the town of Guntersville appeared, surrounded by a levy that kept Guntersville Lake out of the downtown streets. Four grain elevators stood at the dock where barges were tied, bins of grain full and ready to be transported down river to the destination on the bill of laden. Grain slipped off the barges when they left the port, spilling into the lake. Gulls flew overhead, diving for a free meal, circling the elevators, squawking loudly, fighting over who had first rights on the morsels.

Rumor had it that large catfish lived under the dock, feasting on the grain that the gulls missed, growing to a hundred pounds or more. Fishermen were always close by on the bridge leading to the elevators or on a boat, cruising in the wake of the barges.

David and Carrie found the courthouse and asked to see the clerk in the records department. A sign on the door posted the Saturday hours. The office would close in thirty minutes. They didn't have much time.

"We're looking for a woman named Rebecca who is a school teacher in the area. She would be in her fifties. Her maiden name was Hanson. Her mother's name was Carol. Do you know anyone that fits that description? We thought she might have come through your court or you'd know her from paying her taxes. I'm a retired judge and it's important that we find her," David explained in a concerned tone.

"There's a teacher at Guntersville High School named Rebecca Kelly. She's divorced and her mother's name Carol. She came to live with her when she broke her hip. They used to go to church with my sister," the clerk informed them.

"Do you know where she lives?" Carrie asked.

"Wait a minute and I'll find her address from her car tag registration."

A few minutes later, Carrie knocked on the door of the house Rebecca Kelly bought twelve years ago. David was behind her, anxious to see if they'd found the right person. A woman opened the door, a woman David recognized as Harold's daughter. Her hair was shorter and she had gained weight, but it was her.

"Are you Harold Hanson's daughter?" Carrie asked.

"Who wants to know?"

"I'm Carrie Stevenson. My mother was Skye Campbell. She was married to Owen Campbell. We need to talk to you about him."

"Owen Campbell was my uncle. Not that I am proud of that. He was a mean SOB." The woman motioned for them to come inside.

"The place is a mess. I'm working on grades," Rebecca stated.

They settled in chairs in a room decorated with antiques, lace curtains, a wool patterned rug and a green velvet couch with a white cat lounging in the middle. A dining room table held papers, books and a centerpiece of Christmas ornaments, half burned candles and cedar boughs.

"So, what can I do for you?" Rebecca asked as she moved the cat.

"We have reason to believe that Owen and Colin raped a woman and as a result of that rape, a child was born. The child is grown and is now sick, and we're wondering if we can get some information about your father and brothers. I found their graves at the cemetery in Decatur and we need to know what happened to them," David stated.

"Who is the girl they raped?"

"She was my wife," David answered.

"Well, well… I wouldn't doubt your story for a moment. My mother told me horror stories about those two. Mostly we stayed away from them. They lived out in the woods and ran moonshine. Rumor has it Owen killed a man, shot him between his eyes. My daddy believed it and we always figured it was true," Rebecca said from her place on the couch.

"What killed your dad?" Carrie asked, retrieving a pen and paper from her purse.

"He died from Huntington's Chorea in 1967. He was fifty-six. He and my two brothers suffered from it. Luckily, I've escaped. They say I don't have it since I haven't had any symptoms at this age. When my daddy developed it, they didn't know what he had. Then my brothers came down with the same symptoms and they identified it as Huntington's. It's the same thing Woody Guthrie died from. Like Woody, my father was misdiagnosed, considered an alcoholic and a lunatic. By the time he died, he was a vegetable. It was horrible." Rebecca wiped tears from her chin.

"And your brothers?" David asked.

"One developed symptoms at thirty-eight, and the other at forty. My youngest brother has three children. So far, we don't know if they have it. I elected not to have any children and my oldest brother didn't have children."

"The disease must have come from Harold's mother. Her death certificate gave her cause of death as kidney failure but she had to be the carrier. She could have had Huntington's and died from something else. Did you know your grandmother?" Carrie asked.

"No, I didn't, but my mother did. She said the disease came from my grandfather. Would you like to talk to her? She's taking a nap but she's in her room and will be awake in a few minutes," Rebecca asked.

"She is alive?" David asked, shocked.

"She is *very alive* and remembers everything. She'll probably remember you. I'll get her," Rebecca stated, and left the room.

A few minutes, later a woman entered the living room in front of Rebecca. Her wrinkled face revealed years of worry and concern, her stooped shoulders had a shawl wrapped around them over a calico patterned dress that hung to the top of her white socks. Her gray hair, pulled back into a bun, emphasized her light blue eyes. She looked ancient as she shuffled to a place on the couch and put on glasses which immediately slipped to the end of her nose. The cat jumped into her lap. She began to stroke it.

"Rebecca says we have visitors. She says it's someone from the mountain where Owen used to live with that woman he married who was an Indian," Carol Hanson said in a strong voice.

"That would be my mother. Her name is Skye. She's half Cherokee. She married Owen Campbell a long time ago, and I'm her daughter."

"You're Owen's daughter?"

"No, I'm by my mother's first husband. My father died when I was four."

"Was he the one kicked in the head by a horse? I remember when that happened. It was in the paper and made the gossip loop around town," the old woman asked.

"Yes, that was him. Later, my mother married Owen."

"I didn't think much of Owen and figured anyone who was stupid enough to marry that bastard was as backward as he was," Carol said with a bounce in her voice, leveling her eyes to Carrie. The conversation was between the two of them, equals in the room.

"Well, she was married to him for a few years. I agree it was a bad decision. They have one son, my brother Ross," Carrie replied.

And he has another son named Clark, Carrie thought.

"Was your mother the one that threw Owen in the river?"

"That's right. I helped her do it," Carrie stated quickly.

"Helped her kill him or throw him in the river?"

"I helped her take him to the river and I pushed him in with my feet. I was thirteen at the time."

"Wasn't there a lot of snow on the ground when you did it?"

"Yes, it was a cold trip down that trail, pulling his body on the sled. Harder on my mother because she went into labor and had a baby a few hours later. I don't regret pushing Owen in the river. He deserved what he got."

"Well, good for you. Brave little cuss you are!" The woman laughed at the revelation.

Carrie liked the woman. She had spunk. David and Rebecca listened to the two women, trying not to miss a word.

"Owen and Colin raped a girl up on the mountain while Owen was married to my mother. That girl had a baby and it appears that child has Huntington's. We're trying to find the source of the disease and figure it had to be Harold's mother, who would also be the mother of Owen and Colin. Rebecca says you have other information. Maybe you can tell us what you know about the path of the disease."

"I know a lot. Harold's mother was a little loose, if you know what I mean. My late husband, Harold Hanson, was from her first marriage. She loved Harold's father and married him when she was three months pregnant with his baby. His name was John Garner Hanson but he left her when Harold was six or seven. He ran off with some men to take a riverboat down to New Orleans and didn't come back. Word had it he fell off the boat and drowned and everyone believed the story. Then a red-headed Irishman named Clive Campbell came to town and Harold's mother married him. He was a fast-talking man with money in his pocket and liked the women. Owen was born and everything was dandy until Harold's father returned, six years after he left. He felt bad about what he'd done and helped her raise Harold, giving them money and helping her with the little boy." The old woman pushed her glasses up on her face, then continued.

"Then she had Colin. It was obvious John Hanson was the father of Colin. The baby looked exactly like him, but Clive didn't figure it out until Colin was two. He took off when it sank in. Then she died when Colin was six. Kidney failure, they said. She was a looker, a real looker." The old woman embellished the story with her hands.

"So Colin was fathered by the same man who fathered Harold?" Carrie asked.

"That's right. When John Garner Hanson came down with the disease, he remembered that his daddy had gone mad when he was a teenager and saw what lay ahead for him. He went to the woods one day and walked into the river. His body floated up three days later. Harold loved his daddy and it was hard on him. Back then they didn't know about this disease. We had no idea the disease would later strike Harold and then my sons, but it did...it did."

"Did Colin know who his biological father was?" Carrie asked.

"No, I don't think he or Owen ever figured it out. She admitted it to Harold when Colin was ready to go to school and she had papers to fill out. She wondered if she should tell him, but Harold wouldn't let her. I don't know if Colin escaped the disease, for he died when that woman shot him. I figured he deserved what he got, that SOB was a no good womanizer and a thief. I saw that in him when he was a kid. They were back woods white trash, but he sure loved my cooking," Carol said, her voice rising as she revealed her opinion of her husband's brothers.

"Thank you for this information. It helps us understand if the children of Owen *and* Colin will have HD. It helps a lot. I'm happy that we had a chance to get this straight," Carrie said.

"Glad I could help. Thank God Carol escaped the disease. I don't know what I'd do without her," she said, motioning to her daughter.

"We'll be going now. I hope you do well. We may come for another visit," Carrie said as they left.

David and Carrie drove a few miles before Carrie broke the silence.

"Do you realize what this means?"

"I'm not sure. I guess I have to see it on paper."

"Let's stop for some food and I'll explain it to you," Carrie suggested.

They stopped at Bertha's Catfish Café on the outskirts of Guntersville and ordered two meals.

Carrie pulled out a blank sheet of paper and started writing names and drawing lines.

CHAPTER 28

March, 1980

Carrie tried to be excited about *The Daughter*, nominated for an Academy Award for Best Original Screenplay. The movie had generated a lot of buzz and propelled her nephew Clark to the list of best writers and directors in Hollywood. He'd written the screenplay, directed the movie and had a twelve line acting role. Several members of the family had small parts, including her mother.

Carrie knew the family would be involved in the big event but she was glad she lived in Alabama and distant from the madding crowd. Josephine agreed with her, yet she had a vested interest. Judith Scott, the actress who played Josephine, the one who had the facial deformity corrected by Josephine, was nominated for Best Actress. No one gave her a chance against Goldie Hawn, Sissy Spacek, or Ellen Burstyn.

Photographs appeared of Judith, publicity shots for the movie, showing her beautiful face, her blue eyes and curly blonde hair. The photographs didn't reveal the true story. No one would have ever known she had once been horribly deformed. Judith's surgeries were so successful that no scar showed when she wore heavy makeup.

Judith spent most of her weekends with Clark and Josephine, playing with Colette while she healed. During the process, Clark taught her to act for the part of Josephine in the movie. She knew Josephine, her habits, her mannerisms and it was easy for her slip into the roll. The salary they paid her gave her enough money to register for college and after the movie wrapped, she worked on her degree in interior decorating.

Josephine shared Carrie's lack of interest in the Hollywood glamor, the counterfeit smiles, the quest for a perfect body, the perkiest breasts, to be on the list for the "Top Ten Most Beautiful Women in Hollywood." She knew who had work done, she'd operated on most of them.

Josephine and Colette avoided the Academy Awards ceremony, choosing to watch the festivities at home on television. Clark took Skye, his grandmother. It was a sweet gesture and Carrie turned off the TV after they were off camera. She didn't see Morgan and Levi come in. She knew Morgan would be praised for her beauty and the fact she could wear the same dress she'd worn fifteen years earlier. The truth was she'd had it copied to fit her twenty pounds heavier body.

Good for her, Carrie thought then questioned her praise. Morgan had joined the allure of glamor and fascination with the dazzling darlings of Tinsel Town. The next morning, Carrie saw in the paper that Clark and Levi both won. That afternoon, Carrie called her mother to get her take on the ceremony.

"It was okay. I saw a lot of movie stars. We skipped the after awards parties. I was too tired to keep going. Morgan and Levi went but I didn't get a chance to talk to them. Morgan hasn't called much lately. She may be mad about the incident right after Christmas. Maybe she's busy, she and Levi spend a lot of time in New York."

The incident was the revelation by Skye that Owen and Colin had raped a woman in February of 1941 and that one or both of them had Huntington's. Skye overheard the conversation between David and Carrie before she knew how Huntington's disease could affect the descendants of the two men. She revealed the conversation to Josephine who was in the house.

"It's possible both of them had the disease," Skye revealed to Josephine.

As a doctor, Josephine knew about Huntington's and its devastating consequences. If her husband was in line to inherit the disease and he contracted it, Colette was also in line. Panic spread over her. It was three days later that Carrie called to set the record straight, that it was Colin who was the carrier of the HD gene and any children of Owen were safe.

In those three days, Josephine called Morgan and confronted her with the lie that Clark was the son of some soldier who went down on a ship in Pearl Harbor. Morgan had to admit that Owen

Campbell was Clark's father. Then Morgan called her mother and accused her of revealing the secret. Chaos erupted.

"I didn't tell her anything, but the whole family knows. It's obvious, and you need to do yourself and Clark a favor and come clean about it," Skye suggested to her daughter.

When Morgan told Clark that Owen Campbell was his father, he informed her that he had already figured it out.

"I figured it out years ago. The whole family suspected it and we didn't want to accuse you, but it doesn't matter. I love you and I don't care about him. He wasn't a parent to me. He only contributed the sperm. From everything I've heard about him, he was a bum," Clark told his mother.

"Thanks, Clark. Thanks for understanding, and now that the secret is out I'm relieved. Levi had also figured it out, so I guess I was the one who held onto the lie. I'm far from perfect, and I should have trusted you with the truth long ago," Morgan replied.

Later that week, Carrie called Morgan and begged her to let any hard feelings toward her mother be forgiven.

"I agree. I'll call mother and apologize. I love her so much, and after being out there on my own for all those years I want to be in this family, my family," Morgan cried.

Now Carrie understood her mother's words, *Someday you will have to take charge.*

A few days later, Skye missed her weekly trip to the big house on Saturday and Anders found her in bed at her beach house, curled around a pillow in her bed. She was lethargic and in her bathrobe. Her hair had not been brushed for days nor had she eaten much.

"I can't take this kind of turmoil. My children mean the world to me and I can't see them hurt," she revealed when Carrie called in response to Anders' report.

"I know. I'm a mother, too. We have to think of Emma, how her life is shattered, how her husband must feel knowing what's ahead for him. Think of David and how this affects him. We have to be strong for our friends, for them," Carrie told her mother.

"I guess you're right. I'll get out of bed and drive to town and get some groceries. It hurts me to have to deal with all of this, but I will. I will," Skye replied

"I'll call Anders to check on you and you'd better be at the big house on Saturday and do your walk. Take them a cake and pick up your wine for the week. Put it in your pantry if it's more than you need. David would love to have your stash," Carrie reminded her.

Carrie felt better after she had the conversation with her mother but she dreaded her call to Kyle to get a report on Emma. She'd become the go-to nurse for Emma and Kyle. She'd promised Daphne she'd take care of her girls and Emma and Grace were like sisters to her. She also felt the need to be there for David. Shattered and grieving, he acted like he was responsible, but no one blamed him. How could they? He had been a wonderful father to Emma and had nothing to do with the genetic flaw.

Then there was Kyle. He called once a week with questions he should ask the doctor but there wasn't a doctor in their area who had knowledge of Huntington's. Carrie had only seen a few cases, mostly in the psych ward of the hospital before they were shipped off to nursing homes or the state hospital in Tuscaloosa.

If you work in hospitals long enough, you see everything, Carrie realized as she listened for Steve to come home. It was almost seven and he'd had a long day of surgery and examining patients at the clinic. She had been home an hour and was exhausted, but her day wasn't finished. Carrie had to find a volunteer to work at the women's shelter with her tomorrow. She made a few phone calls. She'd help fund the project and volunteered one day a week to work at the center, a job she loved and cherished. Lately, volunteers had been sparse; the newness had worn off and the friend she counted on the most had moved to Nashville.

Carrie had a vested reason to stay close to the women's shelter. She had gotten involved with one of Emma's cases. The Ridings' children and their mother, Patsy Ridings, needed help to escape their horrible situation at home. For two years, Emma worked with the family, trying to get the children away from their abusive father, but their mother lived in fear that her husband would find them. Carrie promised to help Emma get them to Shelby County where Patsy Ridings had a place to live, if she had the courage to flee.

Carrie felt a tightening in her gut. Since Christmas, she had lost weight and had trouble sleeping. *Too much stress,* she said to herself. *Someday Steve and I will make it to retirement and build that house on the coast.* Meanwhile, I still have a lot of responsibilities.

She heard Steve come in bedroom over the noise of the shower.

"Long day?" Carrie asked as her husband put his keys on top of the dresser.

"Yes, a very long day. I lost Gene Werner today. He didn't make it through surgery. Cardiac arrest as I was closing," Steve revealed.

"Oh, I'm sorry. His heart was in bad shape. I'm not surprised," Carrie said over the noise of the spray.

"I need a strong drink, a long shower, and a good night's sleep," Steve suggested.

"Yes, yes you do," Carrie replied.

Three hours later, they fell asleep curled around each other as a soft rain fell on the roof and hit the metal awning over the stoop on the back of the house. The rain sounded like they were sleeping under a tin roof, a sound Carrie loved.

She dreamed about her mother, her sisters and her children. They were all running through a meadow of stars, jumping from one to another, then they all fell and landed in the ocean and Carrie felt herself gasp for breath. She awoke with a start and wondered what it meant.

The rain was still falling. Everything was quiet but something was wrong. She could feel it in her bones.

CHAPTER 29

June, 1980

Emma knew something was wrong in her brain. It felt like her left side did not match her right side. One side wanted to walk forward and the other side wanted to go sideways and neither side won. It was a battle to stay erect and to walk a short distance. When she tried to talk, the words that were in her brain were not the ones she said. Everything was garbled and mixed up in a jigsaw of words that didn't fit the thoughts in her brain.

My brain is messed up, she repeated to herself as she tried to dress. She pulled on her slacks, then her blouse but she couldn't button the front.

Why don't they find out the problem? Or have they, and no one has told me?

Emma surveyed her image in the mirror. Her thin frame revealed she had lost weight and her hair was a mess. She couldn't control her arms long enough to use a brush. She tried again to button her blouse but she couldn't. She looked at her feet and realized she had on two different kinds of shoes. Frustrated, she pulled off the blouse and pulled a sweater over her body.

It bothered her that she was sick. She needed to be a good mother to Dawson, a good wife to Kyle, and she needed to finish her case work, especially the case on the Ridings' children. They needed her to get them away from their father. She was the only one who understood the complexity of their case.

The last of her files were spread out on the dining room table. A new case worker came over every day to help her make phone calls and write notes. She had three cases left and she had until the end of June to work them before she went on medical leave. If she didn't get better, she would retire. That was the latest statement from the doctor. She was ready to be finished with work. She was tired, weary, and worried.

The main case was the children of Patsy and Sammy Ridings. They lived in a trailer park half way between Decatur and Hartselle on Highway 31. The Ridings trailer was in the back of Velma's Trailer Park. Cardboard covered a couple of the windows and a dilapidated porch stood in front of the trailer for access to the front door. The back door opened to a set of wooden stairs with a rung missing.

She'd been inside the trailer a couple of times, back when she could drive. The main room was filthy. Stubbed out cigarettes, candy wrappers and potato chip bags were strewn on the ripped couch. Roaches ran out from under the furniture and up the walls, flies buzzed day-old food on the counter, a dog sat in a recliner as it scratched a flea and cats lived on top of the refrigerator in a basket. The trailer smelled of bacon, grease, rotten garbage, body odor, urine and cigarette smoke.

Living in a filthy house was not a crime, but abuse and neglect are. Bruises on the faces of Sammy Riding's wife and his two daughters revealed his propensity for violence. Gina, the oldest daughter, admitted an act of sexual contact had happened to her. She told one of her girl friends at school about the incident. She also told the friend that her six-year-old brother had a deformity that kept him hidden in the back room of their trailer. He'd not received medical attention for what appeared to be a cleft pallet. These were punishable crimes, but they had to be prosecuted and the matter brought to court before the children could be removed. That was not always the answer to the problem.

Emma wanted to save the children *and* keep them with their mother. She'd sacrifice Patsy Ridings if she had to. She could stay in the house but it would be better if she could get her out with the children. Emma had a plan in mind but for it to work she had to gain the confidence of Gina, the oldest girl. She'd started that before she got sick.

Gina Riding's teacher turned in the report of abuse. Social workers were required to do an investigation but Gina denied she'd told her best friend that her father tried to rape her a week after her fourteenth birthday.

Emma took Gina for a ride when she did the first interview on the case two years ago. They drove to the nearest Dairy Queen.

Ice cream always loosens tongues and endears you to your clients, case workers were told. Sometimes it worked, sometimes it didn't.

Gina Ridings, a smart fourteen-year-old, knew if she admitted what her father did she'd be removed from her home. She was the protector for her sister, brother, and mother, and couldn't leave them. Cases of abuse and neglect were common in the trailer court and Gina had seen a girl removed. She never came back. A few months later, the trailer burned and the girl's mother died, trapped in the bedroom. That scene stayed with Gina.

Emma reviewed Gina's records at school and saw her test scores. *This girl is smart*, Emma realized. *I have to get that family to a better place.* While Gina licked the ice cream cone, Emma pumped her for information.

"I have a report that your father had sexual contact with you. This came from school," Emma approached the subject delicately.

"It's not true. My daddy would never do that," she said.

"Sometimes men do that to their daughters and it is not due to anything you've done. You have a little sister. If he did it to you, he'll do it to her. I also see you have a little brother who's seven. I don't see where he is in school. Where is he?" Emma asked.

"He's at home. He's deformed and we aren't sending him to school. I am teaching him to read and write. He's a good kid. I can't leave him or my sister. I can't leave them and I won't," Gina replied.

"Okay, I understand. What about your mother? Would she leave and take you three with her?"

"She won't cross him. No way. He can be mean when he drinks."

"And he can abuse his children when he drinks. I get the picture," Emma added.

"No you don't. You couldn't possibly know what our life is like. Here you are with your fancy clothes, your leather high heels, and your new car. I'll bet you live in a brick house in town with new furniture and matching sheets on the bed. You couldn't possibly understand how it is to live in a trailer court, in our trailer."

"You make a good point, but you know someday you will have to leave. I don't want you to get pregnant and have your father's baby. That would be a horrible thing for you and for the family."

"I hit him the last time he tried to corner me and I know where he keeps his gun. I told him I'd kill him, and he knows I will," Gina revealed.

"So what are your plans to escape?"

"I don't know what to do. Mother says she's hiding money so we can take the bus out of Decatur, but where would we go?"

"Does she have any family in Alabama?"

"Yes. She has a brother in Shelby County. He lives in Alabaster. The reason I know is he sends us a Christmas card each year and I saved the address. I thought it might come in handy someday. He sent photos of his family and they were dressed in nice clothes, so they must have money. Mother said we might live with him for a while if we got away from daddy."

"Okay, this is good news. I want that address. When we get back to your house give it to me." She did.

Emma wrote the brother. He called her and said if they came to his house he wouldn't turn them away but they could not stay longer than a week or two. He had a family of his own and hadn't seen them in years.

That was a year ago. He didn't send them a Christmas card again.

As a case worker, Emma and her colleagues visited each person on their list once a month. If there was a reason for an emergency visit, case workers might visit several times. They received referrals from schools, churches, and neighbors who witnessed abuse and neglect. Often the visits resulted in a family moving out of the area to avoid an investigation. That was a common way to avoid charges and whole families would disappear overnight. The escaping families lived in their cars, in tents at campgrounds, under bridges, in abandoned apartments, and on the road.

Afraid the Ridings children would suffer more if they left the area, Emma devoted her time to Gina. If she could win her over, she could get them out. She had a place for them to go.

Carrie told her about the women's shelter in Shelby County. Funded by several churches and Jefferson, Shelby, and Walker counties, the shelter was available for women who needed to escape with their children. The house made into the shelter sat on five acres on a one way road in a secluded area. Three rooms had been added to the four bedroom house and the basement space was converted to bedrooms. There was space for nine mothers with children. The local school system added a bus stop at the shelter to pick up the children for school.

Clothes donated by local residents were sorted for the children and women. Meals were served in a large dining room and two televisions provided entertainment and news. The women did the cooking, laundry and cleaning. A game room for the children gave them access to toys they had never seen before and tutors helped them with school assignments. A doctor and nurse examined the incoming residents and were on call for emergencies. The doctor was Carrie's husband and Carrie was the nurse.

If Emma could get them to the shelter they would be free of Sammy Ridings. The shelter provided not only a safe place for them, the staff found a job for the ones who could work. They stayed at the shelter for six months then funding was available for the family to establish themselves in a low income apartment complex. There were several in the three county area. It was the perfect solution for the Ridings family and a chance for a better life.

Emma updated Carrie last month on the case. Her assistant talked to Carrie since she had problems using the telephone.

I can think, I can reason but I can't figure out how to use the telephone, Emma said to herself as she stared at the numbers on the gadget.

The other two cases were not as traumatic. One was a child who needed surgery and she'd found a doctor that would do it free of charge. Another was a Jehovah's Witness case where the parents refused to let their child get a blood transfusion. The child had lost fifty percent of his blood in a car accident and it had affected his cognitive abilities.

She knew how that felt.

Emma lined up her assistant to take her out to see Gina Ridings. Now sixteen, Gina had dropped out of high school and stayed home with her brother so her mother could work. They would go tomorrow and she had one more trip planned for her and her assistant, a trip to the library.

Emma remembered a night after Christmas when she went by Kyle's office. Still driving then, she dropped by unannounced and noticed some library books on his desk. One was entitled "Diseases of the Brain." It was resting on two other books. The book was turned over, its spine on top.

He found what's wrong with me in those books, she realized last week when a trio of good days provided clear thinking. Kyle wasn't a frequent visitor to the library. He brought law books home from work to read, not novels and medical books.

If I don't forget to ask my assistant to take me to the library tomorrow, maybe I can figure out what is wrong with me, Emma thought. She scribbled a few words on a piece of paper and put it on top of her purse.

By late afternoon, the twitching in her face started and her gait started its sideways motion. She took a tranquilizer and her assistant left to file reports at the office. The assistant would be the case worker who would replace her. This was a transition for both of them.

"Emma out, assistant in," she whispered as she crawled in between the sheets in her bedroom.

The next day, Kyle helped her dress. They got a call that Grace had her baby, a little girl, and he volunteered to take her to the hospital to see her new niece. The assistant arrived and Emma told her to look at the top of her purse and read to her what the note said. She couldn't remember.

"It says, 'library go to.'"

"Okay, let's go."

The librarian looked at Kyle's book card and found the same books he'd checked out on January 7th, 1980. Emma checked them out and they drove to the Ridings trailer.

School was out; children were playing in the yards of the trailer park and on the small jungle gym that rested under a large oak tree at the entrance. An above ground pool held a plethora of children, yelling and batting a red ball around in the pool. Several dogs moved out of the road as the assistant drove to the end of the park.

The assistant knocked on the door. Emma was behind her.

"Is Gina in?" she asked the youngest daughter.

"Yes, I'll get her."

Gina appeared, wearing a pair of shorts, a ripped T-shirt and flip flops.

"Can you leaveee for a few minutes? There is something I want to discusses with yourse," Emma said in her faltering speech.

"No, I can't leave. I'm watching my brother and sister while mom is at work. You've lost weight and you sound funny. Are you okay?" Gina asked.

"I'll be okay," Emma stated as they entered the trailer. Emma noticed her assistant looked around the filthy room.

"Where is your mother working?" the assistant asked.

"She's a waitress at the café out on the highway," Gina stated.

"That's a good skill to have," the assistant replied.

"Can she stay in heree with the kids while we talks in the car?" Emma asked pointing to her assistant.

They had contrived this before they drove to the trailer. The assistant would find the boy with the deformity and take photos of him.

"Sure, we can go for a drive if you want to," Gina stated.

"I can't drive but I haveee some… something in the carsee for you," Emma replied.

Once in the car, she gave her a sack with several candy bars, a small bottle of shampoo, two bars of soap, tampons, deodorant and a bundle of clothes. She and the girl were close to the same size.

"Thanks, I can use these," Gina said as she surveyed the things in the sack.

"Look, I am have troubles speak… speaking and have brain disorder. I won't be a case warkers much longererrr. So, listen to meese. When you ready to go I have a place for your all. Call these numbers. This is mine," Emma handed her a card and pointed to the top number.

"Who is the other one?" Gina asked.

"My frees friend Carrie. She knows the probes but lives in Bingham."

"You mean Birmingham?"

"Yes, yes," Emma replied. Her hand began to twitch, her mouth pulled to one side.

"Okay, I get it. You're sick. I'm sorry. Mother has saved a hundred dollars and I've been doing some baby sitting and have about thirty dollars. I'm hoping we can get out of here before July fourth. Daddy always goes on a big drunk on July fourth and starts beating us. I've convinced Mother we have to escape, and she's willing. This time I believe her. You've done a good job of convincing her to leave him. I'll miss you if you aren't around when we make the move," Gina said.

They went back to the trailer and retrieved the assistant. Once she was in the car, she revealed the condition of the little boy.

"He is undernourished because he has a clef pallet and has difficulty eating. Otherwise he appears to be healthy. He has developmental delays that will need to be addressed. He could be a normal kid if we can get him out of there."

She noticed the twitching in Emma's arm.

"Let's get you home," the assistant said as she drove to Emma's house. She put her to bed then took the roll of film to the drugstore to be developed.

The next morning, Emma popped toast in the toaster and tried to pour Kyle a cup of coffee. Most of it landed on the counter and it upset her.

"Damn it. I wants the doctoree to get me fixed."

"They're working on your case," Kyle replied.

"Liar! You know, you know and won't say." Emma threw the toast at him. Kyle dodged it and guided her to a chair in the living room.

"Calm down. I can stay home from work if you need me to. I don't have court today."

"No goes on, I will be fine. I sorry," Emma replied as she sank lower into the chair.

I want to see the books from the library. Why can I think and reason but have no control over my body and my speech? Is the answer in those books?

Thirty minutes later, Kyle left for the office. Emma stayed in the chair in the living room until she was sure he was out of sight.

Then she retrieved the three books her assistant had stacked on the dining room table.

Diseases of the Brain was the first book she opened. She thumbed through it and found three pages that had been turned down at the corner. Then she picked up a paperback book entitled, *Huntington's Chorea, a Family Tragedy*. The third book was one on genetics.

She read the first three chapters of *Huntington's Chorea, a Family Tragedy*. The symptoms of the man in the book exactly matched hers. But he had inherited the disease and neither of her parents had it.

How can I have this if I don't have it in my background? Emma reasoned as she realized she had forgotten to eat. She found a can of soup Kyle opened for her before he left and poured it into a sauce pan. She turned the stove on and resumed reading the book about the family.

Engrossed in it, she realized smoke had filled the living room. She had let the soup burn. She ran to the stove, grabbed the sauce pan handle and the hot soup splattered over her arm and neck. She fell on the soup that landed on the floor. She got up and managed to turn off the stove as she saw Kyle drive up. She was crying and holding her burned arm when he came in the back door.

"My God, Emma, what happened," he said when he found her.

"Hurt, hurt...uh, hurt," Emma cried.

Kyle rushed her to the Emergency Room. They kept her, sedated her, and bandaged the second degree burns. She cried to go home but the doctor insisted she be admitted.

Kyle called David. He drove up the next day and drove straight to the hospital. Emma was sitting up when he arrived. Her hair combed, a robe around her body, she looked good in spite of the bandages on her arm and neck. Kyle was in a chair beside her bed. He looked distraught and shook his head sideways.

"Well, here issy my daddy. Why didn't you tell me I am Huntington's? One doctor in here said so and I knows. Trouble is I don't know hows got it. They have me on anti-psychotic rugs. This disease will be how me dies but they say I live ten more years. I get see Dawson grow up. That is all. I ask see him grow up," Emma burst into tears when she finished.

"I'm sorry you found out this way. It's true, you have Huntington's. How you got it isn't important. What is important is that you will be around to see Dawson grow up and I'll be there for both of you," Kyle assured her.

"Okays, okay. I see Dawson grow up... up to high school grad... graduation at leasty," Emma stuttered.

"I will take you to his high school graduation. I promise you, we will be there," Kyle said as tears flowed down his face.

They visited Emma an hour then had a conference with the doctor.

"I have a list of health care aides. One will need to be with her during the day and you can watch her at night. You need to file for her Social Security disability. I'll back you on that. She can never work again or stay by herself," the doctor advised. He gave him a list of day sitters in Decatur.

Once back at the house, Kyle poured each of them two fingers of Jack Daniels in a glass then put ice cubes in the amber liquid. They sat in the living room.

"This is it. She can't stay by herself any longer. I found these books that she checked out of the library. I checked out the same ones back in January. She traced my steps. She's rational some days, she has to be or she couldn't have gotten these books. But her mobility is shot and she is in danger of hurting herself worse than this."

"I'll stay until your find someone. Please don't put her away," David begged.

"Eventually I'll have to put her in a nursing home. You know that."

"Please, not yet," David pleaded.

Emma came home from the hospital the next day. Her assistant notified Kyle that the medical leave application was approved and brought the papers to him.

Emma's case files disappeared off the dining room table. People from work came by to celebrate her last day at work. Kyle made sure she had a cake and punch for them. Tears were shed and Emma smiled during the party, staying in a chair, trying to control the twitching in her arms, the bandages still covering her arm.

Kyle hired a day sitter and Emma settled into a daily routine. The doctor told them to let her do all she could, except operate things in the kitchen. Emma still answered the phone, talked to Kyle each day when he called from the office, to Carrie and Skye when they called and to various friends.

On July third, the phone rang at four p.m. The health care aide was walking their dog when Emma answered.

"Mrs. Walton, come now, come now. He's drunk and has beaten my mother and sister really bad. I'm calling from a neighbor's phone. He's got a gun and he says he'll use it. He found my mother's money. Come now and hurry. Oh no, I hear a gunshot." The phone line went dead.

Emma looked for the health aide. Then she remembered she was walking the dog. She had to help Gina Ridings, she had to. She had promised. She couldn't remember how to call the police.

She looked out the window and saw the old Packard that Kyle had restored. She looked around for the keys to it. They were on a nail on the back porch. She took them and struggled to get the car door open. She finally slid into the driver's seat and tried to insert the keys in the ignition. On the third time, she got them in. She turned the keys and the motor roared to life.

Remembering how to drive, she backed out to the street and started toward town. There was little traffic. Emma concentrated on getting south of town to the trailer park. Once she realized she was drifting to the center of the highway and swerved to miss a car then overcorrected and ran off the road. She backed up and pointed the car south as she saw the trailer park come into view.

People were gathered at the end of the road. She pulled the car halfway down the gravel lane and got out. She struggled to walk on the uneven ground and found Gina outside in a crowd of people near their trailer. A woman held her back. Angry threats came from the trailer.

"Git away, I'm going to kill anyone who tries to come up those steps," Sammy Ridings yelled from inside the trailer. "I've got my wife and kids in here. If anyone tries to git them I'll hurt them, I'll hurt them bad. Ain't nobody gonna tell me what to do. You hear me? Nobody tells me what I can do," he yelled louder.

"He's inside. He has a pistol. Someone called the police. They're on the way," Gina grabbed Emma and held on to her.

"He's got a gun," Patsy Ridings yelled from inside the trailer.

"He's going to shoot them. He will, I know he will," Gina cried and pulled away, starting toward the porch on the trailer.

"No Gina, no," someone yelled but no one moved.

They had seen this man beat his wife before and knew he was dangerous.

Emma pushed away from the crowd and overcame Gina. She pushed her aside and Gina fell. Emma walked toward the stairs of the front porch, struggling to stay erect.

Gina crawled toward her yelling, "No, no, don't go in there."

A shot came through the cardboard window. The cardboard flew out into the yard littered with trash, an old bicycle, broken toys and weeds.

The shot entered Gina's arm, went through it and hit the hard packed dirt behind her. She screamed then crawled toward the crowd, bleeding and crying. A man ran to her, picked her up, and carried her to someone's car. The crowd scattered as another shot rang out, hitting the windshield of the Packard. Emma continued to the porch.

"Git out of here, I said git out of here. This ain't none of your business, you bitch. You're the one that has got my wife thinking she can leave me. You sorry whore," Gina's father yelled, his distorted face in the window where the cardboard had been.

"No Daddy, no…" someone in the trailer yelled.

They heard a siren in the distance. The police were closer. Emma grabbed the side of the porch and pulled herself up the stairs.

"Let her go, let the children leave," she yelled to the window in a clear voice.

"Git off my property," came out the window with the next shot.

The bullet entered Emma's right eye and traveled into her brain, hit the back of her skull and shattered into several pieces. The force of the shot propelled her backwards and down the stairs. She landed on her back, rolled over and tried to crawl before she collapsed, face down in the dirt.

The police arrived and ran toward the crowd. Two men in uniforms pulled their weapons.

"Call for an ambulance," one of the officers yelled to his partner.

They saw the body on the ground and assumed it was Patsy Ridings.

"He's in the trailer. He has two kids in there," a bystander said.

A policeman threw a tear gas canister in the window.

"Come out with your hands up," he yelled.

"I'll kill all of them if you come through that door," a voice yelled, coughing and spitting.

CHAPTER 30

July 3, 1980

The call came into the Morgan County Sheriff's Department at four-thirty on July third, the beginning of the July fourth weekend.

"Crap, why does someone shoot a person on the beginning of the holiday weekend? I had plans to go fishing," the detective on duty asked the dispatcher.

"I agree it's highly inconvenient but I have no control over the crazies in this area. A woman is down in front of Sammy Ridings trailer and his daughter has been shot. He's holed up inside with a pistol and from what he's yelling, he has plenty of ammo. A black-and-white is out there and they're calling for back up. An ambulance is on the way," the dispatcher replied.

"I'm right behind them," the detective shouted as he ran to his unmarked vehicle.

He sped through the small town of Decatur to Highway 31, turning south toward Velma's Trailer Park where Sammy Ridings, his wife, three kids, two dogs, and an assorted number of cats lived in a broken down trailer. This wasn't the first time the police had been called to a domestic dispute at that address. In fact, he'd been out there last week on a complaint that Sammy shot holes in a neighbor's garbage can.

Sammy liked to beat his wife and kids and when he'd been drinking, he got mean. He also liked to shoot things, any mongrel dog in the trailer park, the windshield of some perceived enemy, the light on the pole at the end of his driveway, the plastic swimming pool next door. But he'd never shot anyone, until today.

The detective figured that was Sammy's wife on the ground in front of their trailer. Too old for her age, battered, wrinkled from years of chain smoking and binge drinking, she had three children who deserved a better life. Rumor had it their youngest child had a birth defect that kept him hidden inside.

The detective pulled up to the trailer in time to see Sammy being led out the back door of the trailer in handcuffs. A young girl was crying and holding her arm. A body was on the ground, covered by a quilt someone had brought to the site. Two children were being cradled by a woman, the youngest was a boy with a cleft pallet.

A rookie on the force ran over to the detective.

"The woman on the ground is not Sammy's wife. See for yourself. This is tragic, tragic," his words trailed off.

The detective walked over to the body. He exposed the head and took a long look at the face. "No, oh my God, no, no…she's dead. How did this happen? How did she get involved in this mess?"

"No one knows. Guess you'll have to figure it out and you'll have to tell the judge. A real tragedy here, a real tragedy," the rookie replied as he shook his head.

CHAPTER 31

July 6, 1980

The funeral for Emma was held at the First Methodist Church
where she and Kyle attended. Most of the citizens in Decatur
turned out for the services. Policemen directed traffic to an
overflow parking lot and the motorcade to the cemetery was two
miles long.

Carrie picked up Skye at the Birmingham airport. They
drove to Decatur and arrived at the church thirty minutes before
the services. Grace, a new mother with a three-week-old baby girl,
attended her sister's funeral with her child in her arms, her husband
beside her. Kyle and Dawson, circled by Gordon and David, kept a
close vigil with each other.

David wept when the casket left the church. Kyle stared at
the metal box, Dawson hung his head and Gordon put his arm
around David. The four of them exited the church together and
rode in the same car to the cemetery.

The graveside services were private. The family and Emma's
coworkers were the only ones invited, but others came. No one
asked them to leave and the overflow crowd stood in stunned
silence as the minister spoke. When the family left, two men filled

the cavity over the casket with red clay dirt. They patted the dirt with the back of their shovels and placed flowers on top and around the area. Some ended up on Daphne's grave a few feet away.

Ladies from the church brought food to Kyle's house as neighbors dropped by and people milled around. By seven p.m., most of the people left. Only close friends and family remained in the house.

"I can't believe this happened. She wanted to see Dawson graduate from high school and Sammy Ridings took that away from her," Kyle said more than once.

"What now?" someone asked Kyle.

"Dawson and I go on. David and my Uncle Gordon will help me with him. We'll do okay. We have to. What else do you do?" Kyle cried.

Carrie and Skye stayed in the kitchen until the last person left. They put the rest of the food in the refrigerator, washed all the dishes, and returned to the living room to say their goodbyes. Kyle thanked them for all they had done then told them again how much Emma wanted to live to see Dawson graduate from high school.

"She would have been able to do that if she had lived. I would have taken her, even if she had to go in a wheelchair," Kyle sobbed.

Once in the car, Carrie told her mother, "Sammy Ridings, in his drunken stupor, took Emma's life and her years with her son and Kyle. But he also took away years of suffering and turmoil for their family."

"That doesn't make it easier. Nothing makes it easier," Skye replied.

Carrie and Skye checked into a motel on the outskirts of town.

"There's something I have to do tomorrow. I'm taking a family down to Shelby County. I heard David volunteer to take you back to Birmingham. When is he driving you down?" Carrie asked her mother.

"I'm not sure. He's coming after me in the morning and we're going to the cemetery together. He has two wives buried there and now a daughter. He needs a friend and I'm going to be that friend," Skye said as she pulled a robe around her.

"He doesn't have a house here anymore," Carrie reminded her.

"I know. He's staying at Kyle's and I'll keep this room until he's ready to leave. We'll drop by your house on the drive down to the coast when he's ready to go home. I've decided to rent an apartment in Fairhope for the rest of the summer. I'm going to hang around with him and Gordon and eat some seafood and get acquainted with the area. I understand you're going to build a house on Ono Island when you retire and I may want a room in it for me. Just a suggestion, now that I'm getting older. Better yet, I can build my own small house. I've already talked to Gordon about buying a lot," Skye hesitated.

360

"I'd be honored for you to have a room in our retirement home," Carrie replied as she took off her high heels and slid them under the chair.

"Now don't get all sentimental on me. I'm not leaving Napa or my beach house. I'm just adding a new place to the list of my travel destinations. David needs me, and you know I like to be needed."

"I approve, not that it makes any difference. You have a mind of your own and I'm not even going to try to boss you around," Carrie replied.

"Good. It's settled. David is looking at house plans and I think I'll look at some, too. I've always wanted a place back here, a small place," Skye said.

Both women went to bed with a heavy heart.

The next morning, Carrie drove to Velma's Trailer Park to retrieve the Ridings family. Gina and her mother packed their meager belongings to leave the trailer where they had lived for ten years. Her arm bandaged, Gina wore a pair of tailored slacks and a cotton sweater. Carrie thought she'd seen Emma wearing those things last year.

Patsy Ridings was dressed in a long skirt and a matching blouse. She looked younger than Carrie remembered. The worry lines on her face had relaxed, her hair was clean and brushed, she had on a nice shade of lipstick and stood taller. The younger children were dressed in shorts, faded t-shirts, and flip flops. Gina and her mother stalled at the door of the trailer.

"God knows I won't miss this place. Oh, I found someone to take our cat and I think the man who owns this trailer is going to junk it. That suits me," Gina said as they walked away.

Her mother looked back at the run down trailer, shook her head, and turned toward Carrie.

"Are you sure he's put away? Is he going to get out and find us?" Patsy Ridings asked.

"He won't find you. He's going away for a long time. He killed a judge's wife. No one on a jury is going to feel sorry for him," Carrie assured her as she put their things in the trunk and motioned for them to get into her car.

They pulled out of the trailer park and turned south. Patsy Ridings sat in the back seat with the small children. Subdued and silenced by years of abuse and trauma, Carrie knew she would require intense counseling to overcome the trauma she had witnessed and the abuse she had suffered.

For a few miles, no one spoke. Gina's eight-year-old brother had not been out of the trailer in four years. He looked around in amazement, at the people, the cars, the buildings on the highway. He saw a cow and pointed to one then a horse came into view.

"Has, has," he said in his cryptic speech.

"I doubt he's ever seen a horse," Gina said from the front seat beside Carrie.

Carrie tried to calculate the harm one man had inflicted on his family and Emma, who was now in a grave. Emma would not see her son grow up, Dawson was robbed of a mother, and Kyle of a wife, even though she was sick. Sammy Ridings took Emma's life, but Emma's poor judgment contributed to her demise. In her state of brain deterioration, she had made a rash decision to storm the house and that decision was the wrong one.

Carrie reminded Gina of that after the funeral when she drove out to the trailer to tell them they were leaving with her the next day. Carrie sneaked out of Kyle's house after the funeral, pleading she needed to go to the grocery store so no one would know what she was doing. She'd promised Emma she'd take care of the Ridings family, and she would.

Carrie drove past Hartselle and looked at her watch. Almost noon, she realized she hadn't eaten.

"There's a Waffle House ahead. Anyone want a waffle?" she asked.

"What's a waffle?" Gina's little sister asked.

"You're about to find out," Carrie said.

She pulled into the parking lot. Everyone got out but the little boy.

"Come on, let's go inside," she said waving her arm.

"He's afraid, he's afraid of everything. I'll bet people will stare at him," Patsy Ridings said as a tear ran down her face.

"So what if they do? He can't help it and he needs to eat. I'll show you the best way to feed him then after the surgery you can teach him the normal way," Carrie said.

"Surgery? Can he be fixed? You know I don't have any money," Patsy replied, choking on the words.

"He can be fixed and I know the right person to do it. There is a plastic surgeon in our family who specializes in his kind of surgery. You're all going to California in a few weeks. You don't need money. It will be taken care of," Carrie told the battered woman.

"And all of you are getting new clothes, a decent haircut, good shoes, and you will have a safe place to live while Gina gets her GED."

"What's a GED?" Gina asked.

"A high school diploma. You're going to need it because I'm going to see to it that you go to college," Carrie informed her as they entered the restaurant.

A huge smile spread across Gina's face as she slid into a booth. Patsy pushed her hair behind her ear, the little girl smiled at a stranger at the counter, and the little boy pulled his hand up over his mouth. A waitress put menus in front of them.

"We all want waffles. Put a double helping of pecans on them and bring us some orange juice and lots of syrup," Carrie said to the woman.

"Yes, ma'am," the waitress said as she wrote down the order.

About Huntington's Disease

Huntington's Disease is a real disease. While this book is fiction, the descriptions of Huntington's Disease are accurate. More than 30,000 Americans have HD, as Huntington's is often labeled. At least 150,000 others have a 50 percent risk of developing the disease and thousands more of their relatives live with the possibility that they might develop HD.

Until recently, scientists understood very little about HD and could only watch as the disease continued to pass from generation to generation. Families saw HD destroy their loved ones' ability to feel, think, and move. The disease has been documented back to the Middle Ages but it gained little attention and support from the medical arena until the late 1900s. In 1872, a physician named George Huntington wrote about an illness that he called "an heirloom from generations back in the dim past."

In the last several years, scientists working with support from the National Institute of Neurological Disorders and Stroke (NINDS) have made several breakthroughs in the area of HD research. HD results from genetically programmed degeneration of nerve cells in certain areas of the brain. This degeneration causes uncontrolled movements, loss of intellectual faculties, and emotional disturbance.

Each child of an HD parent has a 50/50 chance of inheriting the HD gene. If a child does not inherit the HD gene, her or she will not develop the disease. The rate of disease progression and the age of onset vary from person to person.

The Human Genome Project resulted in the discovery of the gene that causes HD in 1993. A genetic test, coupled with a complete medical history and neurological and laboratory tests, helps physicians diagnose HD. Testing is now available for individuals who are at risk for carrying the HD gene and embryonic screening is available. Some people who are at risk do not want to know, while some decide not to have children and continue the disease.

There is no cure for HD. Some medications help control emotional and movement problems. As late as 2008, a drug was approved to help the involuntary movements. At this time, there is no way to stop or reverse the course of HD.

Woodie Guthrie died of HD in 1967. His wife, Marjorie Guthrie, founded a lay organization entitled Committee to Combat HD. Several of Woodie's children have died from HD. His son, Arlo Guthrie, now in his 60s, has no symptoms and has escaped this horrible disease.

If you would like to learn more, contact the Hereditary Disease Foundation at 3960 Broadway, 6th Floor, New York, NY, or the Huntington's Disease Society of America, 505 Eighth Avenue, Suite 902, New York, NY. You may also research online for the thousands of testimonies of HD patients as well as videos of patients suffering from HD.

I have a friend who lived in the shadow of HD. Her mother died from the disease in the 1970s. Her sister developed the disease and died from the malady. My friend is now in her late 60s and has escaped HD, although symptoms and development of a mild case of HD have been documented as late as age 70. There is a lot of research that examines other dementia patients and those with late onset HD cases.